AUTOGRA

KATHY TYERS

L. JAGI LAMPLIGHTER

JAMES CHAMBERS

STEVE RZASA

GABRIELLE POLLACK

WAYNE THOMAS BATSON

DANIELLE ACKLEY-MCPHAIL

PAUL REGNIER

KERRY NIETZ

TEISHA J. PRIEST

JEFFREY LYMAN

REALMSCAPES

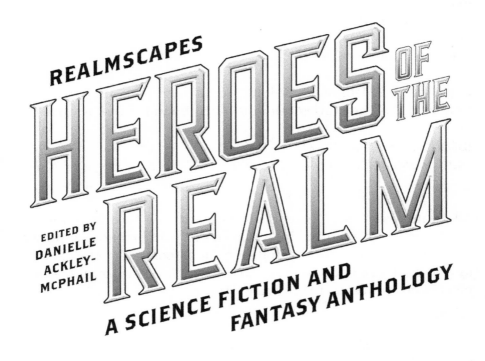

HEROES OF THE REALM

EDITED BY
DANIELLE
ACKLEY-
MCPHAIL

A SCIENCE FICTION AND
FANTASY ANTHOLOGY

REALM MAKERS
Pottstown, PA

PUBLISHED BY
Realm Makers Media
939 N Washington St
Pottstown, PA 19464
www.realmmakers.net

Copyright ©2019 Realm Makers Media
Copyright for the stories remains with the individual authors.

ISBN: 978-0-9962718-4-4
ISBN (ebook): 978-0-9962718-5-1

Cover Art and Design: Kirk DouPonce, Dog Eared Design
Interior Design: Danielle McPhail, Sidhe na Daire,
            www.sidhenadaire.com

DEDICATED TO THOSE WHO SERVE

THE POLICE, FIRE, EMT, AND MILITARY PERSONNEL
WHO SPEND THEIR LIVES BEING HEROES EVERY DAY.

Contents

WHAT IS A HERO?

IN SOME CIRCLES, THE MENTION OF A HERO CONJURES VISIONS OF A SLICK costume, superhuman talents, and maybe a secret identity. In others, perhaps a hero leads the charge against staggering odds, rallying the hopeless into one last stand. A hero might be that inspiring individual who makes the ultimate sacrifice and ensures others might forge on in freedom.

But heroism, even on a smaller, more personal scale, is no less heroic. The disenfranchised outsider triumphs when she summons the courage to speak the truth to those who have cast her out. The brooding criminal exhibits the heart of a hero when he turns away from the self-serving methods that have been second nature for so long, in favor of championing something higher and nobler than himself.

We at Realm Makers root for heroes, glad to swim upstream in a culture bent on dismantling heroism. We love a good story that sweeps you up in its thrill, offers an occasional point to ponder, and maybe casts a little ray of light to see by.

We hope this collection of stories gives you a taste of our passion for excellence in the storytelling arts. May the coming moments of adventure rewards you, because you, the reader, are the hero an author needs in this creative quest called writing.

Rebecca P. Minor
Realm Makers Executive Director

ASHLING AND THE LITTLE PEOPLE

KATHY TYERS

Ireland, about 1000 A.D.

THE DARKNESS WAS EATING ASHLING'S VISION.

He blinked, his sight restricted as if by a long, narrow tunnel as he stepped east along the great *Slí Mhor*. Ancient oaks' shadows dimmed the stony road even further. Just so, day by day, the shadowy grey-brown ring narrowed all he could see.

According to his Da—totally blind now—this was how it began. Da had also been fifteen at the time.

The darkness was winning now.

Ash paused at the end of a long rise and looked back. A cone-roofed tower still showed of the monks' settlement, the meadow or "Cluainn."

Ahead, Da called a soft "ho-o-o" to their pony, Samson. He'd probably heard Ash's steps pause. On a heavy cloth over Samson's back, Da's harp rode in its leather bag.

Ash gazed back a little longer. The monks lived at a broad bend in the great River Siannon. Just days ago, raiders—not Danes this time, but native Irish—had stolen a nearly completed Gospel Book: a beautiful one, illuminated with gold leaf and lapis, with a jeweled cover. Wars were fought for such books.

Ash frowned. It was early afternoon, but the road ahead looked dark, and not just because of the shadows in his eyes. What were the odds they would reach the next town unmolested?

He squinted north next, over the shallow marshland. Everything at the center of his vision was clear, but in the gray-brown ring around its edges, he could only see blurs. His head drooped. He and Da had gone to the Cluainn with such hope—for his eyesight, and for the loosening of his stuttering tongue. Ash had walked all the rounds of the holy pattern, and he'd stammered out all the prescribed prayers. For good measure, he'd even knelt under one of the high stone crosses all night, listening to river reeds swish while Da sang in the monks' quarters.

"Courage, son." Da clasped the red squirrel-fur edges of his harper's cloak. "The sainted Paul carried his thorn. I carry mine. Praise the Light, even when we see it not." His unseeing gray eyes reflected the clouds. "Especially then, maybe."

Ash frowned. In hindsight, it seemed foolish even to have gone to the monks. A recent illness had taken a third of them out of this world.

He turned back to the main road, straining his ears. Surely even book-grabbing thieves wouldn't molest a harper. An honored bard's ridicule was a terrible disgrace. To anyone.

And oh, Da could ridicule.

Finally, Ash let himself think a forbidden thought. Might the Old Ones have cured him, if he'd gone to them instead? The ancient gods—mighty horned Cernunnos, or lovely Siannon, or one of the unlovely others?

No, no. He kicked a stone off the road. He must not regret his baptism. Life was short. In eternity, he would live in perfect Light. The Old Ones were long banished outside the circles of the world— if they ever existed at all, outside the monks' vision of hell.

He drew a deep breath. The air smelled of wood smoke and drying grasses.

"P-praise to the L-Light," Ash muttered, but the words tasted like watery gruel. In the old days, heroes had battled dark powers. Da and Ash sang those songs too. Not usually for monks, but the chieftains loved them.

When Ash sang, the timid stammer didn't plague him. But he hated the stutter in his everyday speech. Truly, there was nothing of the hero in Ashling Harperson.

He hurried to catch up. Samson the pony stepped surely along the Slí Mhor, the ancient road splitting Eire. Da walked alongside, steadying himself against Samson's flank and gripping his walking stick. Between the broad Siannon, the boglands, and occasional islands of firm ground, the raised Slí ran supernaturally straight. Ash stepped over a long groove that suggested that something had been dragged recently—maybe a roadside oak, felled to build someone's hut or corral, and feed a cook fire. The monks had fed the bards stirabout, a thin soup of grain and late-summer greens. Longingly, Ashling imagined a succulent river eel or wild goat stewed with onion.

Actually, he did faintly smell meat. He raised his head and sniffed again. Ahead of them, off to the north, a chain of bog-islands supported dark oak and holly trees. Smoke threaded up from the middle one.

Not good. Ash squinted harder. Da sniffed again.

Out of a holly thicket on the island's near side plunged five ragged men, shouting through tangled beards. Ash's hands went clammy. He grabbed Samson's lead rope and laid his other hand on Da's shoulder, hoping Da didn't feel it shake.

There had been ruffians before. Da knew what to do. Still, Ash's heart pounded.

"Travelers, ho!" The tallest man brandished an axe. Beneath the dirt, his tangled beard looked vaguely red-brown. "Hah, a harper! Look at that!"

The others scrambled up onto the road, bringing a manly stench of old sweat. They shouted and waved their weapons.

"Ye'll be coming with us." The tallest man took another step toward Da. "We can use your skills tonight. We have meat, and honey, straight from the brown-robes' hives."

Da stretched out his arms, hands upraised. "Peace," he called. "We are walking to Duro, to sing and pray. Let us pass, and you'll have our prayers for a year."

"Pray!" There was laughter. Men frowned, clashing axes and pikes. "Peace," someone else snarled.

Ash's vision darkened. They weren't reacting like most ruffians. He glanced side to side. There were eight of them now. "L-leave him be!" he shouted, but no more words would come. He wanted to shout, *He's blind. You aren't so blind you can't see that, are you?*

Coward, he scolded himself. *Useless coward.*

A ruffian grabbed Samson's bridle and yanked the pony's head toward a gap in the oaks.

"Peace, Ashling. We'll eat their food and leave them with a lesson." Da seized the edge of Samson's blanket and followed. Ash had to follow Da, feeling as low as the lowest bog fish. No wonder the darkness was taking him. He never could speak when it mattered. What good would he ever be, tongue-tied and eventually blind?

He plodded through the oaks and underbrush, then out onto grassy tussocks that squished underfoot.

The middle rise concealed a clearing, recently cut. Leafy willow and alder twigs lay wilting all around, and in the fading afternoon light that filtered through the oak trees' twisted branches, Ash spotted ten or fifteen more men, most with axes in their belts. Pikes rested against four rickety-looking shelters built from pale, recently stripped limbs. Willow, Ash guessed. A larger, skin-covered shelter stood behind a much thicker, weathered, free-standing pole. It looked almost like a tree, standing alone and lopped of limbs. He peered closer. Images carved into the pole gave him the shudders. A weathered but unmistakable image of Cernunnos, the ancient horned god, sat cross-legged about halfway up. From the top dangled a painted leather image of the river-goddess Siannon, the sea-god's daughter, with her long hair floating as she drowned. Her face looked white and misshapen.

All the best of the Old Ones were long dead. If they ever existed at all.

Someone pointed to a stump. Ash sat. The ruffians stayed close, picketing Samson. At least they left the harp alone. Another man led Da into the big leather shelter. More images of the Old Ones danced around the shelter's skin door. Ashling didn't know most of their names, but even the beautiful ones felt sinister to him. Demonic. A fire burned close by, under a blackened cauldron. A squat, big-bellied man poked a long forked stick into the cauldron, pulled out a chunk of dripping meat, and strolled into one of the rickety shelters. A woman's voice drifted out.

Ash's mouth watered. He rocked forward to stand, but his guard glowered. He sat back down. Surely they wouldn't starve a harper. Not even his apprentice.

"Ye'll wait," the man grunted.

Ash sat still and tried not to cry. A pile of old, dead branches lay near the fire, and from time to time his guard leaned down and tossed on a branch, careful to miss the cauldron.

Da stayed in the big leather tent a long, long time. The sun had fallen fully halfway from noon when a raggedy woman emerged from one of the other shelters, fished out a hunk of meat for herself, and brought one to him. It didn't smell like goat. Badger, probably. He chewed gratefully, though it was mostly gristle.

Finally, he made himself look hard at the standing pole. Cernunnos stared out into space, seemingly as blind as Da, but demanding tribute. Something already lay like an offering at the pole's foot. Ash tried to squint away the gray-brown ring. When he squinted so hard his forehead hurt, the "something" came into focus.

Jewels flickered with the fire's low flames. The thing was rectangular. He gasped, and then he tried to cover the sound with a belch. The monks' missing book! This was a travesty.

His guard laughed. "Spotted it, did ye? Those *manchan* have bound the sweet Siannon with their ugly new bridge. That terrible thing's ashes will surely please her."

Burn a holy book to a drowned goddess? Hours and months of work—to say nothing of the calves slaughtered for their hides, and scraped for the pages—and—now his stomach really churned—the very holiness of the words inside. How dare they? He'd glimpsed that new bridge near the settlement, a wonder of stout poles and woven wicker. Finally, pilgrims to the Cluainn could make the treacherous crossing without risking boats.

Still, bridging the sacred river was heresy to pagans.

He squeezed his eyes shut. *Help us, Blessed Chríost.* At least in silent prayer, he didn't stammer.

That's when he spotted the leprechaun.

It had to be a leprechaun. A red-bearded ruffian marched a child-high captive with a bag over its head toward the fire. This was no child, though. It wore shining, high-topped black shoes below its breeches, with tiny gold buckles that sparkled at the ankles. Plainly fairy work.

Then the ruffian pulled off the bag, and Ash didn't try to disguise his gasp. Leprechauns wore beards, didn't they? This little prisoner had a big, bald head. Wide eyes carried all the defiance of any Wee One that Ash ever imagined. It—he—also wore weird garments that fit as tight as if someone had painted his skin.

The red-bearded ruffian gave it a hunk of meat and sat down, gripping his axe. "Caught one," the ruffian told Ash sidelong as the Wee One ate like a starved thing. "See, bardling? The Old Ones are real. More real than the brown-robes' Chríost. He's got to give us three wishes for his freedom, and he's not going home until he brings us gold. We'll have a sweet burning to appease the Lady Siannon and her father, and yellow gold for Lord Cernunnos." He pointed up at the carved pole. "And for us, of course." He belched. "Or else we'll drown it in the Siannon, along with a well-burned book. Hear that, leprechaun?" He shoved the Wee One's shoulder.

Ashling glanced at the cook fire, then into the Wee One's huge eyes. He made a slight, helpless gesture with both hands. Baptized he was, but the fairies' legendary powers were terrible. Especially at night. Yet he pitied the wee thing, a captive like Da and himself.

If only he could speak up. Rail at the red-bearded man. Ridicule them all, as a harper ought to be able to do.

Then came the strangest voice Ash ever heard. It sizzled inside his head. "Save the book! I can't reach their weapons."

What? Ash shook his head. What, save the book? What, how?

The voice sizzled again, and in those huge eyes Ash still saw defiance. "In the holy and blessed name of Jesus, help me save that book. We'll reward you."

Ash felt his eyes widen, too. The Wee One had never stopped staring, though its mouth kept devouring the meat. Red-Beard didn't react at all. Plainly, he hadn't heard a sizzling voice.

Was this the Wee Ones' magic? And since when did supernatural creatures use the Holy Name? Ash glanced at the main shelter where Da had vanished with the biggest ruffian. Someone shouted inside, and then Da's voice chanted. He sounded scornful.

Ash missed the words, though, because the voice sizzled on. "We came farther than you can imagine, my friends and I, to study what's in that Book. Help us." The Wee One glanced up into the late-day sky.

A gust of breeze blew smoke into Ash's eyes. He blinked hard. This contradicted everything he thought he knew about fairies.

Hadn't they started leaving the Isle when Patrick brought the holy Word? They hated it—and him—didn't they? Still, one more glance at the monks' book, and the cook fire all too close, made Ash shudder. "How?" he mouthed.

"Be ready to speak."

He shut his mouth and pursed his lips. Speak? Couldn't it have asked him to do something easier? Grab a pike, or reach for an axe? Maybe climb the nearest tree, upside down and backward?

At that moment, one of the ruffians held up the big shelter's skin flap. The head ruffian and Da re-emerged, shaking their heads. "The shame of it. Ye, a harper. Keeper of the ancient ways. A Chríostaí."

Da turned this way and that, taking deep breaths, plainly testing the wind. He frowned, and Ash wondered what he smelled.

Ruffians, probably.

A thread of river-mist blew into the camp from the nearby Siannon.

"Very well, then." The big man clenched Da's upper arm. "Ye shall witness the offering anyway. Vellum crackles well when it burns, and ye shall smell the stench. And then, ye shall sing us the song that we want."

"I shall not," Da said softly. "But I shall sing your shame up and down the Slí, town to town."

Ash swelled with pride, hearing those words.

"Sing it our way." The ruffian glowered in Ash's direction. "And not one word of ridicule, else yer son—and yer harp, too—will be burned with the book. Ye shall smell that, harper. And his screams shall ring in yer ears."

Bile burned in Ashling's throat. The gristly meat threatened to come back up. He'd burned his hand once, on a cook fire. But burn all over? He couldn't imagine the agony. Mock him, Da! Ash wanted to shout. But they had threatened. And Da said nothing.

"This way. All of ye. Bring the leprechaun and the boy, and the abomination." The big man headed down toward the river. A skinny, yellow-haired ruffian grabbed the book and followed him.

"No," a small voice murmured aloud. The leprechaun stood up and shook his big head. "This will not happen."

Red-Beard grabbed up the Wee One and laughed harshly. "Ye'll watch, then, and see what we do to traitors. After we deal with them, it'll be ye and yer gold." He gave Ashling's shoulder a shake. "Get up, boy. No tricks. There's an axeman behind ye. Ye can still burn if ye're bleeding."

The last sunlight faded through tree branches overhead as the rag-tag band emerged, carrying lit torches, at the riverside. The skinny ruffian carried the book upside down and inside out, clenching the covers' corners together. Precious hand-lettered pages dangled loosely as Skinny tramped along. Another ruffian led Samson, and one more carried Da's harp. Hope shrank in Ashling's thumping heart. Here, the broad river valley was broken only by a small island about a quarter mile upstream. The valley was wide, the river-mist rising steadily. A flock of birds settled onto the water downstream.

Closer, on a small rocky rise near the river's edge, dead boughs had been piled. "Stand here," Ashling's guard ordered. He set down the Wee One close by. It stared out over the river, flapping a hand. Skinny stood near the fire, still holding the precious book upside-down. Was that mockery, or was he illiterate? Both, maybe.

The ruffian carrying Da's harp set it down—gently, with the respect due a bard—between Ashling and Da. A soft whinny filtered out of the trees behind Ashling. Samson, probably picketed.

Ash shook all over. Da stood tall, clenching his hands. "You must understand," he muttered in Ashling's direction.

"Silence." A smelly ruffian gripped Da's shoulder. He might maybe have slapped someone else, but not a harper.

A ruffian threw his torch on the pile of boughs. Twigs crackled as little fiery tongues climbed through the dry sticks, and Ashling felt the heat. He could not—dared not—imagine being thrown onto that fire. The pile was enormous. And Da's harp—how hot it might burn!

Da must write these pagans their song! He could do penance later, and write a new one to mock them. Da would not let Ash burn. He would not.

One of the ruffians raised his voice in a harsh ululation. Ashling didn't follow the words, but they sounded evil.

"You must speak." The leprechaun's voice buzzed again. "This won't work if you don't speak."

Ash opened his mouth, but nothing happened.

Skinny stepped closer to the fire, holding the book closed now, brandishing it in front of his face.

An even more bizarre sound, buzzing and sizzling like ten thousand insects, came from the island upstream. Mid-river, something bubbled and boiled. "What's that?" Red-Beard shouted, stepping farther away from the bank.

Something tall and shining rose up out of the misty river. Splashing noises came from it, and from the island.

Ashling's heart pounded in his throat.

A woman, twice Ash's height and wearing flowing green, floated up out of the water, onto the riverbank. She glimmered in the mist, and Ash could see through her, almost to the bank on the far side. Hair like a gold river flowed over her shoulders. Silver gleamed at her slender waist.

Siannon herself, the river-goddess? How could that be? She ought to be dead, if she ever existed at all, outside of hell! Ash shut his gawping mouth, but it fell open again.

"Speak, boy!" the voice buzzed. "Say something! It isn't real!"

Ash stood blinking.

The chief ruffian bowed down so low that his beard dragged the tall grass.

The huge woman stretched out her arms toward the fire, looking plenty real to Ash. Sure enough, her hands were bound at the wrist. The cords looked like braided willow bark. A deep, feminine voice echoed across the river valley. "Bel Bheg, did you call me?"

"Speak up, boy!"

Ash simply gaped. And it got worse. Out of the fire leaped a man, shining like fire, like the sun, with streaming hair as pale gold as the woman's, but only for a second. As soon as his forearm left the smoking fire, the man withered, his skin blackened and crisping, eyes glowing. He had long, tearing teeth.

Hungry. That's how he looked. Hungry. His flaming arm drifted toward Skinny, who backed away still gripping the book. A pony's shriek faded into the forest behind Ashling. Hoofbeats pounded away.

"It's. Not. Real. Boy. Say something!"

His tongue, cheeks, and lips were utterly dry.

The head ruffian backed even farther from the fire. Skinny flung the holy book high into the air, toward the fire-demon. It sailed supernaturally slow, as if it had wings. As it sailed, the demon leaped fully out of the fire and engulfed—not the book—but the skinny ruffian, who shrieked and disappeared. The book fell to the earth.

No one else moved. Ashling shook. The Old Ones were real. *Chríost, save us,* he pleaded silently. *If we're going to die, take us to be with you!*

Da strode toward the fiery man. "Kill us," he cried, "burn the copy, but the eternal—"

Then the creature was on him. It engulfed him, and Da vanished too.

No! Hot tears burned Ashling's cheeks. Da was gone, Ash was going to die too, and the Old Ones were as real as that bonfire. And they were merciless. There was no hope. Yet ... an image appeared in his mind's eye, a shocking picture of Da standing on a green hilltop alongside a green-robed woman like this goddess, but human-sized. They were singing Chríost's praises. Together.

He swallowed salt water and smoke. Was that a spark of hope? Might some of the Old Ones—long banished outside the world—ever bow to the King of heaven? Could even a harper imagine such a glorious thing? After all, there were angels who had not rebelled.

All fear fell away. If he was going to die, he would die singing. For even when he couldn't speak, he could sing.

He dropped to his knees beside Da's harp, and he felt he was finding the words Da had only begun. "Kill us, burn the copy, but the Word will set this island free! Living light, shining far, reaching more hearts than you ever could kill."

The fire-demon lowered its head. It crouched, hands on its knees, ready to pounce.

"Good, boy! We've almost got it! Don't stop!"

Ash didn't steel himself. There was no fear to fight down. After all, the dark would blind him soon enough. He felt huge. Mighty. He stepped toward the goddess and shouted, "Sweet Siannon! Your river will be a highway of that living light. Be free in that light!"

And then the power left him. He was a boy again, trembling on his knees in the mud.

But in an instant, the huge woman raised her arms, and the bark-bindings flew away. She flung her hands wide, and that voice echoed across the water mists again. "Light! Light of heaven!" A blast of frigid water soared out of her hands. Darkness—not light—fell as the fire sputtered and drowned. The demon disappeared, too. Around the fire's smoking ruin, ruffians shouted like drunken men.

Sionnan still glowed. Now the droplets that fell from her hands looked like jewels. "Perfect, boy! Well done! Pick up the book," sizzled in Ash's head. He lunged between stumbling ruffians, snatched it up, and cradled it tightly.

Meanwhile, Siannon held both arms upraised, still flinging gems in all directions. "Living light!" her voice echoed. "Shining far! Rejoice in it, people of Eire!"

The leprechaun grabbed Ash's hand and ran toward the riverbank. He leaped down beside it.

Lady Siannon also turned and seemingly ran, barely moving her legs, out across the flowing river—what? Yes! On top of the dark water. The Wee One followed without hesitating. Ash kept his eyes on the Lady, not the river below his feet. It felt like flying. Time itself seemed to slow. In just a few heart-beats—or maybe just one—they reached the small darkness of the island.

Three other Wee Ones stood amid the bushes, clustered around a box made of silver. The Lady shrank and vanished into the box. "Inside, inside," sizzled in Ash's head. One of them ducked through a door in the ground.

The Wee One he'd followed raised his head, and finally, he smiled. "Well done, boy," he said aloud. "Bring the book, and we'll show you wonders."

➤➤≪≪

They tried to explain. Something about "research," and "getting an accurate sonic fix on it," and that the silver box was what they called a "projector" that shone "images" onto river-mist. Too rapt and too confused to follow or understand what they were saying, Ash stood on a shining silver floor between silver walls, and he gawped. They opened page after page of the holy book and swept a smaller, dark gold box back and forth over the pages. One of them crooned a soft song. Ash didn't understand a word of it. Yet his own Wee One stayed close, smiling and trying to explain, and slowly, understanding pierced the fog.

Angels had visited them, too, a thousand years ago on a far distant world. Angels, shouting glory to the heavens—but the holy birth would happen only once, and only here. They had been summoned to make the journey. Now they would go back, taking the copy they were making of this gospel book. A thousand years' journey? Pah. Apparently, they lived many thousands of years. For them, this journey was just a pilgrimage. Other researchers would come, but they would leave humans alone.

"Mostly," the Wee One added, and Ash thought its eyes sparkled.

Then came a second wonder. One of them held a strangely shaped object up to Ash's head and burbled the same language the other was singing. Then he said, "Yes. Reward. Thank you, boy."

The dark ring shrank. The silvery cave grew brighter. Like smoke blown from a dowsed fire, the darkness blew away. Grateful tears ran down the side of Ash's nose.

But the third wonder was best, for there in the silvery cave stood the skinny, yellow-haired ruffian—and Da. "We cannot heal him," they told Ash sadly. "The blindness is too old, too far along."

Yet Da seemed content, especially when he heard where they had come from, and why. Ash never had seen him smile so broadly. Ah, what a song that would make. "But no monk would believe it," Da whispered. "Nor any chieftain."

"No." Skinny stood against a silvery wall, cringing and shaking. "Never. Chríost, forgive me for all I've done. Chríost, forgive me. Forgive me—"

Da stretched out a hand toward Skinny. "Do you have a name, son?"

"Mac," he said. "That's all anyone ever called me. Just Mac. Son of. Son of no one," he added. His head drooped.

Ash reached out and clasped Skinny's hand between both of his own. "Mac, I'm Ashling." His own steady speaking voice startled him. "A-ashling Harperson. And it's sure you can be forgiven."

At dawn, the Wee Ones set them all back on the Slí Mhor: Ash, Da, and yellow-haired Mac. Daybreak lit the Cluainn as they stood at the same spot where Ash had stood and looked back. He clutched the holy book with both arms.

Mac wrung his bony hands. "Won't ye let me take it back to them? Let me do penance. Else they'll turn me out!"

"No." Ash's own voice echoed in his head, and it sounded as strong as singing. "They'll treat you fairly. Da and I want to do it." And the darkness would not win. Not in his eyesight, and not in this world—or the other world. All praise to the Light!

Mac pushed yellow hair out of his eyes. "But ye'll leave soon. I mean to stay. Take vows. Give my whole life to Chríost."

Da gripped the man's free hand. "Then give us this pleasure," Da said. "If you really want to do penance, help us find Samson and get back my harp."

"I will!" Skinny craned his long neck to look back down the Slí. "Gladly. If the Abbott will let me—"

Stones rattled underfoot. A silver shape streaked into the sky from mid-river, and Ash turned toward it. He raised a hand in farewell. "God grant you a safe return," he wished the Wee Ones, knowing his words had helped save them. "And may they believe you!"

THE TEA DRAGON

L. JAGI LAMPLIGHTER

As Ulysses Prospero lay sweating with fever, his long legs dangling over the edge of a bunk designed for much shorter men, he vowed a solemn vow.

Sweat poured down his face and soaked his waistcoat and jacket as his body fought off the deadly venom. His cravat, which had not been starched since he left Hong Kong, lay limp as a wet noodle. The stench of rotting sturgeon contributed to his nausea.

Through the open door of the deckhouse, he glimpsed the fan-like sails of the Chinese junk, which may once have been red but had weathered closer to burgundy. He could have used a Burgundy right now, Ulysses mused in his nigh-delirium, or, preferably, a shot of Scotch. It was a hard thing for a man to die halfway around the world, away from his family, with not even a drop of liquor to soothe his throat.

If he recovered from this venomous bite, he vowed solemnly, he never again wanted to be more than a day away from the creature comforts of civilization. Adventuring was all well and fine, but the day should end with a warm bath and a smoke.

Outside, the voices of the Chinese sailors rose in alarm, shouting, "Sea monster!"

One year earlier:

"You proved it once and for all, didn't you?" Ulysses Prospero asked as he strolled around Kew Gardens with plant-hunter-extraordinaire Robert Fortune. "That *Thea bohea* is the same plant as *Thea viridis*, I mean."

Ulysses was a dapper young man in his mid-twenties, impeccably dressed in a sculpted, dove grey morning coat, a double-breasted waistcoat of silver damask, and, at his throat, an opulent charcoal paisley ascot. As an amateur botanist, he was a regular at Kew and felt quite honored to be talking with one of the most famous botanists in the country.

"Without question." The tall Scotsman nodded. He wore sideburns and a jacket and trousers of unrelenting black, without an eye to the latest fashions. "The two plants are identical, now called *Thea sinensis*. The difference between green tea and black tea is how they are processed. But there is a great deal of difference between varieties of the plant. Some produce a better green and others a better black."

"And all of these," Ulysses gestured toward where his father and one of his many older brothers examined new rows of plants, recently installed in the gardens, "were your finds, from your trip to China?"

"Indeed, let me acquaint you with them." Fortune rubbed his hands together, grinning.

He moved toward the towering, red pagoda where the plants he had donated to Kew after his last trip now flourished. He pointed out the feathery-fronded *cephalotaxus fortunei*, or Chinese plum-yew, and the *rhododendron fortunei* with its pale flowers, explaining to the younger man exactly what grew there and where he had found each one. Both plants, Ulysses noted, had been named for him.

"It is quite extraordinary," Ulysses exclaimed. Drawing out paper and charcoal, he began to sketch the new arrivals.

Ulysses' father and his older brother Erasmus strolled up beside them. Lucretius Prospero—known to some as the immortal Dread Magician Prospero, whose exploits were chronicled by Shakespeare in his famous play, *The Tempest*—was a tall, white-haired man with a long beard and a gray wool Inverness cape. He leaned on a long length of teakwood topped with a star sapphire, the *Staff of Transportation* that allowed him to return instantly to any place the staff had ever touched.

Erasmus, Ulysses' much older brother, wore a morning coat of green brocade cut in a fashion that had gone out of style before Ulysses was born. His lank dark hair fell over mocking green eyes and a narrow chin. In one hand, he held a long rectangular staff, the sides of which were alternating black and white.

"Two hundred years," Erasmus drawled. "China lorded it over us, setting the price of the most prized beverage in the Empire, and, in one trip, you personally changed the balance of power, Fortune."

Fortune let out a low, gravely sigh. "That still waits to be seen."

"How are your acquisitions growing?" Ulysses asked.

"The green tea flourishes," Fortune explained. "But, as you know, green tea has declined in popularity, due to my discovery that, to please the Western eye, the Chinese had been adding ferrocyanide—for its Prussian blue—and gypsum—calcium sulfate dehydrate, for its yellow color, just to bring out the green color that they felt we Westerners desired."

"But both of those are poisonous," Erasmus objected, "particularly the cyanide!"

"Precisely."

"So the black is in ascendance? I hear you did very well, sneaking into the area where the plants used for black tea are grown and even bringing back a clipping from the bushes of the famed *da hong pao* tea from the monks of the Tian Xin Yong Le monastery."

Fortune sighed. "I did. But these teas are doing less well in India than my greens. The plants are not flourishing."

"Which is what brings us here, my sons," Ulysses' father stated. Turning to Fortune, Prospero said, "It is my hope that we will be able to aid you, and through you, the entire Empire."

"It is certainly my wish that this will be so. I have myself been away from my family many years, and I have not the expertise to catch..." Fortune paused, as they were no longer alone.

A large family came strolling down the garden path, examining the new specimens with noisy excitement. A nursemaid followed, pushing a perambulator containing a squalling infant.

"Is there anything more tedious than an infant," Ulysses mock-shivered with distaste. "All their caterwauling? I realize that we need to reproduce the race, but surely it can be done farther from me."

"You were a particularly ugly infant yourself, all barfing and mewling, and not so long ago," his older brother quipped wryly. "So I can see why you would disapprove."

The nursemaid gave both men a disapproving frown, and the family moved on.

Fortune looked left and right, confirming that the four of them were alone. In a low voice, he said, "Erasmus tells me that you will not laugh at what I am about to say."

"If it is a matter of arcane lore, we shall not," Prospero replied.

"When I returned to India from China, I brought with me ten tea growers, and they brought with them," he paused and then blurted out, "a *luchalung*."

"Green Tea Dragon?" Ulysses looked up with curiosity from where he was examining the rose-like flower of an excellent specimen of Camellia.

"Apparently, the *lung* makes all the difference in the health and quality of the tea. It is what gives Chinese tea its superior taste," Fortune replied. "To successfully complete the theft of Chinese tea, we need a *hongchalung,* a black tea dragon."

"Ah," Ulysses said. "Our oldest brother Mephisto the Beast Tamer is the one you need. He's a wonder at catching supernatural critters."

"Mephisto is indisposed," Erasmus quipped.

"This week?"

"This decade."

"Actually," their father ruminated, "I was thinking of sending you, Ulysses."

"What, *me*?" the young man cried, astonished.

"Indeed."

"But..." Ulysses sputtered. "Surely, you are not trying to dig me out! I am an intimate of the Prince of Wales, who expects me to be on hand to play whist and make cutting remarks about fashion. I spend my days tasting wine and tutting about with exotic plants. I am a dandy, not an adventurer."

"And that is precisely why I thought of you," his father opined. "A bit of exertion will do you good, and because you know your plants."

"I do fancy botany..."

"And you speak fluent Chinese."

"True."

"Very good," Prospero nodded pleasantly at his youngest son, "it is decided then."

"No! Absolutely not! I am not leaving my friends and traveling halfway around the world on a year-long journey to China! I realize that as the *paterfamilias*, I owe you due respect, but...*Are you mad?*"

"As the youngest, only you, of all my children, do not have your own magic staff." Prospero gestured with the long length of teak he carried. "If you go and come back victorious, I will make you one of your own."

⤙✥⤚

Seagulls wheeled overhead, their cries mingling with the clinking of masts and lines. The salty air, both bracing and cool, might have been quite pleasant if it had not stunk of bracken and old fish.

Ulysses stood on the docks, preparing to embark upon his adventure. His gear was already stowed onboard. All that remained was for him to mount the gangplank. Beside him, his eldest brother Mephisto sat on a crate, the tip of his tongue protruding from the side of his mouth as he worked to remove a figurine from his staff, which consisted of a series of wooden statuettes strung together like a totem pole.

"Okay, all ready," Mephisto chirped cheerfully, holding up the one he had just freed. "I am lending you Brokky. Take very good care of him and bring him back to me."

"So this thing," Ulysses looked at the figurine, peach wood with amber chips in its eyes, that looked rather like a mongoose, "will catch the *hongchalung* for me?"

"It will! Just tap the figurine on the head, twice, and Brokky will appear."

"And it's called a brokky?"

Mephisto laughed. "No. It's called an ichneumon, but this one reminds me of Allen Brokken, one of my friends down at the club. So I named it after him."

"Ah. That's ducky then." Ulysses took the figurine and slipped it into the pocket of his exquisite pearl gray traveling coat. "Anything else?"

"You have the bag and the Wardian cases?" Mephisto asked.

"If you understand this all so well, why don't you go?" Ulysses exclaimed, annoyed.

"Sorry," his brother replied. He made a circle with his finger and pointed it at his own head. "Crazy as a bed bug."

Ulysses' response was interrupted by a group of women, carrying parasols and chattering like magpies, who jostled him as they pushed by the brothers and up the gangplank.

"Oh, don't tell me they're coming, too," Ulysses drawled. "Is there anything more useless than a woman? Why even let them on ships? Such a shame that we need them for reproduction, too. Rather hang out with a group of fellows any day."

Mephisto stared after the girls, entranced, a little smile on his handsome yet crazed face. "You'll understand when you get older."

❧❦

The voyage was tiresome yet uneventful. Upon arriving in Hong Kong, Ulysses took his letter of introduction from Robert Fortune to the renowned trading company of Messers. Dent, Beale & Co.. They provided accommodations and introduced him to Sung Woo, who was to act as his servant and guide for the trip inland. Under Sung Woo's direction, Ulysses' hair was dyed jet black and a long braid of hair was attached to the back of his head.

The day before he was to leave the Wuyi Mountains, Ulysses joined Mr. Thomas Harsley from Dent, Beale, & Co. at an outdoor shooting range the company maintained for its employees. Decked out in his new Mandarin robes, he stood sideways, sighting over his pistol at a target.

"I dare say," Mr. Harsley exclaimed, "you do look the part."

"I must admit the duds are quite sensational, pure silk brocade and all." Ulysses paused. "If I may ask, what about my face? Nothing has been said about that."

"Won't matter," Harsley said.

"What do you mean?"

"Didn't matter for Fortune."

"But I don't look even a bit Chinese."

"They won't know that."

"I...fail to follow you." Ulysses took his shot, hitting the target square in the center of the bull's eye.

"Excellent shot!" Harsley exclaimed.

Ulysses reloaded. "How could anyone who looked at me not mark me for a foreigner?"

"Because once you get inland, none of them have ever seen a foreigner. China is a big country, with many ethnic nationalities. If you say you are from far away, they will just assume that people over in that area of China look different. So long as you speak Chinese and conduct yourself as if you are one of them, they will never know the difference. Mandarins are mysterious to the peasantry, anyway."

"And this is how Fortune did it? With his large nose and his towering height?"

Harsley nodded. "He just brashed it out."

⚜

"You must take Chinese name," Sung Woo explained when they headed out. "You now Jao Ching."

Sung Woo spoke English, Chinese, and Pidgin—a language used by dockworkers that was a mix of Chinese, English, and Portuguese. As they walked, the two men meandered back and forth between the three languages.

They strolled through the busy streets on their way to the boat that would take them up the Min River. From there, they would travel by rickshaw through Fujian Province and finally to the Bohea area. The streets were a riot of colors, full of bustling merchants and shoppers. Stalls and hand carts offering strange foods: white balls of rice dough filled with sweet red beans, dried squid, duck, and dozens of other things that Ulysses had never tried before arriving in Hong Kong, and most of which he would not miss if he never ate them again. They passed apothecaries, selling open bins of dried mushrooms or bamboo or mushrooms or live scorpions, vendors with carts offering an array of spiced meat, and cloth salesmen with bolts of red or black silks patterned with dragons or birds.

Some streets were sunny and hung with red lanterns. These smelled of spices and warm rice. Others bore unpleasant odors and housed opium dens, thoroughly unpleasant places that Ulysses would not want to be caught dead in, or alive for that matter.

Merchants offered them goods as they passed. Ulysses bought a few things that he thought might be useful on the trip and paid to have a few other things taken back to his apartments to be packed and shipped back to England.

As he stopped to examine some speckled duck eggs packed in crystals of salt, he was surrounded by merchants pushing their wares. One man kept yelling that he wanted to sell him a dog, or maybe he was offering to *cook* the dog, Ulysses was not sure which and, frankly, did not want to know. Another, an ill-kempt fellow with a crazed look in his eyes, pushed a woman at him, shouting in one of the many dialects that Ulysses did not speak. She was not a young woman; rather she was old and going gray, and yet it looked as if the man was hawking her. Ulysses demurred politely, on both accounts, and pushed his way out of the crowd

"What was that last one doing?" Ulysses inquired of Sung Woo as they approached the boat, "the one who was trying to shove some old lady at me?"

Sung Woo replied blandly. "Selling his mother."

"I say! What?" Ulysses cried. "That's barbaric! I might find women, in general, a tiresome lot, but one's own mother is cut from a different cloth! Mothers are sacred!"

"Opium addict. Makes men crazy. They do anything for more."

"Deuces unpleasant. Awful stuff. Ruins all who use it. Why do your people put up with it?"

Sung Woo gave him a strange look but did not reply.

❧

The first day or so heading upriver, Ulysses was afraid that he would be found out, but, to his surprise, no one seemed to question his story of being a Mandarin on a journey to view the famous tea groves of the Wuyi Mountains. Under his bunk, Sung Woo had packed the heavy Wardian case in which they would put the tea dragon once they caught it.

Wardian cases were a relatively recent invention. A Dr. Nathaniel Bagshaw Ward, who kept cocoons of moths in sealed glass cases, had discovered that some seeds accidentally left within had germinated and could grow perfectly well without any intervention. The grass that grew from the seeds flourished and bloomed for four years until the seal on the case rusted away. Wardian cases—made from iron, wood, and glass—could keep plants alive even over long sea journeys. Those tending the green tea dragon had insisted that it travel surrounded by tea plants. Ulysses intended to do the same for the black variety.

The next part of the trip, by rickshaw, proved tedious, but Ulysses spent the time reading and sketching in his journal until they reached the Wuyi Mountains. Sung Woo, who had grown up in this region, grinned with satisfaction as Ulysses gawked in wonder at the tall, jagged karsts that jutted from the mist like the bones of the earth. The sight was breathtaking.

The two travelers soon arrived at the Tian Xin Yong Le monastery, where Sung Woo introduced Jao Ching as an associate of Sing Wa, which had been the name Robert Fortune used during his travels. The monks welcomed them enthusiastically, providing a comfortable place to stay.

Over the next several weeks, Ulysses and Sung Woo ranged the countryside. Ulysses grew heartily sick of every meal consisting of rice and pickled radish. They learned a great deal more about tea than Ulysses had ever wished to know. In actuality, he was *hongchailung* hunting; however, he dare not tell the monks that he wished to steal one of their sacred dragons who helped keep their tea plants healthy. So, he was obliged to travel all around the steep countryside, visiting tea farms, viewing tea factories, and drinking tea with natives.

The last, at least, was not a burden, as the local tea was truly the best that Ulysses had ever tasted. He just wished that they had provided milk and sugar.

He had been expecting to have to sneak off, maybe in the dead of night, to secretly steal clippings to fill his Wardian case, but to his surprise, the tea growers were eager to press seedlings upon him when he visited the rolling, terraced hills upon which their precious bushes grew. Tea, he learned, was made from only the most tender shoots and buds of the *Thea sinensis* bush. The older leaves were too bitter and acidic. While, so far as he could discern, the legendary "monkey-picked" tea was just a myth, he

was assured by many men, young and old, that virgin-picked tea
had the best flavor.

⊱❧⊰

The trip to the tea factory proved more interesting than he had
expected. Ulysses filled many pages of his journal with sketches
of the process. He used his drawing as an excuse for why he
was constantly looking around, ever keeping a sharp lookout for
tell-tale signs of *lung*. So far, no one had seemed suspicious.

On the other hand, how often did foreigners sneak in disguised
as Mandarin and steal their dragons? He probably could have
strode around openly peering under bushes and behind rocky
crags, asking about the creatures, and no one would have given
him a second thought.

The warm, dry courtyard of the tea factory was filled with the
pleasant, woody scent of the tea plant. Leaves lay drying in the
sun atop woven rattan platters the size of dinner tables. The sun
beat down upon them, "cooking" them. The difference between
green tea and black tea, Sung Woo explained, was this first step.
Green tea was left to stew under the sun for about an hour. Black
tea stayed for twelve hours, stewing in the heat of the day to bring
out its tannins and give it that distinctive darker color.

Next, the tea was brought to the furnace room where it was
tossed about in giant woks, the heat drawing out the sap and
breaking down the vegetable matter. Then the heated leaves were
emptied onto a table and worked over with bamboo rollers. Ulysses
drew two excellent sketches of this portion of the process, even
catching in his drawing the green juices pooling on the tables.
Then, the tea was cooked one last time.

By this time, the leaves were tightly curled, not even a quarter
of the size they had been to start with. It took a tea picker, the
factory director explained, a whole day to pick a pound of leaves.
This process reduced that pound to a handful.

The final step was a table where workers sat separating the
choicest, most tightly wound leaves from the lesser-quality ones.
The best leaves would be sold at the highest price as *pekoe,* the
factory director insisted that these leaves had the richest and most
unique fragrance and taste that lasted longer in the mouth. The
next best leaves were called *congou,* and what was left, known as
dust, would be sold to the general public.

Ulysses noted all these things, and he made the most of the offer to taste the different teas. Of the *hongchalung*, however, he saw nothing.

※⟫⟪⟫⟨⟪

That night, he spoke privately with Sung Woo. "We have been here for days. We've been in the fields. We've been in the mountains. We've walked through the tea bushes and examined the factory. And yet, I have not seen a single glimpse of a *lung*."

Sung Woo spread his arms shrugging. "They elusive. Sometimes, patience required."

Ulysses scowled, pacing. "I told my father that this whole mission was a mistake. I will give it another week. Then, we're heading back, and Fortune can grow his tea without a dragon."

※⟫⟪⟫⟨⟪

The day after the visit to the tea factory, two of the monks took Ulysses and Sung Woo on a day's walk to visit the sacred *Da Hong Pao* trees that produced the most expensive tea in the world. The two-hundred-year-old bushes grew on the side of a cliff, supported by a short stone wall. Beside them, the three characters for Big Red Robe—*Da Hong Pao*—had been carved into the rock and painted crimson.

"Legend say nine evil dragons fight here," the elder monk explained. "They destroy crops, eat livestock, and ruin lives. Immortal, finally, come to confront them and restore order.

"Great battle ensue. Heavens rage. Earth quake. One by one, immortal destroy nine evil lung and make karst from each corpse." The monk gestured in the direction of the nine great karsts known as Jiulongke, Nine Dragon's Nest, whose bare rock cliff-sides towered over the lush green landscape.

This elder monk then fell silent. The younger monk picked up the narration. "Immortal want to celebrate victory with memorial. So people not forget what he do for them. So he give three tea bushes, which he place up here on top of cliffs, far from valley.

"Tea from these bushes help heal empress. In return, emperor send back red silk blanket to protect roots of bushes from cruelness of winter frosts. Thus name: Big Red Robe."

The monks had to hurry back to resume their duties. Ulysses and Sung Woo were left to themselves standing before the rock face from which the *Da Hong Pao* bushes grew. With no one around, Ulysses climbed up and carefully took a small clipping from the back of the bushes. Luckily, tea twigs were particularly easy to root.

"Sung Woo," he asked when he had climbed back down. "I have a question I have been wondering about."

"Ask, Jao Ching," Sung Woo replied.

"You grew up here, and you know my real motives. Why doesn't it bother you that I am stealing tea from your country? For two hundred years, China has dominated international trade through its monopoly on tea. Why are you willing to help me?"

Sung Woo was quiet for a time, contemplating the question. He stood gazing at the famous tea bushes, his hands clasped behind his back.

Finally, he replied, "In my village, three times as many people now as a hundred years ago. The land not support so many. With no prospects and not enough brides, young men go to city for work. This brings shame to their families."

"But," Ulysses rubbed the bridge of his nose, confused, "wouldn't that mean that you would want more customers for tea, to have more work to do?"

Sung Woo continued as if he had not interrupted, "In city, some find work. But many...Far too many...path ends in opium den. Opium destroy my people. Opium sucking the fire from our souls."

Ulysses frowned, puzzled. "I fail to see what that has to do with my question. What does opium have to do with the theft of tea?"

Sung Woo looked as if with sorrow upon a foolish master. "Opium what your England pay for tea."

"You mean *we* bring the opium?" Ulysses cried, aghast.

"Your East India Company brings it from India. We fought war to reject it, but we lost."

"Oh, was that what that was about? *Er...* sorry. I wasn't really paying attention at the time."

Sung Woo lowered his head sadly. "Most Westerners not pay attention to price of their tea, that is."

"In my defense, I was rather young when that war took place," Ulysses replied. "So you are saying you are willing to help me because you want the opium trade to end?"

Sung Woo nodded solemnly.

Ulysses thought about this for a time. With a slight frown, he asked, "You mentioned the men leaving because there are not enough brides. Where are all the girls? Do they go to the city, too?"

Sung Woo had a strange expression on his face, almost as if he were not willing to meet Ulysses' eyes. "Daughters expensive. Sons work. Daughters require dowries. Dowries very expensive. Families not able afford many dowries."

"So...what happens? Many girls remain spinsters? You think if they wanted the lads to stay on the farms and there weren't enough wives, they would just let the spinsters marry without dowries. Wouldn't that make more sense?"

Sung Woo hesitated, as if reluctant to answer. Suddenly, he cried out and pointed up at the rock face, near the *da hong pao* bushes. "Jao Ching! The *hongchalung*!"

➵➤❦

Ulysses launched into action. Grabbing the specially prepared bag from a deep, quilted pocket, he tossed it to Sung Woo, who had drawn out the wooden figurine Mephisto had given Ulysses.

"Release the Brokken!" Ulysses shouted.

Sung Woo tapped the peach wood statuette on its head, as he had previously been instructed. The two men began to imagine that a quick light creature, much like a mongoose, bounded over the rocks. Then, they could see it. It had black and white fur, forming a subtle gray pattern, a sharp nose, and a long pointed tail. Lithe as a weasel, it leapt back and forth, arching and diving, as it darted up the cliff side.

Above, peeking from behind the sacred tea bushes, was a long sinuous creature. It was red and black with a face a bit like a lion's, whiskers like a koi, a long, scaled serpentine body and four legs ending in large talons: the *hongchalung*.

The lung started to retreat, but then it saw the ichneumon.

A dance began. Ulysses could think of no other word for it. The ichneumon arched and hissed. The *lung* hissed back, its black forked tongue flickering as it began to circle. The ichneumon jumped in and out, quick as lightning, nipping the *lung*'s tail. The dragon moved almost like a liquid, turning so quickly, its head always facing its enemy.

The *lung* struck. In a motion that would have many an Olympic gymnast proud, the ichneumon rolled in the air, its tail whirling almost like a propeller as its hind legs twisted halfway around, feet pointing up, to avoid the needle-like fangs of the dragon. It landed, front paws first, its back legs and tail high in the air.

"Go! Get it!" Ulysses shouted, drawing his pistol.

The bushes rustled to his left, but he ignored the distraction, his attention focused on the fight. He wanted to help, but then he remembered that he needed the lung alive and healthy. He was not sure where he could shoot it that would not damage it too badly to survive the trip. Also, while he was ordinarily an excellent shot, the ichneumon moved so quickly, he could not be sure that he would not accidentally injure it, should it suddenly jump in his way.

Recalling that mongoose caught snakes by snapping their spines, Ulysses hoped that Mephisto had instructed the creature not to kill their prize. He was not sure what good a paralyzed dragon would be to the tea farmers of India.

Then, just as suddenly, it was over. The ichneumon struck, grasping the lung in its powerful jaws.

"Come! Let us catch it!" Sung Woo rushed forward with the bag.

"You do it," Ulysses gestured airily, not feeling any particular need to put himself out. He hung back and let the other man do the work. "I'm sure you'll do fine."

Sung Woo began gingerly maneuvering the lung into the enchanted bag. As soon as it was secured, Ulysses tapped the figurine again, returning the ichneumon the way it had come. Inside the bag, the lung writhed, which Ulysses took to be a good sign. Apparently, the ichneumon had not paralyzed it.

A slither in the tea bushes behind him, and a second lung, perhaps the mate of the first, was upon him, its teeth sinking into the meat of his bicep.

Screaming in pain, Ulysses brought up his pistol and shot the gold and green dragon in the face. There was a *whoosh,* and it slithered backward. Whether it vanished into the underbrush or turned into a puff of wind, he could not say.

➤❦❧

The trip back to Hong Kong was nightmarish. It turned out that Wuyi *lung* were venomous. Sung Woo and the monks did the best they could to remove the poison, but Ulysses' arm swelled up like a balloon. The pain was tremendous.

The rickshaw ride back to the river was a blur. Later in life, he could hardly remember anything from this period except for the sheer agony. Every time the conveyance jostled, Ulysses let out a bloodcurdling scream.

The boat ride down the Min River was less painful, but the constant motion of the vessel and the constant odor of bilge water and old fish made him nauseous. He lay in a feverous haze, wondering how deadly *lung* venom was and whether he had any chance of ever seeing London again.

⊰※⊱

He was awoken from a fitful sleep by an extremely irritating noise. The high wailing rose and fell, grating on his already raw nerves, denying him the rest he so craved. Ulysses gritted his teeth and waited for the noise to stop, but it did not happen.

"Sung Woo," he muttered through cracked lips, "what is that excruciating noise?"

"A girl child."

He was going to die, robbed of sleep because someone could not quiet their baby, death by infant caterwaul. Why didn't the parents silence the wretched thing?

"Ugh," he moaned, "How utterly useless."

Sung Woo replied, sadly resigned, "Parents agree with you."

⊰※⊱

Lying in the dark, dying, trying to sweat off the venom in the oppressive heat, Ulysses peered blearily at the Wardian case with the tea seedlings and lung inside. Idly, he wondered what would happen to the dragon if he died. Would the locals open the case, letting it out? Would they bring it back to Dent, Beale, & Co. along with his body? Or would it be trapped inside until the wood rotted or the metal rusted?

Ulysses lay there, sweating and miserable, his arm swollen and aching, missing London, missing the comforts of home. In an effort to make himself feel less miserable, he had changed back into his own clothing. They were close enough to civilization at this point that the crew of the ship recognized him as a Westerner. However, he had had to tear a sleeve off of his shirt because it would not cover his swollen arm. Still, he felt better in his own trousers and waistcoat.

What he would not give for a cold bath.

"I vow," he whispered, his tongue swollen and his voice unfamiliarly thick, "never again. If I live, I never want to be more than a day away from civilization. I don't mind going adventuring, but I want to spend my nights at home."

The boat heaved.

"Sea monster!" voices cried from outside the low cabin. "*Gonggong!*"

Sea monster?

Ulysses tried to raise his head, but he felt too weak. He was not merely going to die. He was going to die and be eaten by a sea monster. Up until now, he had sailed through life with very little thought, callous and carefree. But suddenly, it struck him.

Life was precious.

He had never understood that before. Life was worth living. What is more, it was worth fighting for.

"Very well," he spat, "maybe I am going to die, you son of a monster. But you are not taking anyone else's life!"

Gritting his teeth, he heaved himself from the bed, rolling sideways. His feet began to give way, and he nearly slumped to the floor. But by sheer strength of will, he managed to stand up. Stumbling to his bags, he drew forth his pistol.

❧❦

Outside, the deck was entirely deserted, except for the helmsman, who stood wide-eyed, gripping the helm. Ulysses glanced around, puzzled, even though the motion hurt his head. There had been a whole crew and many passengers, not to mention Sung Woo. Where had everyone gone?

"Where...are they?" he asked, though he was not at all sure that this is what he had managed to say.

The helmsman pointed, indicating the way below deck.

Ah. They had run, the cowards.

Ulysses straightened up and looked around. A gigantic serpent, something like the *lung*, but with eight heads, rose from the water. When it moved, the ship rocked. Ulysses nearly lost his footing and what was left of his last meal. Grasping the mast, he managed to avoid both.

He peered at the creature. Eight heads sprang from a single collarbone. Much of the creature was covered in thick, blubbery scales—which looked to be too thick for him to pierce with his pistol. He regretted not having brought a hunting rifle. There was, however, what looked like a more vulnerable spot right where the many necks met.

Unfortunately, at this range, his chance of punching through even this less-armored spot was low.

If he was going to kill it, he needed to be closer.

Ulysses turned to the helmsman and gestured. "Draw closer. If we get closer, I can kill it."

The man shook his head, too frightened. The boat rocked alarmingly.

"Turn the front of the boat toward the creature!" Ulysses cried. "Or we are all going to die!"

The boat rocked, apparently the creature's tail attempting to wrap around the ship.

Ulysses stepped forward and put his pistol to the terrified helmsman's temples.

"Look, you son of a dog," he said calmly, "the monster *might* kill you, but if I shoot, your death is certain. Turn toward the monster."

More terrified of the crazy Westerner now than of the monster, the helmsman did as requested, bringing the ship around. The main trunk of the *gonggong* drew closer.

Calm as clam shells, Ulysses stalked across the deck, leveled his pistol at the spot where the necks came together, and pulled the trigger.

The shot flew home.

With a bellow, the monster released them, sinking into the water. Whether it was dead or fleeing, Ulysses could not tell.

The helmsman shouted with pure joy.

As soon as it was clear that the ship was safe, the crew and other passengers poured out from wherever they had hidden. When the helmsman told them what had happened, speaking in a rapid rush, the others surrounded him, eyes shining with hero worship. Some knelt at his feet, bowed to the ground, or embraced his legs.

Ulysses still felt hot and clammy, but his fever had broken.

He would live.

Live?

Ulysses whooped like a schoolboy. How he loved life! Truly, it was a gift that he had not appreciated.

Mid-whoop, he froze, his eyes slowly widening.

Life. The gift he had not appreciated.

Several formerly inscrutable comments that Sung Woo had made over the last several days suddenly snapped together, becoming pellucidly clear.

Tedious? Annoying? What a dunderhead he had been!

He turned to the helmsman, gesturing with his spent pistol. "Go back upstream."

"Upstream?" the man cried. He gestured at the others around them. "I cannot. The other passengers will object!"

Ulysses held up his pistol. "I just saved you all."

The man grunted and rushed to do as he had asked. Whether this was out of gratitude or whether he thought that the pistol might have another shot it in, Ulysses did not inquire.

❦

He stood by the bow of the ship as it sailed upstream, his nails sinking into the wooden rail, listening for the sound he was afraid he would not hear.

After about two hours, there it was! The piercing wail was weaker than when they had passed on their way downstream, but Holy Jesus, it was there.

"Sung Woo," Ulysses handed the other man his pistol, "See that they don't leave without me." Then, leaning close, he whispered, "It's not loaded."

Sung Woo nodded, resigned.

Ulysses leapt over the side, splashing through the waist-high water. Coming to the shore, he ran up the steep slope, leaping from rock to rock. It took him nearly ten minutes to reach the top of the low hill.

There, lying on the bare rock atop a thin, soiled blanket, wailing as if her life depended upon it—which, in fact, it had—lay a tiny, naked infant.

Looking down into the face of the tiny baby girl, Ulysses thought it was the sweetest sight he had ever seen.

"How could I have overlooked the glory that is infants?" he asked, pulling off his jacket, wrapping the tiny child in it, and lifting her into his arms. "My precious one!"

⟫⟪

Some months later, Ulysses Prospero disembarked in Calcutta along with the Wardian case containing the *hongchalung*. His father and two of his brothers waited on the docks.

"Well done, my son," the Dread Magician Prospero lay a comforting hand on the shoulder of his youngest son. "You have done your country a great service."

Ulysses, his arms full of a bundle wrapped in a blanket, replied, "And China, too, as I understand it. Our selling them opium is doing nobody any good. I fear what we as an empire have done to the young men of that nation will weigh heavily upon our souls one day."

"And not just as an empire," his father said sadly. "Two of your older brothers hold positions of trust in the East India Company. Part of this is their doing."

"Is that why you sent me?" Ulysses asked, surprised. "You felt our family was at fault?"

Prospero nodded his head solemnly.

"Well, I'm glad you did. I needed to be dug out. It was a fantastic place, Father. The noise, the color, the food! But crazy, too! Most of it in the least afternoonified. Do you know that I learned that they consider girl children such a burden—due to the need for dowries—that they kill them at birth, and then they don't have enough women for their men to marry! It's madness!"

His father stroked his beard. "What else have you learned during your journeys?"

"Two things," his son replied solemnly. "That home is far more precious than I had realized, but that life is the most precious thing of all."

Prospero raised an eyebrow, impressed. "You have done well, and I will keep my promise. Have you decided what you want in a staff?"

"Indeed," Ulysses replied with a grin. "I took a vow. I don't mind adventures, but I never want to be more than a day away from a hot meal and a bath. Can you make me a way of getting home quickly?"

"Certainly, I..." A frown creased Prospero's brow as the bundle in Ulysses's arms moved. "What is that you are carrying, my son?"

"Ah, this?" Ulysses's face broke into a huge smile. He drew back the blanket, revealing the sweet face of the sleeping little girl. "This is my new ward, Baozang. It means treasure."

"A ward! That is a bold step!" Prospero gazed at the sleeping little girl. His eyes twinkling, he held out the sapphire-topped, teak length of the *Staff of Transportation*, which could return its bearer to anywhere the staff had touched in an instant. "Here, son. This is yours now. It will allow you to do exactly as you have asked. I will make myself a new staff."

Ulysses' face lit up. "That is a princely gift indeed, and I will cherish it." Waking with a stretch, the tiny girl reached for the staff, cooing. He gazed down at her, his face filled with fondness. "But Baozang is my greatest treasure of all."

THE FIRE-PROOF MAN IS DEAD

JAMES CHAMBERS

From the New Alexandria Post,
September 9th, Evening Edition:

POSEIDON'S PRINCESS RESCUES FERRY PASSENGERS AND CREW

*A mystery woman saved dozens of lives, including
a thirty-person tour group from the International
Phrenological Conference, when a steam engine
explosion set the Paumonok Sound Ferry to sinking at
3:15 p.m. this afternoon. The explosion punched a hole
in the hull below the water line and drew the attention
of nearby boaters and fishermen, who mounted imme-
diate efforts to aid the endangered passengers. Many
quickly became trapped underwater due to the ferry's
rapid sinking. Boaters reported the intervention of an
extraordinary, as-yet-unidentified woman who swam
through the choppy sound with what one fisherman
called "the speed of a shark." Mistaking her for an
overboard passenger, boaters attempted to fish her
out only to witness her dive beneath the ferry moments before it miraculously rose and righted itself.
Divers, attempting to free passengers trapped
below, surfaced with incredible reports of the woman*

apparently breathing water and holding the ferry afloat—an incredible intervention that allowed all crew and passengers, many of whom had been submerged, to abandon ship for the safety of nearby craft, thus avoiding a disaster that could have exceeded that of the infamous Canarsee Strait ferry crash. One diver reported that the mysterious "Queen of the Sea" smiled and waved to him...

⊰❧⊱

"They're roasting alive in there—and we just stand here?"

At the edge of a wall of infernal heat, Digly Nohaptong gaped at the conflagration consuming the Hopewell Ladies Garments Factory. Super-heated glass shattered as flames licked the windows and smoke columns unraveled from the roof, smearing the sky above the Muhheakantuck River. At street level, the New Alexandria Fire Brigade worked steam-powered pumps to hose water from hydrants and tanks onto the burning building while the Bucket Volunteers Corps conveyed river water via human chain. To either side of Digly stood Ed Kobeski and Wilbur Smithers, holding their young colleague back from the factory's main doors, engulfed in fire. The three-man Rescue Aid Auxiliary Crew awaited survivors who so far hadn't emerged.

"We go in there, we die, no doubt about it," Wilbur said.

"It's a hard choice, but it's wise," Ed said. "At least here, we're ready to help anyone who makes it out. Once the firefighters get the burn under control, they'll go in with protective gear."

Digly shrugged free of his partners' grip but kept his distance from the fire. "For heaven's sake, they're all women and children in there!"

Ed nodded, his expression grave. "It's all that penny-pinching bastard Hopewell's fault. Ought to be in the stocks down at Henderson Square, you ask me."

"My sister worked there two months last summer," Wilbur said. "Hopewell nailed shut the emergency exits to keep his employees from sneaking out for coffees or whatnot on company time. The city should've shut him down ages ago, but he greases too many palms."

In response to a piercing shriek from inside, Digly stepped toward the building.

"Easy." Ed renewed his hold on Digly's arm. "Waiting here is a hell of a way to start your duty, but it's part of the job—and it's better than dying on your first day. You want to get in there, save people, show what you're made of, I know, but we go in, they'll just have to dig three more graves."

"I feel useless," Digly said.

Thirty yards down the block, a crowd gathered behind a barricade established by New Alexandria's finest.

"They're so... quiet and calm," Digly said.

"They're waiting for loved ones to appear," Wilbur said.

"There has to be something we can do," Digly said.

His partners frowned. A knot of wood exploded, launching a burning coal over their heads. The three men ducked.

"Fellas! Hey, fellas!" A white-haired man in a threadbare suit and shoes with loose soles hailed them. "You're the Rescue Aid Auxiliary ain't you? Why ain't you rescuing no one?"

"Get back, old man!" Ed said.

"Anyone sets foot in that building will roast alive," Wilbur said.

"Come on, now, fellas, there's women and children in there! You can't stand around and let 'em perish, can you?"

The old man jogged toward the doors. With cries of protest, Ed and Wilbur grabbed at him, but he slipped through their grasp, shoved Digly aside, and disappeared into the flames.

"Suicide!" Wilbur said.

"Who is he?" Digly said.

"A crazy man," Ed said.

"A dead man more likely," Wilbur said.

The fire surged. Walls collapsed and crashed. Fresh screams followed. Then the old man appeared in the doorway with two girls slung across his shoulders. Snakes of flame nibbled at his clothes. Soot blackened his face. He laid the girls on the ground then raced back into the factory. The stunned Rescue Crew dragged the girls clear of the heat. They wiped ash from their faces and offered them water while they examined their injuries and burns.

The old man returned, carrying two more girls and leading a group of six women. All of them gasped and coughed in the fresh air as they stumbled away from the burning building. Ash and soot painted their faces. The old man brought out three more groups of women and children, and the Rescue Crew provided them with water, bandages, and balms. Teary reunions began by the police line as onlookers embraced their rescued loved ones.

The sixth time the old man entered the building the front wall collapsed after him.

Cries of terror rose from the crowd. Tense moments passed, during which the fire brigade finally contained the flames, sparing neighboring buildings, but the man did not return.

"Do you think he's dead?" Digly said.

"He's got to be superhuman to have survived going in there at all," Ed said.

"No way out now," Wilbur said.

A roar of triumph rose from the crowd. The three men spun on their heels. Several yards down from the ruined door, burning lumber stirred and tumbled as the old man leapt clear of the fire, cradling a girl no more than 10 years old in his sooty arms. She clung to him as he rushed her to the Rescue Crew. They cleaned her, salved her burns, and tended her wounds until her mother appeared to scoop her up. The woman cried with joy and thanked the old man, kissing his ashy face.

The morning edition of the *New Alexandria Post* boasted the headline "Fire-Proof Man Saves Youngest Dressmaker." The whole city buzzed with the story.

⇒⟫⟪⇐

"He entered the fire with no protective gear and emerged unhurt?"

Left eyebrow raised, Morris Garvey leaned on his desk, surrounded by stacks of rumpled files, piles of newspapers, and schematics for new machines upon which he'd scribbled copious notes. The din rising from Morris Garvey's Steam Sweeps and Machinations Sundry's many workshops and laboratories drifted into the office, a dampened but unmistakable background buzz of science, invention, and industry.

"Six times, Mr. Garvey. He saved most of the factory workers."

"Very interesting, indeed, Digly. I applaud your thoughtfulness in telling me almost as much as I applaud the fine rescue work you did yesterday."

"I didn't rescue anyone. My boss wouldn't let us go in."

"You would've burned to death if you had. Staying clear meant you were on hand to give critical first aid to the factory workers the old man brought out."

"Not how I thought Rescue Crew would be."

"Reality rarely equals our ideals. The right choice often is the hardest one. You'll learn that fast now you've outgrown my Sundry Troubleshooters. Grown-up life isn't only about getting mixed up in the middle of things and reporting back about it."

"I can't say I don't miss that."

"You did fine work for me and Machinations Sundry, Dig. You and all the other street urchins and former chimney sweeps of your generation. You helped me more than you know."

Digly smiled. "Not like we had much choice after you put us all out of work with your steam-powered sweeps."

"That's progress. Society matures just as we all do and must make our fortune in this world."

"Fortune's what I think that old man had in mind."

"How so?"

"After the survivors left, I hung around to watch the NAFB wrestle the fire. They mostly doused it by midnight, but parts of the factory still burned when the old man came back. I was studying the collapsed door frame, wondering how to prevent such structural failure in the future when he walked right into the wreckage. Before I could raise an alarm, he vanished into what remained of the flames. Minutes later he came out carrying a *safe*."

"You mean a cashbox?"

Digly shook his head. "A five-foot-tall safe, parts of it still glowing hot."

Garvey eased back in his chair, thoughtful. "An entire safe?"

"Like it weighed no more than the littlest dressmaker. He ran off with it into the night. I reported it, but no one believed me. Ed and Wilbur accused me of sour grapes. But that's not true, not one bit."

"I know it's not, Dig. Your reputation with me is sound."

"Why would he go back for that except for, well...?"

"For the money? Maybe."

A knock at the door interrupted the conversation, and an athletic girl of fifteen came into the office. One of Garvey's Sundry

Troubleshooters, she wore a yellow dress with a leather waistcoat and a black cap, her blonde hair tucked up beneath it.

"Mr. Garvey, sir, I have some news."

"Yes? Go ahead, Sheila, don't keep us in suspense."

"It's the Fire-Proof Man, sir, the hero of the factory fire. He's dead."

✦✦✦

Garvey led Digly up a stairway canted precariously from the wall. The building, a relic tenement from an early construction boom, slouched like a grandmother curled beneath a shawl. On the fifth floor, police officers guided the two men to apartment 5D, where a third guarded the open door. A trio of reporters at the corridor's end, notebooks in hand, press credentials pinned to their suitcoats, rippled with excitement at Garvey's arrival.

"Mr. Garvey, what's your role here?" one said.

"How can a man be fire-proof, Garvey?" another said.

Garvey waved to them as he entered the apartment. Inspector Daniel Matheson greeted him, and Garvey introduced him to Digly. The corpse of the "Fire-Proof Man" lay on the floor in front of a tattered wing-back chair, sightless eyes staring at the cracked, moldy ceiling.

"Not that it isn't always a treat to see you, Morris, but this hardly seems a case for your talent," Matheson said in his rolling Texas drawl.

"I hope you're right, but Mr. Nohaptong and I may have information helpful to you." Garvey gestured at the body. "How'd he die?"

Matheson sighed, lifted his Stetson, and smoothed his hair. "Won't be a hundred percent until the coroner reports, but it looks like he was conked on the head several times."

"I wouldn't be surprised," Digly said. "The factory practically fell down around him."

"How did you reach your conclusion, Inspector?" Garvey said.

"Lumps on his scalp." Matheson handed Garvey a pair of paper gloves from his pocket. "About five good-sized goose eggs and a depression in his skull, possibly a fracture. Could be a concussion. Maybe blood trapped on the brain. Seen it a few times, fellows thrown by bulls or kicked by horses, feel a little woozy, but then they drop dead a day later."

After slipping on the gloves, Garvey knelt and pushed his fingers through the dead man's thin hair, touching his scalp. He felt barely any lumps or depressions.

"His scalp is smooth," he said.

"What?" Matheson knelt and checked for himself. "Well, I'll be. I examined his head not an hour ago and felt big lumps, clear as day. Maybe the swelling went down?"

"Dead men don't heal." Garvey stood and yanked off the gloves. "Regardless, you ought to hear what Mr. Nohaptong witnessed at the scene of the fire."

"That so? Well, spill it, young fella," Matheson said.

Digly explained about the safe to the incredulous Inspector Matheson.

"Well, now, that sure puts a different saddle on this horse. Only one problem, though. We haven't found any safe here. More important, what did our dead man want with it?"

From the New Alexandria Post,
September 18th, Morning Edition:

RUNAWAY BALLOON! FLYING FOX MAN SAVES CHILDREN

An astounding airborne rescuer saved the lives of three children trapped in a runaway hot-air balloon during yesterday's East Side Harvest Market. The children, ages 6, 9, and 11, set aloft alone when anchor ropes snapped as they awaited schoolmates boarding the gondola of a balloon ride sponsored by Maury's Tall Building and Construction Corporation. Groundworkers failed to regain control of the balloon when gusts pushed its dangling lines beyond their reach. Only the arrival of what onlookers described as a "human flying fox" or a "gargantuan bat" prevented the balloon lofting out to sea on the high easterly winds. The Flying Fox Man reportedly glided through the air, arms and legs outstretched to extend a brown cloak like the membranous wings of mammalian gliders. Landing in the gondola, the Fox Man took control of the balloon, piloting it on a descent that ended safely in Henderson Square, interrupting a public demonstration of phrenology at the Morgan Gazebo conducted by the International Phrenological Conference. After anchoring the balloon and freeing the children, the Fox Man climbed a nearby tree, launched himself into the sky, and glided away before officers of the NAPD arrived...

⊰⊱

Garvey shivered as a morgue attendant wheeled a gurney to the center of the room at Inspector Matheson's request. A woman stood by, grim and quiet, brunette with streaks of gray, wearing a neat blue dress and a tweed waistcoat, wire-rim spectacles perched on her nose. The attendant peeled the sheet back from the body, revealing a middle-aged woman with lusterless brown hair and thin lips, pallid flesh, her eyes closed. Garvey flashed Matheson a curious glance.

"Meet 'Poseidon's Princess,'" Matheson said. "Our homegrown 'Queen of the Sea' collapsed on Grandlocke Street after halting a runaway Peruvian cargo ship before it rammed the piers. NAPD officers recognized her from the ferry accident. They tried to save her, but she died on the spot. Two hours ago, her skull bore unmistakable signs of blunt force trauma. Now it's smooth as a baby's bottom. Sound familiar?"

"Like our Fire-Proof Man," Garvey said.

"My thoughts exactly. Now, Morris, bear with me, but all those vanishing bumps got me thinking, and, well, I asked Ms. Canterbury here for her opinion. She's up from Baltimore for the International Phrenological Conference—"

"Phrenology!?" Garvey scowled." You're wasting my time, Dan."

"Heh, I knew you'd say that, but hear us out, is all I ask. You know very well you and I ride the same trail when it comes to phrenology. It's bunk with no place in police work—uh, no offense there, Ms. Canterbury—but this maybe ain't what it seems."

Unaffected by Matheson's description of her work, Eliza Canterbury smiled. "The good Inspector is correct to consider a phrenological explanation. Phrenology is often misunderstood, Mr. Garvey. The shape of one's skull holds great influence over one's personality, thinking, and abilities. The contours and irregularities—the bumps, depressions, and ridges—all hold potential to unlock the worst in people, an excellent aid for identifying criminal personalities."

"None of that is accurate, scientific, or true," Garvey said.

Matheson chuckled. "Play nice, Morris."

"A rarely discussed aspect of phrenology, however, is the potential for these features to unlock one's greatest strengths and most noble urges. Perhaps you're familiar with the case of Lucia Gomez, Martyr of the Rio Grande Flood?" Canterbury said.

"Of course, and I've no doubt as to Miss Gomez's heroics during the flood, but the feats attributed to her—dragging fifty workers to safety with a single rope? Moving boulders to dam the rushing waters? The stuff of legends, nothing more."

"Did you know boards from washed-away houses struck her head prior to her incredible interventions?"

"What does that matter?"

"Witnesses said several boards hit her in succession from different directions. The waters pulled her under. They assumed her lost. Only later did she commit her marvelous life-saving acts. It's my belief the blows to her head altered the shape of her skull and unlocked vast powers within her."

"Coke and ash," Garvey said.

"Don't be so swift to dismiss it," Matheson said. "I still lived down that way at the time of that flood. More than one fella I trust backs up those stories, and the Gomez woman dropped dead a few days afterward."

"Are you seriously suggesting our recent wondrous oddities achieved greatness after knocks on the head?"

"Like Miss Gomez," Canterbury said, "they too have both died soon after exhibiting their powers. What if once their bumps and bruises begin to heal, they can no longer contain or put back in storage the power set loose inside them, leaving it to overwhelm and kill them?"

Garvey sighed. "Nonsense to bolster a branch of pseudoscience that belongs on the same trash heap as spontaneous generation, bloodletting, and ear candling."

"That's a matter of opinion," Canterbury said.

"It most certainly isn't. We're through here, Dan."

Shaking his head, Garvey left the room. Matheson hurried after him down the corridor.

"Now, wait a minute, Morris," Matheson said. "You set all this in motion, after all."

Garvey stopped dead. "And how did *I* do that?"

"You and that Digly kid told me the Fire-Proof Man stole Hopewell's safe. Well, we recovered the safe from an alley near his apartment. Aside from money, all he took was a New Alexandria flag, the very first ever flown above City Hall. Hopewell's great-great-grandfather sewed it, and the city gifted it back to him. We've got no idea what the Fire-Proof Man did with it, though. Equally intriguing, it turns out Princess Bathing Beauty robbed the Paumonok Ferry of a collection of paintings by our city's very own Damian Whitley, shipping from an estate on Two Forks Island to the port for overseas transport. Divers confirmed the shipment's gone from the wreck. Who could've taken it but this aquatic mystery woman? That ain't all. I'm keeping it quiet, but last night some lowlife stole the jeweled lenses from the gaslight atop the Broxcorton Building. That light's been dark since before I settled in this city because the access hatch rusted shut and lightning strikes fused the metal. Only way someone got up there was, well, wild as it sounds, by flying—like our Flying Fox Man. My bet says he turns up dead within the next few days."

"Well then shouldn't you be out looking for him while he's still breathing rather than wasting time with fairy tales?"

"I've got half a dozen men searching right now. Listen, I know you don't dwell on it, but this city counts on you. New Alexandria wouldn't be what it is today without Morris Garvey's steam-powered chimney sweeps and half a dozen other gadgets you've invented. Half the people in this city are alive thanks to your ingenuity heading off catastrophe. Voodoo. The Cult of Bast. Contaminated reservoirs. Magical assassination attempts. You saved us time and again. My gut says we got another big dust-up brewing. These flash-in-the-pan heroes are part of it. All I ask is you give it some serious thought."

"What makes you think I haven't?"

Upon returning to his office at Machinations Sundry, Garvey found Digly Nohaptong waiting, an edge to his stance.

"What is it, Dig?"

"A man threw himself in front of the Roald Street evening trolley to stop it running over a child, and... well, the trolley car exploded when it struck him. Parts everywhere! Thank the heavens, the car had just started its route and carried no passengers. The conductor only survived because the man caught him—one-handed, no less—as he flew out the window."

"Another mystery hero."

"Except I know this one, and he's no hero. Brannon Short. Used to shake down me and the boys for pocket change. Now a brute bully's got power like that? It's not right, sir."

"Any chance he stole something in the confusion?"

"I don't see how. The crowd practically threw him a parade. People gathered up parts for souvenirs. Not even the driver seemed very concerned about the demolished trolley car. They're all far too infatuated with these fire-proof men and sea queens if you ask me. They hustled Short into McTaggart's Pub for a celebratory drink."

"When was this?"

"Only as long ago as it took me to run here from Roald Street."

"Excellent. There's still a chance for us to act. But we must move fast!"

➳➳❦❦

The pair watched McTaggart's until closing time when Brannon Short stumbled from the door, a drunken, off-key song springing from his lips. Several other men exited with him, singing along to finish the chorus then going their separate ways.

Garvey and Digly followed Short, who doubled back after a few blocks and returned to Roald Street, where trolley wreckage remained strewn on the road. He kicked an iron gear and sent it clattering into the quiet. Another kick sent a piece of pipe clanging after it so hard it bounced once and embedded itself in a brick wall.

"Is he trying to wake the dead?" Digly said.

"He's raising a ruckus to make sure no one's around," Garvey said. "The trolley route normally starts here. Even at this hour, there should be a crowd and street vendors. But until the Transit Authority cleans up the street, protocol reroutes cars to the next stop, Booker Street."

"Which means everyone has gone down there to catch the trolley."

"Leaving Roald Street abandoned."

"Are you saying he wrecked the trolley to brush off the crowd?"

The crash and tinkle of breaking glass answered for Garvey.

Across the road, Short hummed as he punched a shop window, shattering it, the third in a line of broken glass plates. He punched a fourth then moved on to the shop of Miller and Miller Imported Curios, where he cracked his knuckles before ripping the ironclad shop door off its hinges. He entered. Minutes later a second-floor window erupted with shards of glass and wood splinters. A black box followed, arcing through the air then thudding in the middle of the street, cracking cobblestones amidst trolley debris. Short leapt from the smashed-out window and landed beside the battered safe.

"Another thief!" Digly said.

"Shh," Garvey said.

Short made a fist of his right hand then blew on his knuckles. Sporting a wide grin, he punched the center of the safe door, plunging his fist through squealing steel and into the compromised container. Its contents clattered inside until Short brought out his hand, holding a wooden box. He popped the lid, smiled, then snapped the box shut, and jogged away, downtown. Garvey and Digly tailed him along a circuitous route all the way to Meer's Gardens, a neighborhood lined with rows of neglected brownstones.

Short climbed the stoop of a sooty house and let himself in.

"Now what? Digly said.

"We watch."

Morris jogged to the house, Digly alongside him. They searched the exterior, as dull and characterless as all the other homes on the block. Garvey led them along a narrow alley between the brownstone and its neighbor into a small, cobblestone yard overgrown with weeds. Dim light from the brownstone windows fell upon the pavers. Voices came from inside. Garvey and Digly kept close to the shadows and spied in through the windows.

Short sat at a square table with three chairs in a dingy dining room. He held his head in his hands and moaned. The wooden box sat open and empty on the table. The shadow of another person fell upon it, and then he stepped into view, a pair of embossed leather gloves clutched in his hands. He wore a finely tailored outfit. His gaunt, aquiline features cut sharp lines in the harsh glare of the gaslight.

Short groaned and shook his head.

"I know it hurts, Mr. Short." Window glass muffled the man's voice. "Perhaps if we'd had more time to prepare your body would better attune to the power, but we needed to move fast while the phrenology conference provided us cover. The greater the power, the higher the price. If you survive the next few hours, you'll consider it a bargain."

Slamming a fist on the table, Short growled.

"Do something, Samir!"

"There's nothing I can do. I explained the risks. You accepted them with the power and the money as I accepted the commission that led me to employ you."

Short surged to his feet, knocking over his chair and upending the table. The wooden box flew off and cracked against the wall. The aching brute raised his fists.

"You knew!" he cried. "You *knew* this would happen and tricked me."

Retreating, Samir stumbled against the overturned table, reaching into his pocket.

Short snarled and seized him in a bear hug. The thin man's feet left the ground.

Samir grunted and wheezed. He wriggled one wiry arm free, drawing from his pocket a steel doctor's hammer, its wedge-shaped head gleaming, and then he struck Short three times on his skull. The strongman howled and released his grip. He and Samir fell to the floor.

Short rolled onto his back, clawing at his temples. Samir struggled to catch his breath.

"Let's get in there now!"

Garvey held Digly fast by the shoulder. "No, wait."

"Wait? For what?!"

Glass shattered inside the house. A third figure appeared in the dining room. Agonized, Short ignored the newcomer, but Samir's eyes widened. He scrambled to his feet, still gasping.

"Now!" Garvey said.

Unleashed, Digly vaulted the back steps two at a time and hammered his weight against the back door, which crashed inward with a bang. Garvey followed him inside, into the dining room, where Eliza Canterbury stood with a revolver leveled at Samir.

"Watch it, she's armed!" Digly said.

"Lower your weapon, Ms. Canterbury," Garvey said.

"Garvey! You insufferable skeptic! Stay where you are!"

Canterbury fired a single shot into the floor between her and Garvey. Wood splinters fountained. Short yowled and rolled onto his side.

"Why are you even here, Garvey?" Canterbury said.

"I'm here because of Lucia Gomez."

"What has got to do with anything?"

"When I told you I knew of her story, I didn't tell you I'd already investigated it through contacts in Texas, who shared with me that she too engaged in an odd theft soon after rescuing the flood victims. Authorities covered it up to protect her heroic legend. Interesting knowledge in its own right. But what positively fascinated me was that you were also in Texas at that time and consulted on her autopsy, promoting your positive phrenology bunk. You didn't share that with Inspector Matheson, did you?"

"So what? It's no secret. I've done nothing wrong. Not like Samir, who doomed those poor, naïve people he made into heroes so they would rob for him." She directed her pistol at Samir. "I'll bloody well have that Mallet now, Samir."

"I'll never give it to you," Samir said.

"Don't think I won't kill you to take it."

Canterbury cocked the revolver's hammer.

"All this over a hammer?" Digly said.

"Not just a hammer," Canterbury said. "The Spurzheim Mallet, forged by phrenology's greatest advocate, tuned to the vibrations of the human mind, a tool for unleashing the greatest powers hidden in the human psyche. I've been chasing it around the world for years."

Digly raised an eyebrow at Garvey. "You said there's nothing to this phrenology bunk."

"The Mallet's not what it appears, Dig. It's a magic artifact and deadly powerful but it has nothing to do with reading the bumps on your noggin. Now, Canterbury, listen, put the gun down. You're in over your head."

"I'll shoot you too, both of you," she said.

"No, you won't," Samir said.

He struck the Mallet against the floor. It created a hollow thump and rang with a steely vibration that filled the room like the hum of tuning fork.

In response, Short thrust himself to his hands and knees, bellowing in pain and fury.

He staggered to his feet and charged Canterbury. She fired her gun three times, each shot passing through Short's torso, none slowing the brute. He grabbed her gun hand, crushing bone and steel in his grip. Canterbury shrieked. Short gripped her throat and squeezed, snapping her neck. He cast the body aside and grabbed for Samir, who ducked beneath his reach. Blind with rage, Short flailed his fists. Samir dodged them, struck the side of Short's head with the Mallet, and then retreated to a corner. The ring of the hammer filled Short's skull. Wailing, he arched his back and clawed at his head—then collapsed to the floor, dead.

Garvey leapt over the corpse.

The reedy Samir turned, the Mallet in one hand, a dagger in the other.

Garvey slapped the dagger to the floor and grabbed Samir's other wrist, deflecting the Mallet aimed at his head. The two men grappled, but soon Garvey overpowered him. He and Digly tore Samir's fine jacket and used it to bind him. From one of the pockets, Garvey fished out a chunk of Carnelian carved with the face of a cat.

"Is that real?" Digly said. "Does it mean...?"

"Yes. Samir works for the Cult of Bast."

"How did you know?"

"The robberies and rescues each represented one of the four prime elements. Fire at the factory, water for the ferry, air for the Broxcorton crystals, and finally...," Garvey opened the wooden box on the table, revealing leather gloves, "...gloves that once belonged to the architect who designed New Alexandria's underground gas and water conduits. It represented earth. The Cult hoped to use their deep, elemental connections to the city in a magical assault. They've wanted revenge ever since I thwarted their attempt to spark an international incident here."

"But the Mallet?"

"That I didn't suspect until Canterbury turned up. Even most phrenologists consider it a myth. By whatever means it grants such amazing powers, I doubt it's due to dings in the skull. You heard it sing, saw its effect when Samir struck the floor rather than Short's head. I'd guess it infuses magical energy via vibrational alterations that realign the body's own power, ultimately too much for a human to contain for very long. The bumps on the head simply structure the ritual or perhaps let one program the powers assigned."

"So, what now?"

"Now, Dig, you fetch a cop and get word to Matheson. We need this house staked out. If I'm not mistaken, Samir's employers will soon be coming by to collect their prizes."

✦

Four hours later, with Samir and three members of the Cult of Bast in custody, Matheson and Garvey regrouped at Police Headquarters.

"Any word on our flying fox man?" Garvey said.

Matheson shook his head. "Maybe he got lucky and survived." He plucked up the Mallet from his desk. "This really creates powers with taps on the skull?"

"Not exactly," Garvey said. "It uses vibrations. To make it sing, you strike something with it. A skull works as well as anything else."

"Harder the head, the better, I suppose. Real shame about Ms. Canterbury. She should've been less hard-headed about phrenology and taken a few lessons from you and science. What do you think she wanted to do with the Mallet?"

"I'm sure I don't know, Dan."

"Well, one thing we do know for sure is New Alexandria owes you again, my friend."

"I live here, Dan. This is my home, my city, as much as yours or anyone else's. It's made all of my successes possible. There's nowhere else on Earth I'd rather live. This city doesn't owe me a blasted thing."

THE GARRISON HOLDS

STEVE RZASA

I WANT NOTHING TO DO WITH THE WAR BETWEEN BRITAIN AND THESE United States. My calling binds me to remain aloof from the conflict, as shambolic as it is.

That does not mean I will stand idly by as men spill each other's blood over trivialities.

Word reaches me at the *Camden Light* newspaper, early in the morn of the twenty-third of September, 1814, of impending doom for a small fishing village.

"Tobias!" Duncan cannot decide whether to shout or whisper my name outside my bedroom door, even as he pounds with his fist. His muffled cry is no less urgent. "Tobias, *wake up!*"

I slip from bed, don a pair of trousers stained with printer's ink, and fling the door aside. My apprentice, blond curls in disarray and set aglow by the wavering light of his candle, stares at me, as awake as if it were midday. "There's a barge left Castine not long ago. British soldiers, armed to the teeth. They've made landfall at Saturday Cove!"

Such news will do our militia no good. Saturday Cove is twelve miles up the road toward Belfast, a half hour even by their fastest horses—and the bulk of the volunteers are on foot. Duncan knows I am the only one capable of reaching the village in time.

He stares at the medallion hanging from a chain around my neck.

I tuck it into my shirt and reach for my long coat, made in highwayman's fashion with a tall collar useful for obscuring my face. A dark kerchief tied atop my head completes the disguise. "Is the militia alerted?"

"They are. A boat's put out into the bay with a handful aboard. More are gathering by the meeting house."

"That is the best they can accomplish."

I take the back stairwell of the *Light*'s two-story wooden structure, stepping lightly into the yard between neighboring buildings. Would that I had more time, I would have preferred to make my departure from a more concealed location, such as among the elm trees a few blocks distant.

The medallion exudes cold like the surface of Megunticook Lake in a deep freeze. Its mere touch lances through my chest. *Breathe.* I take two steps and concentrate my thoughts on the eagles that frequent Camden Harbor, majestic wings carrying them aloft.

I soar into the dawn.

Mist shrouds the inlets and clings between the treetops. Fields are covered in green gauze. The landscape passes in a blur, as wind whips around me, yet does not touch my flesh. The medallion does not grant me true wings; rather, it alters what the scientist Cavendish deems the gravitational constant.

Thus, I can fly a hundredfold faster than a man can walk.

I grasp my pocket watch, feeling the seconds tick by. Saturday Cove lay but a few hundred yards away.

The boom of musket fire tells me I am too late to prevent the skirmish.

I dive into the forest, skirting pines and brushing needles into emerald clouds. My landing tosses gold and crimson leaves. Saturday Cove is a motley collection of sturdy cabins. The tranquility of the village's morning is juxtaposed with fishing craft aflame. A pall of smoke hangs over the houses, blown hither and yon between them. Soldiers in red uniforms fire into the windows with rigid precision, the crash of broken glass their reward. Their opponents, however undisciplined, are unparalleled marksmen. A British infantryman takes a hit to the shoulder.

I hear the hammer of a musket drawn back, a few yards to my left.

I can see a palisade in my mind's eye, a long fence of towering wooden posts whose ends have been sharpened to imposing teeth. Such a flight of fancy is fuel for the medallion's influence.

The musket discharges. There follows a spark, then another, then yet another, as gunfire from around the village smashes into the unseen wall I have erected. Flattened discs of lead litter the ground along the line, for the musket balls have entered the wall just far enough to be drawn to earth by a force of gravity many times what a man experiences when he jumps from his horse.

The trees and smoke provide perfect concealment as I hurry along the edge of the forest, casting barricades between the two sets of combatants. I catch sight of a woman wiping her hands on an apron, flour following in a dust cloud, as she berates two British fleeing from her house. Another pair of soldiers accost a young man, bereft of weaponry, with bayonets held ready to skewer his bowels.

I flick my fingers and a giant hand conjured by my imagination, though invisible to the naked eye, plows them away from their intended victim. He takes advantage and runs for cover.

Shouts from the water's edge draw my attention. There lies the barge, soldiers maneuvering a dark object on its prow—a swivel cannon. More shouts. Fishermen emerge from hiding, muskets and fowling pieces at the ready, determined to charge the withdrawing and bloodied British.

The fuse lights on the cannon.

I leap to the roof of a house, its windows broken and interior silent, crunching onto tiles as the cannon's *boom* thunders across the cove. There is no time to provide a wall strong enough. Instead, I see the metal curve of a barrel's hoop.

The cannonball veers from its trajectory toward the fishermen and embeds itself in the wall of the house.

Elation warms me against the morning frost as the British withdraw, their boats filled with pilfered goods but also stained with blood. The villagers cheer. Taunts follow the repelled invaders into the bay.

No one has seen my interference, perched as I am above the smoke and mist. I make ready to fly off before the morning sun can burn the concealment away.

A crushing blow hurls me into the tree line.

I smash from trunk to trunk, leaving broken branches in my wake. I cannot right myself. Thoughts are a jumble, and thus, the medallion's effectiveness neutralized. I pray the Lord to clear my mind of fear and confusion. Bits of the fifty-first Psalm spill from my lips.

The ground harkens.

I envision a pillow stuffed with feathers. It cushions my fall, though I fear I shall spend the remainder of the day counting contusions. If, of course, I survive my assailant.

He floats to the ground as gently as one of the myriad leaves I've knocked asunder, a wraith clad in the gray of storm clouds— breeches, coat, cloak, and all. His face is covered by a featureless mask as if he is hiding behind the morning mist. The breeze off the cove rustles a wild tangle of chestnut curls, incongruous with the foreboding visage.

"It heartens me to see you have not lost your zeal for your calling, Tobias." Zebulon Fitch removes his mask. He is all smiles and flinty brown eyes. Would that I had met him on a New England road, passersby on horseback, I would have exchanged friendly greetings with so pleasant a fellow.

"I knew you would respond," he says. "What better way to draw you into action than by threatening lives, be they on either side of a conflict."

"Stand down, Zebulon." I feel faintly absurd, demanding his surrender whilst I force myself upright upon trembling elbow. "The Ashen have no claim to this region."

"I was under the impression my brothers had no desire to rule this land. Influencing the outcome of the war between England and America, though, is far more enticing."

He makes no sense. "The war is already coming to a close. Have you not heard? Ambassadors from Washington are in Ghent as we speak, discussing peace terms with their peers."

"Peace terms." Fitch chuckles. "The English masses cry out for the conquest of these states. Have not their soldiers sacked the capitol? Far safer for John Quincy Adams and his ilk in Europe than the smoldering ruins of this failed experiment. Yankee Doodle has gone topsy turvy. If you think the Ashen will stand idly by as this opportunity to steer the course of history passes, you are more the dolt than I ever imagined."

"If you're to kill me, be done with it. I do not fear death. My eternal home awaits."

"And here I assumed we would lack an opportunity for your tiresome preaching." Fitch shakes his head. "Let this serve as a warning: the Ashen are in New England now. Interfere with our plans, and more than you, the vaunted representative of the Garrison, will die. You know our ways—so-called 'natural' disasters are much preferred to the revelation of our respective societies and the powers our medallions share."

The whole time, I have marshalled my strength and let the medallion's power built until I fear my breath will expel in icy feathers. I lash out, nothing but the world's greatest hammer in my mind, but Fitch is as agile as a fox hunted by the hound. He leaps. The tree behind him explodes in splinters.

"A promise is a promise, Tobias!" Fitch dons his mask and soars away, lost among the clouds.

Whilst I am left to pick my way home, slowly, minding the forest lest I am seen by my waking countrymen.

⊰⊱⊱⊰

"You came out at the little end of the horn on this one." Duncan hands me another cold, wet cloth. "It was a snare."

"Yes. And I the willing rabbit." I wince as the cold touches my skin. Bruises aplenty, indeed. "But his intent was not to kill me. It was a warning."

"A warning of what, though?" Duncan leans against our press. The stench of printer's ink fills the *Camden Light*'s office, mingling with the aroma of paper. Shelves line the walls, filled with past issues and blank sheets. "That he will cause an earthquake? Hardly the stuff to make the British army cower."

"Not in the least. No, this would have to be more direct. Something to fan flames of anger against our country."

"Or he could be mistaken. The Ashen are not known for sharing their plans. If he had wanted British soldiers dead, he could have shot them himself and cast blame for the deed on another man. That raid this morning might have been his own provocation."

"Likely, that. He'll want a grandiose gesture, though. Zebulon Fitch may be many things, but incorrect is not one of them. Taxation for the war effort weighs heavily on England, but with

France defeated, their full might has turned against us." I pick up one of our prior issues, stacked on a shelf, fanning the page for Duncan to read. "Thousands of soldiers sent to conquer New England. Washington put to the torch. We are turned back on every front."

"We." Duncan snorts. "You mean those who want to keep fighting Mr. Madison's war. Would that I had a penny for every boat I've seen trading contraband with the English."

"And vice versa." I shake my head. "Speaking of the devil, what say we make haste to the harbor and speak with Malcolm?"

Duncan scratches the back of the neck. He investigates the tips of his shoes. "Malcolm and I have been... at odds."

"This wouldn't have to do with your courting of one Isabelle Montgomery, would it?"

"Seems it would."

"Never mind, then." I straighten. The motion only exacerbates the tightness of my muscles. But it is better than being hit in the morning's crossfire or subject to the full wrath of an Ashen agent. "I have someone else whom we can question."

❧

Many a vessel line the piers of Camden's harbor. Too many. One would think a storm threatened Penobscot Bay and the captains had all sought refuge. Gone were the days their ivory sails carried goods to points across the Atlantic. Between the three years of the Embargo Act prior to the war's outbreak, and the British blockade of American ports since 1812, legitimate trade was stifled.

That being said, I tip my hat at the crews of vessels who are offloading barrels from ports unmentioned. Doubtless, they bought them from the very officials who occupy the eastern reaches of Maine. Doubtless still, they will set off with fish and sundry items to sell in return.

One young fellow has his nets drying on the ground, his boat pulled halfway from the brackish harbor. Asa Richards is a sturdy, weathered man with a long, solemn face more suited to a priest, yet his smile is earnest. "'Lo there, Tobias."

"Asa."

"Hear there was a clamor up to Saturday Cove. The militia's been out—two hundred men."

"So I understand." I prop one boot on the gunwales of his boat. I discover another sore spot in doing so. "A pity you lack fish to feed them."

His expression sours. "Through no fault of mine. Our new neighbors in Castine took the entire catch—hake, cod, haddock. Peter Oat and I stayed their unwilling guests for the better part of the day and a restless night. They had the gall to give me a single guinea for my troubles, while the good sailors of the Royal Navy feasted on *my* catch."

Asa's neck goes red as he recollects the confiscation. "I heard tell they offered to pay you handsomely."

"He'd have made a traitor out of me, and I'll not have that on my tombstone." Asa spits onto the mud. "I hope that Lieutenant Robbins and his lot vomit up every last morsel."

An unappealing visualization, to be sure. "They were raiding from Castine, I take it."

"That they were." Asa produces a knife and cuts through a rotted line. "Some of the sailors were spoiling for a fight, let me tell you. Their captain is a hero of the war with France. Has himself a gold medal from the king and everything. It's his frigate wallowing over there, when it's not prowling the bay. Thirty-eight guns. A French capture, every inch of her."

I'd caught sight of the imposing warship from the slopes of Mt. Battie, during more than one late-day walk. More disturbing, though, was the realization that yet another veteran of England's bloody war against Napoleon was now freed of his duties on the Continent and had come to America to apply the same disciplinary action.

Footsteps pound on the bank. Duncan is at a run, face red, hair blown back. "Tobias!"

"Excuse me and my overeager apprentice." I nod to Asa. "Thank you for your information."

"If you're bound and determined to write about our new neighbors, spit in their eye for me," he mutters.

I take Duncan by the elbow. "Perhaps we'd best keep our voices down."

"Sorry. Yes. I spoke with Malcolm."

I glance over his shoulder. "Is that why you're running? I see no signs of pursuit."

"You're a jester, you are," Duncan murmurs. "He was up to Castine last week, on a ... visit to a friend of his."

"Duncan, I don't have the slightest care what forbidden cargo your brother was shipping or how much he was paid." I do, however, care if Asa Richards overhears us discussing the very thing he believed made a man a traitor, despite most of his fellow seafaring townsfolk doing the same. I take Duncan by the arm as we leave the waterfront. "What of it?"

"He says the British officers have taken several homes as their own. Headquarters and such. The locals were grumbling about vandalism, especially in the insult carved in a window by one officer's diamond ring—a Union Jack, with the American flag flying upside down underneath."

I grimace. "A nation of states in distress."

"But it was the statement carved with it that riled him more: 'Yankee Doodle Topsy Turvy.' As you said."

"The very words from Fitch's mouth." I feel a fresh, cold twinge from the medallion, as if it spurs me to action. *Rest easy. In due time.* "Good work. Come. We have a paper to prepare for next week. A pity the skirmish this morning was too far past our deadline for the recent issue."

"Perhaps later. Widow Wagner is looking for you."

I peer up at the few houses along Bay View Street. One in particular, a rundown edifice with peeling white paint, seems to hound my steps. "Then I shall not keep her waiting."

❧❦

The home of the widow Alisa Hope Wagner is two stories tall. Black shutters rim windows facing out over the harbor. Curtains are drawn back. The slate stones balanced for the front steps rock underfoot, as if I'm stepping aboard Asa Richards' boat. I rap my knuckles on the door.

"Come in!"

The voice is angelic, if rasped by age. The door creaks open. In need of grease—

Metal flashes.

I see the knife tumbling end over end in the same heartbeat that I engage the medallion. A swift swipe sends it veering to my left, a mere foot from my nose, curving toward a new gravitational center. Then I halt it inches from the wallpaper, lest it produce an unsightly tear.

"A fine catch." Alisa Wagner sits in an overstuffed chair that threatens to swallow her spindly frame whole. Morning light from the nearby window makes her skin like marble. She wears black—always black. There's a tiny portrait of her late husband in ivory on the brooch pinned beneath her chin.

"Your tests of my skill with the medallion would be more of a surprise did they not occur every visit." I pluck the knife from the air and close the door. "You wished to see me?"

"If I wished to see you, it would take the same mud our Lord and Savior put in the eyes of the man he sent to the Pool of Siloam." She gazes upon me, yet her line of sight is to my right. "Your smell is enough to identify you—ink, paper, sea spray, mud. Wipe your boots."

I oblige before joining her in the parlor, hat clasped behind me. "Then I trust you know where I've been."

"Since the talk about town this morn' has been of Saturday Cove, I surmised as much. The stink of whatever they put in their lye for washing clothes confirms it. How did you fare?"

"Zebulon Fitch appeared. Not to kill, but to warn me—and perhaps, taunt. The Ashen have something planned for the British at Castine."

"Hmm. The rumors from the Garrison prove true, do they?" She folds her hands. "Elizabeth! Fetch me my paper, girl."

A silent young woman with auburn hair hurries into the room, a copy of the *Camden Light* in hand. She nods and smiles. "I have it here, Mrs. Wagner."

"Leave it and brew us tea."

She curtseys and is gone like evaporated mist.

"She has read me the hints you dropped," Widow Wagner says. "In the missives you relay from Portland and Boston. What is not said, between the lines of what is … yes, the Ashen are on the move, wishing to fan the flames. Fitch? Arrogant pup. You know your duty."

"I can confirm he was in Castine recently."

"Then why do you stand here prattling? Go. Stop him."

I hesitate before replying. She pounces like a wolf on a sickly lamb. "What bothers you?"

"There is so much more I could do. Sinking the ships of the Royal Navy while they lay at anchor would be simple." I snap my fingers. "A loose board here, a crushed hull there—"

"No. The Garrison has spoken. We are to take no active role in the war. We are only to prevent the Ashen from causing greater havoc."

"So, we hide."

"We persevere." She flips her brooch around. There is a crude rattlesnake carved on the reverse side. "What do you wield?"

I dig the medallion from under my collar. Dented, silver, tarnished by time and the skin of those who have used it before me, like the inside of an oyster's shell. Brass is visible underneath, where the surface has chipped away, and the tiniest black patterns are inscribed. The handiwork of angels, to hear the old-timers speak of it. "The strength of God, lent to men."

"For what purpose?"

"To keep it safe from the hands of sinful men, and to curtail the deeds of those who have already misused the medallions—the Ashen." I turn the medallion over. The same etched rattlesnake glares up at me. "I serve the Garrison."

"It's best you not forget." Widow Wagner sinks into her chair. "I trust your judgment when it comes time to act, Tobias, but never forget your hidden state. We dare not slip into the trap of arrogance to which the Ashen have succumbed."

I will not forget.

But the temptation remains.

Three days of watching produces no results, except to heighten my frustration.

Castine is a subdued coastal village, its sheltered harbor packed full of Royal Navy vessels. Chief among them is *HMS Furieuse*, the warship of French birth to which Asa Richards alluded. Her masts are wreathed in fog, as yet another dreary day comes to a close.

The crimson coats of soldiers drift through Castine's muddy lanes. Others are clustered atop the hills surrounding the town, where elaborate breastworks are under construction. I perch in a cluster of pines a quarter mile away, spyglass giving me a much closer look, albeit one interrupted by mists.

Soldiers everywhere, like rats in a ship's hold—on the docks, at the gangplanks, positioned around the deck of *HMS Furieuse*. A pair shares swigs from a hidden flask; another is intent on polishing the bayonet affixed to his musket. None are paying close attention to their surroundings; indeed, the gangplank watchmen guffaw at a fisherman's jest.

As with the previous two nights, the captain's cabin glows a warm yellow against the subdued blues and shadowy blacks. Captain William Mounsey is bent over his desk, quill pen flicking away at a sheaf of papers.

There have been no indicators of attack. No whispered rumors as I tread Castine's streets. No mention of Zebulon Fitch, save that he comes and goes from the port with the intermittency of a seagull.

None of which will help me put paid to his plans, whatever they may be.

There's a splash in the water, off to my right. I whip the spyglass in that direction. Nothing—wait. A pair of shapes, moving through the mist. Boats? I cannot make out who drives them.

Enough of this waiting. I tuck the spyglass into a coat pocket, adjust my collar, and summon the medallion's powers. I tuck and fall, letting the rush of cold air slap me awake before I swoop through the damp night air.

I lose sight of them. Yet, as I slow my headlong rush and the air grows still again, I hear the water slapping against their hulls. There. A wake.

I dip low to the waves, behind the boats, staying several hundred yards away, lest I provoke musket fire. They are twin fishing craft, common to any number of villages in the region. Their hulls are full of mounds of—is it tarps? Kindling? Both?

Yet absent people.

They move of their own accord, not drifting, but under power as surely as if strong young men were at the oars. Both are headed for *Furieuse.* I close the distance, itching for a better look.

Flame erupts from both, the brilliance and heat startling. Their paces accelerate.

Furieuse is but three hundred yards away.

A shout goes up from her deck. Bells clang. Mounsey whirls around, his chair tipping onto his floor. He is topside in a flash, blue coat donned. "Put out the boats!" His voice booms. "Push them astern!"

The sailors and soldiers scurry, but even as ropes squeal against their divots, I know they won't be able to get them down in time. Should the boats reach *Furieuse,* they will either catch the frigate alight or explode, spreading the fires. The end result is clear.

Fitch means to blow the frigate's powder magazine.

Dozens, if not hundreds, could die, and a blaze spreading with such ferocity, embers flung far afield by the explosion, would be catastrophic for the gathered ships and Castine itself.

I marshal the medallion's powers, drawing away some of its strength that gives me flight, forcing me nearer the waves. To push them away would be subtler—yet they move too quickly. I imagine a great scoop lifting them from the harbor, seawater and all. It will be seen but there is nothing to be done about—

The *crack* of a musket's discharge pierces my concentration. A fiery pain slices across my leg.

Flight fails me. I strike the water, air forced from my lungs, dunking headfirst. All is dark, save for the writhing glow of the flaming boats above me. I choke down a mouthful of the bay before powerful strokes carry me to surface.

Gunfire is now the sound of the night.

From whence does it come? Flashes of light, on all sides, flinging musket balls at the upper deck. A soldier drops, blood spattering Captain Mounsey. He ducks, reaching for the fallen man. Wood splinters and men seek cover, brandishing their weapons but seeing no target.

Fitch. He must be hiding, muskets held aloft with his medallion's power. He's lured me into another trap and sets before me two obstacles. The intent is clear—he makes me chose.

The fool underestimates my capabilities.

I shoot from the water in a spout rivaling the greatest whale's, my attention already split between the two boats, which are now less than a hundred yards from Furieuse and, in what must appear sorcery, accelerating. I dive for them, my boots scraping the surface, and grit my teeth as the medallion's strength pulls them into the air.

I cannot ignore their mass, though. The strain of exerting the medallion wears on me—muscles burning, bones straining, lungs gasping. Pull them free. Higher! Faster!

Water sprinkles the deck and the crew as the boats clear the masts by mere feet.

But the gunfire continues, and now that I have made myself a willing target, Mounsey gives the order: "Shoot the devil!"

I swing the boats below, absorbing the first salvo without incident, then spin them once, twice, before letting them sail through the air, clear of the ships in harbor and far from the docks, toward open water on either side.

And toward the flashes of light from bewitched muskets.

I drop to the deck, landing in the midst of four soldiers and Captain Mounsey himself. The redcoats are reloading; one slashes with his bayonet, but I dodge his attack, sending the weapon into the depths of the harbor. A brief adjustment to gravity in a semi-circle tosses the quartet onto the pier—doubtless, they're unable to swim.

Mounsey levels his pistol at me and cocks the hammer. "Fly, fiend."

"Captain, I am not your enemy, nor am I of the devil." I keep my hands at my side, making no threatening moves. "You must flee from here. Your life is in danger."

"From the likes of Satan? I shall take my chances."

More flashes, behind him. I instinctively rip Mounsey's gun from his grasp. It fires, sending a burst of flame and smoke toward the sails. I yank him aside, spinning him with the medallion's power.

A fusillade blows apart the railing where he stood moments before.

I lash out, combing the flashpoint for the sensation I know is there—the stabbing cold of another medallion. Like a successful angler, I reel in my prey.

Fitch slams onto the deck.

I strike him across the head before he can rise. He is prostrate before Mounsey, who stares, hand on the hilt of his cutlass.

"This man would have your nation destroy ours and take the lives of your men to prolong the war," I say. "I am here only to prevent the shedding of blood, including yours."

"You claim no allegiance, but your words tell me you're a Yankee." Mounsey still has a sword but does not draw it. "What assurance have I of your intentions?"

"Only the evidence I lay at your feet." I kick Fitch in the ribs. He moans. "This is the man who sent the fireships and who attempted your assassination. How else could guns shoot from the sky, or a boat appear from nowhere on the waters? Believe me or not, it doesn't matter. But trust my word that the people here were not involved."

Mounsey kneels. He seizes Fitch by the hair. The blade rasps free of its sheath and shines beneath Fitch's neck. "Speak. Is this true?"

Fitch spits a bloody gob. "You have no idea the power I wield. What you saw was child's play compared to—"

Mounsey withdraws the blade and slams Fitch's nose against the planks. "We'll hang him at first light."

"Sadly, you've not the jurisdiction." I hop into the air, dragging Fitch off the deck, and before Mounsey can reload or shout a command, sweep us both away into the darkness.

⊱❧⊰

I meet the Ashen on a spit of land called Green Ledge, scarcely two hundred feet across. Three Ashen in gray cloaks and hoods wait on one end, spectral, as I drop Fitch at their feet.

"Your action is thwarted," I say. "The covenants apply. Leave this region."

One lifts his hand. Fitch rises, held invisibly like a rag doll, eyes blinking. "No," he murmurs. "No, wait! I shall—"

Crunch.

His neck twists at an impossible angle. A medallion emerges from under his shirt. The man snatches it from the air.

"Your triumph," he hisses, "is temporary."

They fly into the night, taking Fitch's corpse and his forfeited medallion with them.

I shiver as the damp chill settles into my bones. "But my vigilance, gentlemen, is unwavering."

Where Monsters Wait

Gabrielle Pollack

THE MARKER RESTED AT THE END OF THE FIELD.

The man who stood beside it each night was missing.

Lyric Ashburrow hovered a few yards away, watching the dark stone that was so old even the stars must have forgotten who set it there. The highland grass rippled and turned around her like green waves before a tempest, and a grey sky hung flat and sad above the hills. It would storm later, as likely as not.

A whisper of grass on the other side of the hill, out of time with the wind, made her skin prickle. She slid into a crouch.

The rustling grew closer. Someone breathing, hard.

"Lyric! Lyric? You out here?"

Lyric shot up. "Felix?"

Her little brother stumbled toward her, round face bleached. "Lyric! I've...I've been killed!" The twelve-year-old beanpole collapsed into her, sending them both to the ground. "Oh, I can feel it!" He flopped. "Tell Aunt Ellie and Uncle Charles I love 'em."

Lyric pushed him off. "You're not dyin'. It's only Monday."

Felix stopped his dramatic flailing. "What is that supposed to mean?"

"It means you haven't even had time to get into danger since the week started."

"You're gonna regret that those were the last words you ever said to your poor ol' brother!" He curled up into a ball with a moan. "Oh lore, let it be quick!"

Lyric rolled her eyes. "What happened?"

"You know Skip's sister?" he asked.

"Angel?"

"Aye, her. She went and kissed me! So I'm dyin'," he said with no further explanation.

Lyric couldn't help it. She laughed.

"It's not funny!"

"You...you think a...a kiss is going to do you in?" Lyric asked between snickers.

"Atlas said if I kissed a lass, I was gonna keel over! He says he's seen it happen!" Felix was sitting up now, glaring.

"Aunt Ellie told you not to believe Atlas." She wiped a tear out of her eye. "You take people too seriously."

"But Atlas—"

"He's a trickster and a fibber." Lyric stood and hauled Felix to his feet.

"But he's right about some things," he said.

A cold weight settled into her stomach. "About the weather, maybe. Not much else."

"But he guards the Marker, too," Felix said. "Say, where is Atlas?" Felix peered at the rock.

Lyric shook her head. "We should go home." She grabbed his hand.

"But where is he? He should be here by now." Felix stepped toward the stone.

She wrenched him back. "Come on."

"But we need to find 'im! What if the night monsters get past while he isn't lookin'?" Felix asked.

"No one's seen monsters but Atlas. You're too old to believe silly tales like that."

"But Atlas said they're real! And they're crazy for blood, and—"

"Atlas fibs."

"But he's a Ceasefire! A Ceasefire wouldn't fib!" Felix shot back, round cheeks growing red.

Another chill tightened her arms. Ceasefires were warriors who carried darklighters, the rulers of all beasts, inside their veins. The fighters who used these ethereal creatures were legends, not men like Atlas. "Aunt Ellie doesn't think so. Besides, a real Ceasefire would never stand watch over a tiny, boring town because of a few creatures. They serve armies and kings."

"But Skip says Atlas has black blood! Skip's seen one of the cat monsters, and—"

"And Skip is yet another boy you shouldn't be listenin' to, especially about Atlas."

Felix closed his mouth with a snap, face scarlet.

Now she'd gone and made him mad. But Aunt Ellie was never happy about Felix's fascination with Atlas and his ideas. He should know better by now.

With another tug at Felix, they headed across the hills toward home.

The village of Glipperwick sat in the comfortable hollow of two hills, full of stone houses spaced by stretches of half-cobbled paths. Grass, banished from the roads by sporadic traffic, hugged the corners and cracks of homes, waving to their brothers in the fields. Herdsmen and women ushered a few stray cows and horses through the streets, each heading for their own barn. A lawman stood on a ladder in the nearby square, placing a glowing star inside the town's lone lamppost in preparation for the night.

Felix paused at the beginning of the street, shading his eyes. "See 'im?"

"See who?"

"Atlas," he said.

"He can take care of himself," Lyric said.

"I think you're just tryn' to hide your worry."

"My what?"

"About the monsters. Adults like you always go on acting like they're not scared. But I know you better than that. You may be all grown up with your sixteen-something years—"

"Seventeen," Lyric interjected.

"But you're still bothered."

Lyric glanced down the street to make sure no one was listening. "Felix, the monsters are a legend. Everyone says so."

"Only because they don't want to believe the truth. Remember that tale? When all the village people were so comfy with the way things were that no one believed that messenger's warnin' till they were bein' killed by the bandits? It's like that."

"These are monsters, not bandits."

"Still the same." His eyes were all wide and serious. "You can't just ignore them monsters because you don't like 'em."

"Keep that mouth of yours shut. You don't know what you're—"

"Lyric!" A woman with an apron tied tight over her matronly figure waved in their direction.

"Good glory," Lyric murmured.

Mrs. Syren bustled across the street toward them, the flush in her round cheeks telling Lyric she'd been quite busy spreading gossip. Mrs. Syren grabbed Lyric's shoulders. "I've been searching all over for you." She peered around Lyric. "Hello, Felix darlin'."

Felix gagged as soon as she looked away. Lyric stepped on his foot. "What have you got today, Syren?" she asked as Felix flinched.

"Oh, it's about that Atlas, dear. I do think he has truly gone mad this time."

"His madness doesn't have anything to do with me, now does it?"

Mrs. Syren shook her head. "Of course not, but I thought you'd want to know what has happened! Cynthia said Mary saw Atlas out the corner of her window, stumbling around like a drunk. Of course Mary didn't go out to see. But Lara, the cobbler's wife, said her husband shooed him off their property later because he'd taken up leaning against the house, scaring away the neighbors."

"Because Atlas is scary," Lyric said flatly.

"Oh lore, yes. Considering sending the man to the loon house they are, for all his talk of them creatures."

Felix stepped around Lyric. "But they can't! Then the monsters will—!"

"I'm just repeatin' what I heard, young master. No need getting angry." She leaned close to Lyric. "But you don't believe his tales, do you lass? No proper lady would ..." Her eyes gleamed like she was a starving cow standing before a trough of muddied corn.

"Of course not," Lyric said.

Syren bobbed her head. "I had no doubt, no doubt at all. Just wanted to warn you. Can't have two crazies in town, can we? I think one mad man is enough to deal with." She laughed.

"You mean mad woman," Felix muttered as they walked away. Lyric didn't scold him. She stayed away from Atlas when she could, but that didn't mean Syren had a right to tear him up so.

Their aunt and uncle's house sat a few hills away from town. It was a blocky little dwelling, patched together with rounded bricks and mortar. A haze of smoke escaped its thick chimney, and a warm light leaked out the murky windows. Lyric's stomach growled.

By the time they reached the door the wind was throwing such a tantrum that Lyric's red braids slapped against her face. She threw open the door and nudged Felix inside, expecting the warm rush of home, accompanied by Aunt Ellie's singing and the faint smell of spices, to overwhelm her.

But when a gust slammed the door shut behind them, Lyric heard no music.

Atlas rested on a long cot in the middle of the room where a usually spotless carpet sat. The fellow was dark and lanky with disheveled black hair. He lay on his back, eyes squeezed shut in that look Felix had last summer when Uncle Charles pulled a great thorn out of his foot. Aunt Ellie, a thin woman bearing the expression of a soldier on a mission, knelt beside him.

Aunt Ellie looked up. "Lyric, take Felix to his room."

Felix's mouth hung open. "Is that...?" He reached for Atlas, but Aunt Ellie quickly stepped between them. "Why's Mister Atlas here? I thought you said he was loony."

"Of course he is, but he's...sick. And we can't leave a sick man to die by that cursed boulder." She waved the two back. "Now go on!"

"Sick? What's he got?" Felix was on his tiptoes now, trying to see over her shoulder.

Lyric grabbed Felix and dragged him around the cot and into the hall. She shoved him inside his room but paused in the entryway. Uncle Charles wasn't back yet. Her aunt might need help with Atlas. "Aunt Ellie, should I—?"

Atlas sat up. His eyes were over-bright, and sweat shone on his forehead. Lyric jumped, but Aunt Ellie recovered quickly and shoved him down.

"I...I have to go back."

"Not torn up like that you can't," Aunt Ellie said.

"But—"

"No buts." She patted his shoulder, then plastered a wet cloth over his forehead. "Now stay here while I fetch you a glass of water." She heaved herself up and wandered into the kitchen. Atlas closed his eyes.

Lyric moved into the room and knelt beside the poor man. A thick wad of bandages covered his ribs and left arm. Blobs of black had stained the fabric like someone had poured ink on his middle. Wet, crumbled-up bits of rag surrounded the bed. They were black, too. Even the floor they had walked over sported dots the color of pitch.

Normal people didn't bleed black. They bled red.

Aunt Ellie returned. "Lyric."

Lyric jerked. She'd been staring.

"This is not a sight for a young lady's eyes. Back to the room with you."

"But I...I can help. I've stitched up a man before." Lyric reached for the bandages. The dark stuff couldn't be real.

"I said back to your room."

"I'm seventeen. I—"

"Do as I say." Aunt Ellie's tone was tight, as if she ordered Lyric out of a bull pen instead of away from an injured man.

Lyric slipped away and shut the door behind her. She ignored Felix's expectant look.

Atlas had Ceasefire blood just like Skip had said.

Did that mean Atlas wasn't a liar? Would the monsters come?

She scrambled toward the window. The storm clouds were descending, nearly as black as whatever she'd seen on Atlas. Dusk was coming with them.

"What did Auntie say about 'im?" Felix peered out the window over her shoulder.

No. There had to be some other explanation.

The hour passed as slow as a three-legged turtle. Uncle Charles came home and poked his head in to greet them but didn't say they could come out. Lyric's skin tingled as the storm darkened the sky outside their window. Rain pounded against the glass. She couldn't hear her uncle and aunt murmuring or Atlas' groans. No monsters came, either.

"They aren't going to let us out, are they? Without dinner, too," Felix pouted. He'd been pacing for the last few minutes.

"Stop or you'll wear through the floor," Lyric said.

"I don't hear 'em talkin' anymore, do you?" Felix pressed his ear against the door.

"They'll come when they want us."

"You know, it's almost like they're hidin' something." Felix tried to peer through the crack between the door and its frame.

"None of your business if they are," she said.

"You're right, likely as not. If I was a good *old* person like you, I'd sit right back down and never wonder about it again," he said. "Ah well. Too bad I'm not old." With a mischievous grin, he slipped out of the room.

"Felix!" she hissed. He didn't answer. She stepped into the hall. She was going to tie him up and throw him in a corner once she caught him.

Felix stood beside the kitchen door. It was cracked open, and a thin shaft of light fell into the hall. Felix put his ear against the wood and waved Lyric forward. She mouthed for him to come back. He didn't.

Then she heard her aunt's voice.

"What do you think attacked Atlas?"

"Just a wolf." Uncle Charles' low, soothing voice drifted through the gap like a healing balm.

Lyric glanced at the cot. Atlas lay still, breathing steady. Most of the blood—or whatever that black stuff was—had been cleaned up. Lyric tiptoed around him and grabbed Felix's arm.

"But wouldn't a wolf leave bites? And those marks...they're deep."

"I'm tellin' you. It was just a wolf."

"My father had run-ins with wolves at the farm. None attacked like this," Aunt Ellie said.

A chair creaked as their uncle shifted.

"And what about...?" She hesitated. "What about his blood?"

"What about it?" Charles asked.

"It's black. Only Ceasefires have—"

"Blood comes out real dark sometimes."

"But not like pitch. Look at these rags!"

"It's black from the wound, likely as not. Whatever got him might have left some poison in his veins," Uncle Charles said.

"But you said it was a wolf that hurt him."

Uncle Charles didn't answer.

Lyric and Felix exchanged worried looks.

A long roll of thunder shook the room. Atlas moaned and moved restlessly in response. Lyric dashed toward the hall. She glanced back to make sure Felix followed.

The senseless boy had moved beside the cot, staring at the wounded fellow like he was a two-headed unicorn.

Lyric took the distance in two strides and grabbed his ear. "If you don't come with me, I'm gonna make sure you never leave your room again."

"But Auntie's right. His blood..." He trailed off. "It's black." He was staring at the bandages. They had been replaced and bore fresh dark spots.

"That's nothing to you. Come—"

Atlas' green eyes opened. He blinked once. Twice. His face brightened when he caught sight of them. "Lyric. Felix." Atlas slowly propped himself up on his elbow, grimacing all the way. "A right nice thing you did, taking me in after that little bugger... took a swipe at me." He tapped his bandage.

"We weren't the ones who patched you up, mister," Felix said.

"It's Atlas." The guardian struggled into a sitting position. Even in the dim light of the dying fire, Lyric could tell his lips were unnaturally pale. "I owe thanks to your aunt and uncle, then. I really do appreciate..." He tried to get his legs under him but collapsed back onto the cot. "...them helpin' me," he gasped.

Lyric held out a hand. "You shouldn't get up." She tried to force her voice to stay steady. Should she get Aunt Ellie? Atlas was going to hurt himself if he went on like this.

He ignored her. "What time is it?"

"Never you mind. You—"

"Night's come on," Felix spoke over her.

She glared at him.

A roll of thunder cut off Atlas' curse. He tensed like he was getting ready to stand again.

"You're not goin' anywhere," Lyric said.

"Say again?"

"You're hurt, and Aunt Ellie wouldn't—"

"You know as well as I do I need to be by the Marker at night," he said. "I have to keep the creatures that did this…" He motioned toward his bandaged arm. "…out of Glipperwick."

Lyric shook her head. "There aren't any monsters. Everyone knows so."

"And you believe their rubbish?"

She didn't reply, and his face fell. He turned to Felix. "Lad? Would you mind helping me to the Marker?"

"You're not right in the head," Lyric said. "You need to rest."

"I know I'm not all there, but the monsters—"

"There aren't any!"

"Then I guess a Ceasefire has been wastin' his nights for a long while, hasn't he? And these little scratches came from an over-eager hound dog?" His eyes flashed.

Another roll of thunder shook the room. It sounded like the deep scream of something terrible.

No. It was her imagination. There weren't any monsters. Not here in Glipperwick.

"If the monsters have been comin' around for so many years, why has no one seen them?" Lyric asked defensively.

"The Ceasefires managed to keep them at the edge of the meadow and out of sight. Any closer and they put the village at risk."

"Then…" Lyric fumbled for another defense. "Then why haven't you shown everyone you're a Ceasefire?"

"What do you think would happen if I revealed who I was? We're rare. Kings and commanders snatch us up faster than a hawk grabs a snake. They wouldn't care about your village or the monsters," he said. "And do you think your people would believe me with centuries of lies hangin' over their heads? You've seen my blood, and even you aren't convinced."

His words seemed true, but they had to be excuses. Atlas was sick. He didn't know what he was saying.

Felix slipped under Atlas' arm and helped him to his feet.

"Felix! Put him back," Lyric said.

"But what he's sayin' makes sense." Felix's brown eyes were wide. "Better to go out and face them monsters than be caught in bed by 'em."

"For the last time, there are no monsters!" she spoke louder than she meant to.

"Shhh. Auntie will hear!" Felix said.

"You're right. She will." Lyric marched to the entrance of the kitchen.

"Please, Lyric!" Atlas called after her. "You can't tell 'em. They'll stop me from going!"

Lyric grabbed the door.

"I can't stop the monsters from here. I'm not strong enough. They'll get through to the town, and there won't be anything left," Atlas pleaded.

He sounded so...earnest. Lyric squeezed her eyes shut. No. He was mad. He was lying.

But what if he wasn't?

"I know it's a scary thing, believin' there's something wrong in the world. Something dark. But you can't fight it without opening your eyes and believin' it's there."

Lyric didn't want to think about the creatures in bedtime tales that ate children and kidnapped maidens and tore apart villages. She didn't want them to be real. She wanted to crawl under her warm bed covers and know that she'd wake up in the morning because the monsters didn't exist and never had.

But what if she was wrong?

Lyric shook her head. What would Aunt Ellie say if she knew Lyric was considering such thoughts?

But did it matter what her aunt, or even all of Glipperwick, said? If the monsters *were* real, a town's denial wouldn't stop them.

The kitchen door creaked open. Aunt Ellie stared at her, completely unaware of Atlas and Felix. "Lyric! I thought you were in bed. The storm isn't scaring Felix, is it?"

"No, I..." She had to tell Aunt Ellie about Atlas. She should.

"What is it?" she asked.

Lyric took a deep breath. "Aunt Ellie?"

"Yes?"

"I just wanted to tell you that..." Her gut bottomed out. "...that I looked in on Atlas."

Aunt Ellie's eyebrows rose. "And?"

"And..." A set of rags sat on the table beyond her aunt, crumpled and shining as black as the starless night outside.

"Lyric?"

"And he's lookin' all right," she rushed. "So you don't have to worry about him."

"Is that so?"

Lyric nodded.

"Thank you for checking on him. Now go on back to bed," Aunt Ellie said.

"Yes ma'am."

Aunt Ellie closed the door, leaving the three of them in the darkness. Atlas and Felix stared at her like stunned foals.

"What are you two lookin' at?" she snapped. "We don't have any time to waste now, do we?" She grabbed one of Uncle Charles' old coats and draped it over Atlas. He nodded his thanks.

She scurried to his side, drawing his other arm over her shaking shoulders. This was a downright terrible idea. Sauntering into the worst storm since she was born.

To face monsters.

While dragging a half-dead man with them.

"Don't worry. I'll keep you safe," Atlas whispered. At least, Lyric thought he did. When she looked up, he was staring at the door. Lyric and Felix helped him to his feet. He made them pause to retrieve his short dagger before pulling him outside.

The wind slammed the door shut behind them. The rain pelted their faces and the wind stole their breath. Felix and Lyric lowered their heads, but the tempest seemed to give Atlas new strength. He closed his eyes, letting the water run down his face. Then they trudged over the hill and through the mud-slicked town toward the Marker, the once-friendly grass lashing at their legs.

Even with Atlas' renewed energy, Lyric's shoulders ached halfway across the rolling fields beyond Glipperwick. The rain soaked her hair and slipped down her forehead into her eyes. They navigated by bursts of lightning and half moved by instinct.

They were partway up the last hill when lightning struck the field only a few miles out. The Marker's silhouette loomed black against the light. Dark shapes lurked in the field beyond it. Another flash. They were moving.

The monsters were here. Atlas was right.

A burst of orange lit the field. The flame caught on the grass for a brief second before drowning in the rain. They breathed *fire*!?

Atlas squeezed her shoulder. She kept walking, the deafening thunder and the sting of rain pounding at the edge of her perception. This couldn't be real. Everything moved quickly, too quickly.

A shadow dashed past them. Lyric twisted, but the darkness hid whatever it was she thought she saw.

They reached the rock. Atlas let them go and leaned against it, wiping the rain from his eyes. Felix grabbed Lyric's hand.

The dark shapes lurched closer but were still too far away to make out anything more than bright eyes and mouths full of fire. Growls, hisses, and screams like those of a panther reached their ears between peals of thunder.

Atlas bowed his head and opened his hands, palms up as if to catch the rain. Mist nearly darker than the night itself flooded out of his black-veined fingers.

Atlas' darklighter. A Ceasefire's weapon. The king of monsters.

The rain paused, hanging in the air. A bolt of lightning a mile off froze mid-strike, painting the field in white light. The monsters halted.

A thrill rose up in Lyric's chest like she was the one holding the darklighter. They were going to win.

Then the mist vanished, and the world went dark again.

"Something's not right," Atlas said.

"You think a few hundred monsters woulda said as much," Felix shouted over the wind.

"No," Atlas said. "There aren't enough." He met Lyric's gaze. "Did you see any others?"

"Others?"

"When we were walking to the—"

A yowl rushed over the hills. It took Lyric a moment to realize it came from behind then.

From the town.

"They've already made it past the barrier." Atlas lurched away from the rock. He crumpled.

"Atlas!" Lyric fell to her knees beside him.

Atlas struggled to rise. Lyric slid under his arm to help. "I can't reach that far, not like this," he said.

Another roar rolled over the thunder. What was the monster doing? Had it found someone? *Oh glory, let it not be Aunt Ellie and Uncle Charles.*

They were too late. She'd taken too long to believe him, and a monster had gotten through.

Unless…"If I draw the monster back here, could you use your darklighter to banish it?"

Atlas' grip on her shoulder tightened. "Yes, but…"

Lyric guided Atlas to the rock. She slipped his dagger out of his belt, hands shaking. "Ward off the ones here. And don't move. You too, Felix." She shrugged away and dashed back toward the village.

"Lyric, no!"

Lyric plunged over the first hill. She didn't have a plan, but she could not…*would not…* let this night count for nothing. She'd believed in the monsters once. Now she'd seen them. It was time to act.

The town rose in its hollow. The buildings towered in strips of dark shadows, looming above the single, star-lit lamppost glimmering in the square.

Lyric dove into the streets. The mud caught her, and her shoe slipped off. She kicked away the other as she reached the square, pausing under the glow of the star.

Lyric wielded Atlas' dagger with fingers thick and clumsy. The tiny blade was half as long as her forearm and wouldn't be able to hurt a monster.

But she didn't have to hurt the monster. She just had to get its attention. She needed to give it a strong reason to pursue her, not the sleeping villagers.

"I hope you're right about this, Felix." Lyric bit her lip and slashed her arm. She clapped a hand over the cut. Red welled over her fingers.

Nothing happened. She cursed. How could she expect a creature to smell blood in this torrent? She turned, searching for yellow eyes or flames.

A growl, over her shoulder. She whirled.

A cat-like face with two sets of eyes slid into the light, blinking. The creature crouched low, shoulders pointed and rippling beneath thick skin. Its nose twitched.

She gasped and backed away. It advanced.

She took off down an alley. The creature roared. Lyric slid around a corner, dashing through town for the hills. All she had to do was make it to the Marker. To Atlas.

She pounded up the incline. The creature thudded behind her, gaining. The Marker loomed above the hills like a dark lighthouse. Atlas and Felix were nowhere to be seen. She risked a glance over her shoulder.

The cat-creature pounced.

Lyric dove to the ground, tumbling. The monster sailed over her. She scrambled to her feet as it turned. It gathered itself to jump.

"Atlas!" she cried out. She couldn't see him. She hadn't made it close enough. She was too far away for him to help.

The creature charged. She shielded her face, dropping the dagger.

An unearthly chill rushed over her shoulder, and the rain froze mid-fall. The mist-like form of Atlas' darklighter twirled and twisted, dancing around her. Atlas knelt a few yards away, shaking hand stretched toward her monster.

The mist collected in a rush, solidifying to form solid black eyes and bared teeth.

A massive wolf stood beside her.

The wolf tilted its head back and howled, its cry echoing in a realm only monsters could hear. The cat-creature hissed, ears flat against its skull.

Then it ran. The darklighter wolf dashed after it, snapping at its heels.

Lyric yelled in triumph.

The creature raced past the Marker, disappearing into the grass. Atlas' wolf stopped. It sent up another howl.

Then the world sped back up. The lightning vanished. The rain fell, and thunder caressed the hills. The bright eyes, the fire, it was all gone.

Atlas collapsed. Lyric barely made it to his side before doing the same.

"S-sorry I took your dagger," she said.

Atlas closed his eyes. The black under his skin was receding. "That was...a stupid thing to do. Heroic...but stupid," he managed between breaths.

"You're the one who made me come out here." Her voice shook.

"My mistake."

"I'm not doin' it again, if that's any comfort," she said.

"Good," Atlas breathed. They laid there for a moment, letting the rain slid down their faces. Lyric closed her eyes, and a shiver, some remnant of the conflict, tickled her spine. The monsters were real now. She couldn't deny it, even to Syren.

Atlas opened his eyes, a phantom of the darkness in his veins swirling in their pupils. He blinked at the sky.

"The village is going to think I've gone mad," Lyric murmured ruefully.

Atlas smirked. "Better to believe the truth and have few friends than a lie and have a dead village, aye?"

Lyric couldn't help but return the smile. "You're insane."

"You only figured that out now?"

Felix's head popped up over the grass where he'd apparently been hiding. He stared toward the field, mouth hanging open. "And you said a girl's smooch was gonna kill me," he whispered.

Lyric burst into a laugh. Atlas joined her, shoulders shaking. He held his ribs but made no effort to restrain himself. Like monsters before his darklighter, the last shadows of the night fled before their mirth.

WILL O' THE WISPS

WAYNE THOMAS BATSON

Part One: The Hitchhiking Ghosts

To SAY FIFTEEN-YEAR-OLD STOKER GRAVES WAS INTERESTED IN GHOSTS would be akin to describing Mount Everest as a wee bump. More accurately, Stoker Graves was irresistibly fascinated, relentlessly compelled by, and hopelessly obsessed with ghosts. Those who didn't know any better blamed his creepy compulsion on his cemetery-evoking last name. Others attributed it to the death of Stoker's mother on his seventh birthday and the subsequent alleged hauntings of the Graves' eldritch Victorian home. But the truth of the matter was that Stoker's peculiar preoccupation was all Walt Disney's fault.

When Stoker was just five, his mother and father took him to Disney World in Orlando, Florida. Of all the fantastic rides, Stoker's favorite was the Old Haunted Mansion. Rather than being frightened by the glowing, translucent beings, young Stoker was enchanted. From the glow-in-the-dark spider that tickled his neck to the ballroom full of dancing ghouls—Stoker loved it all. His parents used to joke that the famous Hitchhiking Ghosts had come home with them from the trip—in Stoker's suitcase.

Maybe they had. Since that time, Stoker had become a self-made ghost expert. He'd read everything he could on the subject and even started his own club at school. Students' Paranormal Observation and Omniscience Klub—or SPOOK. Only in existence for a year, SPOOK had made the papers, a national magazine, and scores of blogs and websites. Stoker and SPOOK had even received some fan mail. Most everyone found Stoker's adventures and discoveries very entertaining. That was the difference between most people and Stoker: most people thought ghosts were entertaining flights of fancy or misunderstood natural phenomena. Stoker was convinced ghosts were real. To ignore the supernatural, Stoker believed, was to invite disaster.

When Stoker learned that his school's sophomore class was taking a team-building trip to Camp Letts during a week in early October, he was, well... stoked. Creepier than Crybaby Bridge, grosser than the Goatman, and more mysterious than Marietta Mansion, Camp Letts was the big daddy of all Maryland ghost stories. Camp Letts was the home of the infamous Edgewater will-o'-the-wisps.

Stoker was the first one on the bus to Camp Letts that obnoxiously warm-for-fall Tuesday morning. He bounced on the seat, waiting impatiently for the other students to board so that the bus could finally leave. A feminine shadow sat down next to Stoker and asked, "So, Spook-Boy, do you think will-o'-the-wisps are real?"

Spook-Boy. Stoker shook his head. This was Stoker's best friend: Maria Delarosa Espinosa Definesta Santiago Ramirez Cortez. But Stoker called her Trixie. Maria always said it was because he could never remember her full name, but Stoker insisted that he called her Trixie because she had absolutely huge eyes like Japanese Anime and Speed Racer cartoon characters. Trixie could be trusted to call him Spook-Boy on occasion, but she didn't tease him maliciously. And she would never—ever—ridicule his passion for the supernatural.

Maybe Trixie didn't really pick at Stoker because of her own rather unusual habits and interests. Trixie, you see, wasn't just lowercase "g" goth-like so many burn-out poseurs. She was legit. Queen Goth.

Hair dyed jet black—at times spiked, teased, or swirled in bizarre waves. Huge burnt umber eyes floating in moats of dead-of-night mascara. Black lipstick. Black fingernails. Black leather jackets, trench coats, and jeans. She wore a gigantic black cross on a cord of black leather around her neck. The rings on her fingers were all hideous bats, spiders, and skulls, scary enough to make little kids cry—proven on three separate occasions. And, if Stoker were honest, he'd admit that sometimes, Trixie scared him a little too, just for very different reasons.

"I think they're real," Stoker said. "I'm sure of it. They've been appearing at Camp Letts since 1954: misty, spectral globes of ghostly green, blue, or purple fire. I can't wait!"

"I can!" came a shrill voice from behind their seat.

Trixie rolled her eyes and quickly inserted a pair of earbuds.

The squeaky voice was Russell "Squirt" McAfee. At sixteen, Squirt was a year older than his fellow sophomores but was about as tall as the average fourth grader. His parents had even held him back a year, hoping for a growth spurt, but to no avail. Jocks and bullies teased Squirt cruelly, calling him things like "half-pint, shorty, small-fry," and, of course, "Squirt." In the history of William Harrison Revenant High School, Squirt was the only student to spend the night at school... in a locker... courtesy of certain members of the football team.

"C'mon, Squirt," Stoker said. "The will-o'-the-wisps may glow in the dark and make creepy raspy sounds, but they rarely hurt anyone."

"Rarely?" Squirt echoed. His wide green eyes appeared above the seat back. "You call three deaths 'rarely'?"

"Three deaths since the sightings began," Stoker replied. "In that span of years, you'd get more deaths at a theme park."

"I doubt it," Squirt muttered. "Not like the three at Letts. Those were bad, Stoker. Really bad."

"Granted, those were some pretty gruesome deaths," Stoker replied. "But local law enforcement deemed them tragic accidents only indirectly related to the will-o'-the-wisp sightings."

Trixie yawned loudly and removed her earbuds. Other students continued to fill in the bus seats. "Are we there yet?"

"Funny," Stoker replied. "What's taking so long?"

Flustered at being ignored, Squirt snorted aloud, two parts angry warthog and one part dog sneeze. He reached over the seat and tapped Stoker's shoulder. "Don't forget the dozens of campers who've reported strange bite marks right after will-o'-the-wisp sightings!"

"Bite marks?" Trixie echoed. "That's probably just bed bugs." She laughed, and the rapid-fire, "He, he, he, he, he, he, he" never failed to fascinate Stoker.

"I don't care," Squirt said. "Bed bug bites or ghost bites—I don't like it. Not one bit."

"Pipe down, pipe down!" The Civics teacher, Mr. Nemchek, commanded. "All of your sleeping bags and gear are loaded, so we'll be departing shortly. Remember, stay seated while the bus is in motion. Listen, I know it's warm, but keep the windows up. The driver assures me that the air conditioning will kick in strong once we've been driving for a little while."

Groans, sighs, and a few rude comments answered that announcement. The last few kids filed by. Three of them were blonde girls—sophomore pom squad—and they sneered at Trixie as they passed.

"Big enough cross?" Cherisha Jordan asked. She was the queen bee of the so-called popular girls.

Trixie looked up from her phone, fixed Cherisha in a simmering glare, and replied, "It's not as big as the cross Jesus carried for us. If you want, I could tell you more."

Cherisha rolled her eyes and pushed on toward the back of the bus. "Who needs all that religious crap?"

"*Deus te abençoe,*" Trixie replied in Portuguese. *God bless you.*

The bus crept off the high school campus and at last pulled out onto the highway. Stoker settled back into his seat. "My luck, we won't see any will-o'-the-wisps."

"My luck, we will," Squirt said.

"And my luck," Trixie said, replacing her earbuds, "you two won't stop talking and interrupting my jams."

"Still listening to all that Jesus music?" Squirt asked.

"Yeah, why?" Trixie growled back. "You got a problem with Christian music?"

"Well, no," he said. "It's just kind of weird. You're kind of weird."

"Squirt, that's the nicest thing you've ever said to me. Now, please, shut up."

Stoker sighed. He, Trixie, and Squirt were SPOOKS's founding members back in ninth grade. Seven other kids had joined in this year, but Stoker wondered how long the club would last without finally capturing evidence that would categorically prove the existence of ghosts.

He wiped a trickle of sweat from his forehead. Way too hot for this time of year, he thought, digging into his jeans pocket for his phone. The weather app pronounced the high to be 86 degrees. Stoker gazed through the bus window. The sky was blank and white, the sun glaring, but there was little to suggest a storm. The app agreed: only fifteen percent chance of precipitation.

Stoker sighed again. The best will-o'-the-wisp sightings had occurred during or directly after thunderstorms.

Part Two: The Crab that Got Away

But the weather forecast was wrong.

The first night at Camp Letts, while Stoker and the other tenth graders were at an assembly in the dining hall, towering black clouds bubbled up from the east. A strange stillness fell over Camp Letts outside, while inside, the guest speaker, an Australian marine biologist named Dr. Kay Cooper, held her audience in rapt attention.

"Now, take a look a' this creature," Dr. Cooper said, non-chalantly loading the next slide into the projector. Punctuated by a few high-pitched squeaks, a collective gasp rose up from the tenth graders. On the vast screen, a close up of a bloated toothy horror had appeared. "Looks like something from a creature film, doesn't it?"

"What is it?" someone called out.

"That's just it," Dr. Cooper explained, "the experts in my field were positively flummoxed at first. Ya' see, this handsome beastie washed up on a Texas shore in 2017 after that nasty willy-willy, er hurricane called Harvey walloped the coast. Turns out, it's a fangtooth snake-eel, usually stays deep sea. But when a strong hurricane moves across the ocean's surface, it can cause up-welling—a fair powerful force, bringing bottom water and all kinds of critters all the way up to the surface. We've discovered a few new species due to storms like Harvey."

"Hey, Stoker," Lambert Gold whispered hoarsely from a few seats away. He was the only sophomore to start on the varsity football team. "Whaddaya think? Would ya date her?"

Stoker's stomach churned. "Who? Dr. Cooper?"

"No. The fang eel thing!"

Stoker rolled his eyes, but Trixie fumed. "Lambert, why would you want Stoker to date your mom?" she quipped.

Lambert squirmed in his seat. "Lucky you're a girl," he said.

"How about something a wee bit cuter?" Dr. Cooper asked. She switched the slide to a torpedo-shaped fish with huge eyes and oversized fins. "This little fellow is a species of flying fish from my neck of the world. Flying fish don't fly, they glide. Some glide as far as 650 feet before dropping back into the water."

Stoker leaned over to Trixie and said, "I'd date that one."

The presentation went on, and Dr. Cooper began revealing some live specimens she'd brought for the assembly. Just after nine o'clock, still mesmerized by the Aussie marine biologist and her creatures, the students didn't notice the wind chimes stirring outside the hall. And then at 9:16 p.m., at the very moment when the guest speaker held up a blue crab for the students to see, a lightning bolt knifed down just outside the hall. The blast of thunder set off a dozen car alarms in the parking lot and the lights went out.

Students and teachers alike jumped at the crash of thunder, and general chaos ensued. Screams rang out. Students ran hither and thither, knocking into tables, chairs, and each other. The storm, however, was far from finished. The wind blew at gale force, slamming doors and tearing limbs from trees. Rain pelted the windows like handfuls of gravel. The lightning was like nothing Stoker had ever experienced before. Flash after blinding flash, cloud-to-ground strokes hit home as if a dozen Zeus-wannabees were throwing down and Camp Letts was the bull's eye.

"This is incredible!" Stoker shouted above the thunder. He stood on a chair and cheered while most of the other students hid beneath the lunch tables.

"You're scaring me, Spook-Boy!" Trixie yelled. "Lightning flashes lighting up your face like that, you look like some kind of mad scientist!"

"Yeah, get down, clown!" commanded Lambert. "You're a freak, ya know that!"

Flash-bang! A window-rattling thunderclap followed a blinding bolt. It struck so close to the dining hall students screamed and shrieked anew, and everyone ducked. Stoker stumbled down from the chair and took shelter with the rest.

For the next hour, while the storm raged, teachers and counselors did their best to quiet and comfort the students, but few could hear them. The wind howled and wailed, sheets of rain continued to assault the hall, and the thunder was nearly incessant.

Beneath the table, Trixie's hand somehow found Stoker's, and he didn't mind in the least. He felt like they were at a drive-in movie with the storm as the entertainment. Of course, Stoker knew if he ever mentioned to Trixie that it felt like a date, she'd probably punch him in the jaw.

After a relentless two-hour cacophony, the storm careened away west. Lights all around the camp began to blink back on, in-cluding—finally—the cafeteria's lights. The guest speaker moved frantically to and fro throughout the hall. Throwing his hands up, he yelled, "Has anyone seen my blue crab?"

Squirt let out a yelp, and there was a tremendous thud under the table next to Stoker. Stoker and Trixie immediately released each other's hands and spun around. Squirt was there. He yelled again, bounced up, and hit his head on the table a second time. He rolled out from underneath and took off running down the aisle.

"Hey!" Lambert yelled, pointing at Squirt. "I found the crab! It's pinching half-pint's butt!"

Part Three: Hazel's Mark

The next morning at breakfast with Trixie and Squirt, Stoker noticed that most of the teachers were huddled by the dining hall exit.

"What's happening?" he asked.

"Some of the kids are goin' home," Squirt said.

"What?" Stoker asked. "Why?"

Trixie looked up, eyes wide. "You're kidding, Spook-Boy. You mean you don't know?"

"Know what?" he demanded.

"Ghostlights," she said. "Will-o'-the-wisps, or whatever you call 'em. Some kids in Ensign Cabin 3 saw some of 'em last night. Scared them pretty bad. They called their folks to go home early."

"Aww, mannn," Stoker grumbled. "I missed it."

"Cheer up, bro," Trixie said. "There's always tonight."

"Stoker," Squirt said. "What are you going to do if you see a will-o'-the-wisp?"

"Get pictures, of course," Stoker said. "But really, I want to try to catch one. More than one if I can. I bought these Specter Nets from paranormal experts online."

"So, you're going to be a Ghostbuster?" Trixie asked, rolling her eyes. "*Muito engraçado.*" *Too Funny.* "Spook-Boy, the Ghostbuster. Who ya gonna call?"

"That's my favorite movie," Stoker said.

Trixie laughed. "Only the nineteenth time you've told me that."

"Attention students!" The husky voice belonged to Mrs. Kiering, the well-liked Biology teacher. "The storm last night left quite a mess all over the campus. Camp Letts staff needs the time to clean up the instructional areas, so we're canceling first session classes. You're free to visit the gymnasium or the game room or even hang around here until 10:45 a.m. If you need to go back to your cabin, make sure you have a chaperone or a teacher with you."

The formerly quiet cafeteria erupted in cheers, whistles, applause, and a few random "Rock ons!" and "Heck yeahs!"

"C'mon," Trixie said, yanking Stoker up from his seat. "I want to show you something."

"Can I come, too?" Squirt asked.

"*Biscoito sagrado*, Squirt!" Trixie exclaimed. *Holy biscuits.* "You look like a lost puppy dog. Of course, you can come."

"Woof!" Squirt barked, panting happily.

"You need help," Stoker laughed.

Trixie led the boys across the cafeteria to a set of double doors on the east side of the facility. Outside, a deep deck surrounded the building and overlooked the Rhode River.

"Wow," Stoker exhaled. "Now that's a view."

The climbing sun painted crimson, violet, and orange smears across the sky. Slightly leaning trees framed their view, and the water was as reflective and still as mirror glass.

"Not that, Spook-Boy. What do you think, I'm some kind of romantic?" Trixie picked her way through a few rocking chairs that lined the deck and went to the side of the building where several old bronze plaques hung, almost blending into the wall. Trixie paused at one toward the middle of the wall and said, "This is what I was talking about."

Stoker followed, and Squirt said, "What's up with the rocking chairs? It's like Cracker Barrel on steroids."

Stoker laughed but drifted closer to the wall.

Trixie said, "Take a look."

Stoker read the plaque. Camp Letts had been founded in 1906, but in 1954, the grounds had been virtually destroyed by Hurricane Hazel, the most destructive storm of that year. The raging tempest had ridden up the east coast and pounded the Mid-Atlantic for days on end. The damage had been extensive and not just to the campgrounds. The storm had so churned up the Chesapeake Bay that all the tributaries had been inundated with silt and bay mud. A massive six-year dredging operation had mostly cleaned out the rivers and creeks, but Hazel had left her mark.

Part Four: Wings and Teeth

Later that afternoon, Stoker and Squirt were canoeing out on the Rhode River with a group of about fifteen other students. The sun was high and warm, the breeze light and comfortable, and the tide was coming in.

"If it isn't the dynamic duo of Freak-Boy and Squirt!" Lambert yelled as his canoe floated up nearly alongside theirs.

"Having a nice romantic boat ride?" Billy Barker asked from the back of Lambert's canoe. Barker's head looked like a red sea urchin with beady little dark eyes. "You must be on a date since you're in the canoe together, har har!"

"Leave us alone!" Squirt shouted, shoving his oar into the water to paddle away.

Stoker used his paddle to slow Squirt's attempted escape. "Billy, did you burn out one of your last two brain cells?" Stoker asked. "You and Lambert are in a canoe together, too."

"Wait," Billy said. "What are you sayin'?"

"I'm saying you two make a cuter couple."

Red-faced and swearing-mad, Lambert jammed his oar into the water and cruised even with Stoker's canoe. "You know, freak," he hissed through gritted teeth, "being at the bottom of the food chain like you are, you really ought to keep your mouth shut."

Stoker swallowed once. He seemed to always forget just how big Lambert was. Buzz-cut blond, tall, broad, and muscular—he looked like the stunt double for Ivan Drago in Rocky IV. Still, Stoker had always had a reckless streak. "Bottom of the food chain?" he echoed. "You only know that because you copied my biology test last week."

"Think you're so smart, geek?" Lambert countered. "Funny, you don't even know how to row right. Check this out!" Lambert slapped his oar down so that the flat of the paddle splashed a tidal wave at Squirt.

"Hey!" Squirt complained. He was soaked.

"What?" Billy asked, making a pouty face. "You don't like the water?" He took his oar and pushed down on one corner of Stoker's canoe. It started rocking and, before Stoker could help, Squirt fell backward and toppled over the side. His life vest floated on the surface. Squirt was gone.

Lambert and Billy rowed away as fast as they could. Stoker threw his arm into the water to grab for Squirt, but at first he couldn't see his friend at all. The water was still so cloudy from the storm.

Stoker called out a weak, "Help!" No canoes were close enough, and he didn't see any of the teachers. Stoker was about to dive in when Squirt came up sputtering and splashing.

"Get me out! Get me out!" Squirt yelled.

Careful not to fall in, Stoker hauled Squirt back into the canoe.

"Fainting phantoms!" Stoker gasped. "You nearly scared the life out of me. Dude, were you completely ignoring the instructors when they showed us how to put on the life vests?"

"S-something," Squirt muttered. "Something is down there!"

"What?" Stoker asked.

"I don't know... I saw teeth. Teeth and wings."

Teeth and wings, under water? Stoker frowned. "I want to see this for myself."

"No, you don't," Squirt said. "Trust me. Please, let's just get off the water."

Stoker nodded. He and Squirt paddled quickly back to the dock.

Part Five: The Night Stoker Graves Died

Stoker wore his backpack to the night hike. It was heavy, but it was the only way he could bring his special "ghost camera" and, of course, the Specter Nets.

Teachers and camp staff marched the students in a long, single-file line up a narrow path through the woods. The forecast for the evening was again benign, but the heat was still there—eighty degrees even after sundown. Stoker hoped for another storm, wondering—as he had been all day—why thunder boomers preceded most orb sightings. Stoker sighed and kept trudging up the path.

Wondering where Squirt and Trixie had gotten to, Stoker glanced back over his shoulder. No sign of them. Maybe they—

Something grabbed Stoker's upper arm. "BOO!" Trixie yelled, leaping out of the woods.

A sharp finger poked Stoker's stomach. "I'm a will-o'-the-wisp," Squirt moaned. "You are doomed. Doooooomed."

"Ha! Got ya, Spook-Boy!"

"Very funny, guys," Stoker said. "But I'm not in the mood."

"Grumpy tonight, huh?" she said. "Well, even if we don't see any ghosts, at least we get s'mores. C'mon."

"S'mores?" Squirt echoed. "Suh-weet!"

A few minutes later, they arrived at the bonfire. Mr. Frampstetter, the Algebra teacher, had stoked up a towering blaze of about seven inches. At least it was still enough of a fire to melt a few marshmallows. While the students smashed layers of chocolate, graham crackers, and marshmallows together, Mr. Frampstetter told a ghost story.

"He should stick to math," Stoker whispered to Trixie.

"Yeah, you could tell a better story in a heartbeat," she replied, licking marshmallow off her fingers. "Or he could just talk Algebra. Then I'd be frightened."

The teacher's tale wound on and on, and Stoker busied himself by scanning the woods. The bonfire area was pretty well enclosed by the forest. The only view was straight up through an undulating gap in the canopy. No stars, Stoker thought. The night sky had taken on a murky quality. A flash lit the clearing.

"Put away the phones!" Mr. Frampstetter growled.

There were a few more impudent flashes and playful laughs from the teens assembled there. Even Mr. Frampstetter grinned.

Stoker stopped grinning. A cool breeze wafted through the clearing. A barely audible rumble registered in the distance. "No way," Stoker muttered, fishing his phone from his backpack. He hit the weather radar app and waited as the green outline map filled in with digital color. A lot of digital color. A lot of red. *Uh, oh.*

Stoker leaped up and bounded to the teacher. "Mr. Frampstetter," he said, "we better get going. Another storm is coming. Almost here."

"Stoker, I said put away the phones. Wait, what'd you say about a storm?"

"Look!" He showed the display—all angry oranges and reds—to the teacher, who went ghostly white.

Mr. Frampstetter darted over to Mrs. Kiering, who was bagging up the s'mores supplies. They whispered hurriedly.

"Sophomores, listen up!" Mrs. Kiering called out. This was her 'I mean business' voice. The teens went silent. "There is another major thunderstorm on its way. We need to get—"

FLASH-BANG!

For a split second, every single face in the group shone with bright light. Real terror, Stoker thought, his own heartbeat kicking a few notches higher than usual.

"Okay, line up!" Mrs. Kiering called out over the receding thunder. "Straight line back down the path. Follow the camp staff. Let's go!"

Flashlights popped on and, in a not-so-straight line, the students began stampeding from the clearing. Stoker felt a drop of rain hit his nose. More lightning flashed. More thunder.

Trixie took both Stoker and Squirt by the arms. "Time to go!" she said.

Between the noise of the teenagers squealing and jostling as they marched and the more and more frequent thunder, it was nearly impossible to communicate. But someone, Lambert maybe, cried out above the din. "Look! In the forest! Strange lights, coming this way!"

Stoker skidded in some dead leaves and didn't see anything at first.

"There's one!" someone yelled. "There's another!" "Oh, my gosh, they're all over the place!" That sounded like Mrs. Kiering.

That was all it took. The students screamed and shrieked, taking off in all directions with teachers chasing.

At last, Stoker saw them. One after another, vaporous glowing orbs began to appear. The ghost lights bobbed and weaved through the darkling forest with a kind of lazy, ethereal grace, illuminating raindrops in their pallid colors.

Squirt saw them too. "Will-o'-the-wisps, they're real!" he cried. "I'm outta here!"

"No, wait!" Stoker called. But it was too late. Squirt tore off toward one of the paths. "Trixie, go after him. Make sure he doesn't trip on a tree root and break his neck!"

Trixie sprinted away after Squirt.

Stoker stared into the woods. Glowing spheres surged up the hill, coming in from all directions now. Honest to goodness will-o'-the-wisps, bobbing and weaving through the trees.

As Stoker stared at the ghostly forms, he noted that they were not the perfectly round orbs he'd always imagined. These were more like masses of electrical energy shrouded in ethereal light. Each one shifted and pulsed. There was something familiar about the way they moved. Stoker turned in a small circle, taking pictures of every will-o'-the-wisp that was within range.

A blood-curdling scream erupted from the woods off to Stoker's left. "Ahhh! It's got me, it's biting, tearing me! Help!"

Stoker sprang toward the direction of the voice. He followed a path that fell steeply down a hill. He skidded down the incline and almost ran into one of the glowing intruders. It writhed and churned in the air—attacking someone. Stoker couldn't believe it. It was Lambert.

"Help me, Stoker!" Lambert begged. "I'm bleeding! Do something!"

He didn't care much for the bully, but Stoker wouldn't leave him to this fate. He snatched a Specter Net out of his backpack and flung it at the spirit. The net spiraled and tore the ghost right out of the air and pinned it up against a wide tree trunk.

"Th-thanks, man," Lambert said. "I owe you one—dude, look out!"

Stoker ducked just in time. A bluish ghostlight whooshed overhead. With a yelp, Lambert sprinted away. When Stoker turned, he saw dozens more will-o'-the-wisps pouring down the hill toward him. And the rain had picked just this moment to open up. He had no choice but to run for it. He charged recklessly down the hill, following the path but slipping, sliding, eating spider webs, and getting scratched by branches.

Stoker turned a hard corner, took one step, and put his foot in a dark red puddle. It splashed up his pants leg and smeared on his shoes. It looked like blood. Stoker ran for his life. He exited the forest and searched for lights—the safe kind.

"There!" he cried out. "The boathouse!" It wasn't far—100 yards, maybe. A football field. A pitching wedge. Ten school buses. That's it. But to Stoker, the boathouse looked like it was a hundred miles away. Wet, muddy, and all uphill—no easy task. Stoker looked over his shoulder and pounded up the slope. The ghost lights, more of them now, were closing in. He heard their eerie swishing sounds, saw their creepy writhing movements.

But he didn't see the branch.

The storm had broken off a gnarled limb from some high tree and hurled it to the hill. The branch caught the cuff of Stoker's pants leg, and he went down hard. He felt the burning of broken skin on his chin. He rolled to a knee, but it was too late. The ghost lights swarmed closer. They were nearly upon him. Stoker screamed as the first bites cut into his arms. He tried to fight them off, smacking and raking his arms recklessly. But then, of all things, his lips felt strange. They began to tingle, feeling as if they were going numb. And it was getting harder and harder to breathe. Writhing ghostly lights and then smothering darkness were the last things he saw before his heart stopped beating.

Part Six: Shock

Lambert Gold stood at the top of the hill, flanked by Trixie, Squirt, and Mrs. Kiering. "Where, Lambert, where?" the teacher demanded.

"Last I saw him, he was still in the woods. This way!" He bounded down the hill, his flashlight bobbing and weaving like the will-o'-the-wisps themselves.

The rest of the group fanned out and moved at a cautious hurry. Two-thirds of the way down the hill, Trixie screamed, "Here! He's here! I don't think he's breathing!"

Mrs. Kiering and Squirt arrived next, followed by Lambert, who looked down on Stoker's body. "Oh, no," he whispered. "They got him."

"Lambert, run—I mean sprint—to the medical station!" Mrs. Kiering commanded. "Tell Dr. Conroy to bring the defibrillator!"

"I'm on it!" Lambert was gone in a flash, cutting diagonally across the hill.

Trixie mashed her lips down on Stoker's, and Squirt yelped, "What are you doing?"

"Rescue breathing," she huffed. "I lifeguard every summer. I'll do CPR, too."

Mrs. Kiering knelt by Stoker and took up his limp hand. "C'mon, Stoker, get back here!"

Trixie began chest compressions, counting out thirty and then giving two more rescue breaths. "Mrs. Kiering," she said, "there's something wrong with his lips. They're all puffy."

"His hand is swollen too," the teacher replied. Then she yelled, "Trixie, you're a genius! Stoker's having a reaction. Keep up the CPR. I've got an EpiPen in my backpack."

The teacher unslung her pack, nearly ripped open a zippered compartment, and took out the epinephrine injector. She jammed it into the meatiest part of Stoker's thigh and held it there for a slow three-count. Mrs. Kiering removed the device and blurted out, "Where is that doctor? Stoker doesn't have much time."

Part Seven: Stoker's Legacy

Stoker felt the strangest sensation, something like a thousand fingers gripping his body and pulling. It reminded him of the undertow on a day of rough ocean surf. He opened his eyes and blinked raindrops. He saw a man's face, no one he knew. But Trixie was there and Squirt and Lambert and Mrs. Kiering. But there was someone else standing behind them all. A tall feminine form, shrouded in writhing light, stood there, staring.

"M-Mom?" Stoker whispered.

The woman smiled. Then she held up a suitcase, stuck out her thumb, and was gone.

"Stoker, you're alive!" Trixie exclaimed. "*Graças a Deus!*"

Stoker coughed once, trying to speak, but growing darkness blotted out all vision, all thought.

❧

Stoker awoke again sometime later. He lay in a hospital bed. His father, Trixie, and Mrs. Kiering sat around him.

"You sure picked the hard way to solve the mystery, kiddo," his father said.

"Mystery...what...mystery?"

"The Edgewater will-o'-the-wisps," he said. "They're eels. They bit you, and you had a terrible allergic reaction."

"Eels!" Stoker exclaimed. "Not ghosts? I don't believe it. Eels?"

Mrs. Kiering explained, "As far as I can tell, these eels are a new species. I want to do more research, but the few sources I checked had nothing like them. Unlike flying fish, these eels have strong enough wing-fins to propel themselves and change direction. Nothing else like these in the world."

"Hazel," Stoker muttered.

The group answered as one, "What?"

"Hurricane Hazel," Stoker whispered. "Churned up the Bay. Remember what Dr. Cooper said about upwelling? The eels are probably deep-sea eels that the hurricane deposited in the Bay and its tributaries."

"That's crazy cool," Trixie said. "Spook-Boy, that's brilliant."

"And the storms," he went on dreamily, "so much electricity in the air, bolts hitting the water..."

"Must have triggered the eels to surface," Mrs. Kiering said, "and take to the air."

"Maybe the lightning supercharges the eels," Stoker pondered aloud. "Maybe it intensifies their ability to bioluminesce."

"Your allergic reaction might explain the other deaths too," Trixie said. "Unless the other victims were just scared to death. You were lucky."

Stoker's father said, "And you have that Lambert kid and Mrs. Kiering here to thank."

"Lambert?" Stoker croaked. "He helped save me?"

"He did," Mrs. Kiering replied.

"Awww, man, I'm never going to live this down," Stoker muttered. He shook his head and looked up at his teacher. "Thank you, Mrs. Kiering. I guess words don't mean a whole lot when a life is saved, but thank you. If I can ever return the favor...like if a Bunsen burner sets fire to your room or some chemicals have a bad reaction and explode..."

"Uh, let's hope nothing like that ever happens," Mrs. Kiering said with a gentle laugh. "I'm just grateful that you're alive. But, I was wondering, if the glowing eels turn out to be a new species, would you be willing to share the credit for their discovery?"

Stoker laugh-wheezed. "I could care less about the eels. You can have them. I just want to find—"

"Ghosts," Trixie and Mr. Graves said in unison. And then, they all laughed.

"What's all this ruckus?" A nurse came in and ordered everyone out. "Young Stoker needs his rest."

Alone in the dark hospital room, Stoker unleashed a loud sigh of disappointment. "They weren't really ghosts," he muttered. "I still have no proof."

Then, he remembered his mother. Smiling, Stoker Graves fell into a deep, peaceful sleep.

THE DEVIL IN THE DETAILS

DANIELLE ACKLEY-MCPHAIL

THE NAKED LIMBS OF THE GNARLED OAK TREE REACHED HIGH ABOVE Camden Finn as if to snatch the stars from the sky. The night was harsh, the air dry with the extreme cold. All around, snow glittered on the ground...everywhere *except* beneath *The Tree*.

Camden shuddered and edged back. He was new here in Basking Ridge. The odd kid out; the weirdo.

His mother had always taught him to be accepting of others. That different was just different, not wrong. Of course, she was as different as they came.

He wished the other kids' mothers had taught them the same thing. Somehow everyone at school knew he'd been sent to live with his Grandmother Camilla because Mamma wasn't right in the head. Or that's what they'd said, anyway, before they dared him to touch the cursed tree with a history of hangings...both lawful and otherwise.

Around him, the light breeze grew more forceful until it rattled the branches overhead, making them moan and sigh and wail. Camden shivered again and jerked back further. The sound echoed his last memory of Mamma, both screaming gibberish and sobbing as if her best friend had died, all while being strapped into a strange, white jacket. Reaching not for him, but for her favorite oak tree; the one she kept getting caught climbing naked, until the day the ambulance had come to take her away.

Camden couldn't really blame anyone for calling his little family weird. Heck, he'd be the first to admit it. After all, he'd been a part of it for thirteen years. But all they saw was the unacceptable behavior at the end. They weren't there when Mamma told him about the spirits of the trees with such love and longing in her bright green eyes and a sad smile on her lips. They weren't there when she walked among the grove behind their house talking and laughing softly as if visiting with old friends. Yeah... still crazy, but harmless and sweet, and you could almost believe her. Sometimes it sounded to Camden as if the trees murmured back, though he never could make out any words himself.

He didn't remember her being that bad when he was younger. Quirky, fun, not as concerned with the things other parents made a big deal about. But as he grew older, the situation changed. She became less focused, complaining that her legs burned, scratching at them until they bled. Clothes became unbearable to her and her obsession with the trees took on a frantic edge. There were times he worried he'd become just like her. There were other times he hoped he did.

He missed his mother fiercely.

She would have laughed at this dare. Heck, she would have hugged the darn tree. It was oak, her favorite kind.

For nearly half an hour Camden stood there in the bitter cold, trying to get up the nerve to move closer and touch the bole. He just couldn't do it. Something deep inside him fought the very concept. As if before him lay true madness and to press his skin against it courted such within himself. He was, however, both fascinated and horrified by the chain-link fence wrapped so close around the tree that the bark had begun to swallow it. Beneath the links, he could see great, gaping scars from where the superstitious had tried to bring the old tree down.

In the distance, a revving engine broke the spell on him. Camden jumped and spun around, his eyes scanning the road. The other kids had taunted him, telling him a speeding black car would get him if he drew near the tree. He bet one of them had talked an older sibling into coming out and pranking him if he proved braver than they thought he'd be.

Squaring his shoulders, he turned back to the oak and, before he could talk himself out of it, he lurched forward, slapping his left palm against the bark. Seconds later he yanked it away, overwhelmed by a desperate sense of grasping, of some essence— somehow oddly familiar—clinging to his.

He landed on his butt as he stumbled back, vigorously rubbing his palm down the rough cords of his pants. The skin itched and burned as if little runnels of acid etched its surface. Peering at his hand, he very nearly screamed. For a brief instant in the starlight it seemed the pattern of the bark had clung there, shaping the skin.

Again, the revving of an engine, followed by the squeal of tires on asphalt.

Camden scrambled to his feet. With teeth chattering and the muscles across his shoulders knotted, he hurried in a limping jog across the field away from the road. Compulsively, he kept looking behind him, almost missing the blaze of the car's headlights as he noticed the brisk wind dancing in his wake, brushing away his footprints.

Maybe Mamma wasn't the only one going mad, he thought as he scrambled even faster to reach the trees at the edge of the meadow as the car pursued him.

⊱✦⊰

Camden was back. He couldn't help it. The tree drew him. Called to him…a forsaken soul alone in the meadow. He could identify with it.

There was little to nothing left of the snow, except some dirty, knobby piles sheltered from the sun. Weeks had gone by since he had touched the tree. He'd told the others but they'd called him a liar. His hand still tingled, but otherwise looked normal, leaving him nothing to show for his daring.

His classmates, led by Antony, the school bully, kept egging him on, demanding he bring them some kind of proof, being too chicken to follow him out here to see for themselves. He couldn't imagine what kind of proof he could bring that they wouldn't just call another lie.

He'd never had a cell phone, a situation his grandmother hadn't bothered to rectify. It hardly mattered, though…he'd yet to psych himself up enough to even cross back beneath the tree's branches.

He caught himself rubbing his palm against his leg, something he'd been doing since that first fateful night. The skin still looked like normal skin, if a little rougher and more calloused, only every so often it seemed to shimmer a grey-green shade, like the mossy bark of an oak tree. He had to be imagining it. He'd looked up the legends surrounding the tree and all they mentioned was some crackpot notion that if you touched the tree your hand would turn black if you ate at a diner.

Who came up with this crazy stuff?

With a final look at his hand, Camden turned and headed home.

❧❦❧

Weeks went by. The barest hint of spring had begun to chase away winter's chill. Every time Camden turned around he would swear there was a black car somewhere nearby, windows tinted illegally dark, but then he would look again and it would be gone. He told himself not to be stupid and did his best to forget about the tree and all the legends he'd read about, as his classmates seemed to have done. They taunted and bullied, but had apparently lost interest in the challenge they'd issued.

Left to himself, shunned even by the outcasts, Camden spent a lot of time knocking around his grandmother's place, hanging out in the vast yard. Never quite feeling welcome there any more than he did at school.

He began to notice something quite peculiar while striving to stay out of her way. There was no wood. No trees in the yard, no white picket fence. In fact, hers was wrought-iron, beautifully ornate, but cold and hard. Even the house, he learned, was poured concrete, and the garage at the back of the property was a stark, cinderblock building with large metal doors locked tight. He had tried to peer in the dusty windows, but his grandmother came across him poking around. Her gaze, when he caught her eye, was stony as she sharply pointed him away.

Though she generally seemed to ignore him as much as possible—while providing his care within the letter of the law—from that point forward he felt constantly watched.

When he went to sleep that night, he dreamt to the sound of tree branches wailing, dreams that did not bear remembering.

❧❦❧

"That's private property you keep skulking around, you know," Grandmother snapped at him one morning, just around the spring equinox. She stood in front of the kitchen sink washing dishes, as stiff as one of her wrought-iron fence posts. "Stay away from that infernal tree. You keep away from that meadow or I'll let the sheriff deal with you."

Camden nodded but said nothing. He flinched as she whirled on him, grabbing his arm and shaking him. "Do you hear me, young man?"

"Yes, Grandmother," he stuttered, shocked by the strength she wielded, despite her seeming age. This was the first time she had ever touched him.

His grandmother *hmph*ed and turned away, her expression hard and etched with bitterness.

Until they had come for his mother, Camden hadn't even known he had a grandmother. Though she did her duty and took him in, she clearly did not seem at all pleased about it. She was his father's mother, according to the social worker. His father... there was something else Camden had never had, at least not in any practical sense. He had passed away early on before Camden had been old enough to remember him. Even so, by the stories Mamma had shared, and the love she'd clearly felt, Camden found it hard to believe his father had come from this harsh, unfeeling woman.

He wondered exactly how many days until he turned eighteen and had no one to answer to but the law.

Lowering his head, he pretended interest in his cold breakfast until Grandmother threw down her rag and left the room. That was when he caught himself again rubbing his palm against his leg. He brought his other hand up and ran his fingertip along where the tingling had begun to burn. His palm was rough and thick, but he could feel his veins prominently, branching like roots beneath the skin.

Shuddering, he drew his finger away, cold chills coursing through him.

Camden dreamt of his mother. Her lithe form, her delicate features, the sense of wildness about her, and the slight edge of madness in her gaze that he had for so long denied the existence of—eased, if not banished, only when she draped herself among the tree branches, bare skin against bark, not quite one with the tree...but longing to be—but most of all he dreamt of her desperate grasping for the branches as she was pulled from it that very last time. Of the panic in her gaze as the strange men restrained her, of the hopelessness that dimmed her gaze while Camden watched the vehicle containing her drive further away.

He woke, gasping, and all he could think of was that damned chain-link fence wrapped around the gnarled oak...so reminiscent of the restraints binding his mother.

Camden could do nothing for her, but the tree...that was different.

Though every impulse screamed at him 'No!,' a wild, crazed idea took root. Quietly, he climbed from bed and drew on his clothes, not bothering with socks or shoes. With gentle steps, he crept to the window and slowly slid the sash open. A firm push popped the screen from the window. Camden grabbed it before it could clatter to the pavers below and leaned it against his bedroom wall before climbing out and sliding the window shut behind him.

In the moonlight, his shoulders itched more than his palm ever had. Ignoring the sensation of being watched, he made his way across town until he came to Antony's house. He knew which bedroom belonged to the bully because he often tossed things at Camden as he was walking by. Not bothering to be quiet, Camden rapped on the glass.

He heard a thud, then watched as the window opened, revealing Antony's scowling face.

"You are so dead, dickwad..."

Camden ignored him. "Give me a bolt cutter and I'll give you the evidence that I touched the tree."

Antony smirked. "Yeah...right."

"Give it to me, or I'll tell everyone you were too much of a wuss to touch the tree yourself."

The expression on the bully's face grew even uglier, at odds with his tousled hair and pajamas. When he came through the open window, Camden braced himself for violence, but the other boy just crept around to the garage and disappeared inside, coming out a moment later with the bolt cutters.

"Have the proof tomorrow, or I'm kicking your butt...and either way, I'm telling my dad you stole these...."

Antony's father was the sheriff.

Camden just took the tool and turned away, hurrying off into the night in the direction of the meadow—and The Tree.

The moon sat heavy and full in the sky, bathing the meadow in a pale, blue glow seemingly everywhere except in the area around The Tree. He couldn't help but think of the name he discovered when researching the legends...The Devil's Tree.

He shivered. Though the air of madness surrounding the oak scared the piss out of him, instinct told him the essence of the tree was not evil. Steeling himself, he approached the bole, gaze locked on the angry scars left by frightened mortals, the metal links yet binding and cutting the tree.

Dropping to his knees, he wedged the snipping end of the bolt cutters against the first link, cringing as the steel cut more into the bark than the fence. A sharp pain shot through his left hand, but he continued to leverage his weight on the handles of the tool, half murmuring apologies, though he scarcely knew why, or to whom. With a sharp snap, the first link gave way. He sensed a satisfaction not altogether his own. The meadow seemed poised in anticipation, a hush descending to blanket out the hum of usual night sounds.

As he started on the second, the gunning of a distant engine reached his ears. Straining until pain screamed through his hand, Camden struggled even harder to cut through the links. He was barely three-quarters of the way through when bright lights pinned him to the tree. With all his weight he got through all but the last bit of fence before he heard the squeal of brakes behind him, and felt the sting of rocks thrown up from the still-hard ground.

"Get away from that tree, you devil spawn!" Venom dripped from his grandmother's words.

Again Camden was reminded of her unexpected strength as she shoved him away from the final link before he had cut all the way through. He managed to keep his grip on the bolt cutters but lost his balance. "You will not release her now! You will not set the devil free to corrupt more good men like my Tommy!"

Tommy. That was his father's name.

Some small part of Camden noticed the roar of a second car approaching, but most of his focus stayed riveted as he realized the 'devil' his grandmother spoke of was his mother.

She wasn't making sense, but now more than ever Camden was driven to strip the iron fence from the tree. He eyed the final link, which held together by the barest sliver, so slight he dared wonder if he would even need the bolt cutters to break it free.

His grandmother stood over him, her eyes ablaze and no small measure of madness dancing around the edges of her expression. Camden was certain he spied loathing for him in her gaze. Her chest heaved and outrage etched harder lines into her face than those already there.

"Why did you even take me in?" Camden asked.

"That she-devil stole my only son, but you are half his and by God, I *will* see the demon half run out of you."

She moved forward as if to strike him. Camden set his left hand behind him, bracing for the blow. He gasped as his flesh came down on a gnarled root. Heat blazed through him from the point of contact until he seemed to swell with it, weariness draining from his limbs as strength filled him as it never had before. In the moonlight, his skin seemed subtly ridged, like an echo of the oak bark beneath him, a state that struck him as both strange and fitting, if a puzzle for later. For now, there were other things to deal with.

He did not raise a hand to his grandmother, but he did climb to his feet, flexing his toes in the dirt and grass as he tightened his grip on the bolt cutters.

Tension crackled on the air as she took a step closer, brandishing a crowbar she must have carried from the large, black Cadillac still running behind her.

As she moved, a second car drew up beside the first, strobe lights sending wild pulses of color across the meadow. The door clicked open and the sheriff's voice called out, "Camilla, you will stop right there..."

For a moment, she looked like she would resist, but slowly the tip of the crowbar lowered to the ground. Feeling nothing but pity for the bitter woman who confused love with hate, Camden looked away, meeting the sheriff's gaze.

"This is my land, my tree, my fence! I want him arrested for destroying private property."

"He's your grandson..."

"He's a hellspawn!"

Before the sheriff could move to intervene, his grandmother swung the crowbar with all her might. Calm as he had never been calm before, Camden dropped the bolt cutters and raised his right hand to intercept the wicked hook descending on him, the strength of the mighty oak shoring him up. Wrenching the tool from her grip, Camden reversed the hook and yanked with all the power at his disposal on the chain-link fence, snapping the final link and tearing the overgrown fence from the trunk of the tree, sending bark flying.

Grandmother flinched away from the sprung metal links, screaming a piercing scream as she tore at her hair and fell to her knees.

As the chainlink fell away, a surge of power swept through the meadow. Grasses plastered to the ground and the tree's new-minted leaves danced in the moonlight as Camden lifted his gaze to the oak's gnarled crown. His mouth fell open and his eyes went wide. He could just make out a glimmer of bright green and Mamma's cheery smile. He marveled that her smooth, light brown skin blended with the oak's bark as she lounged in the upper branches as if she belonged there. Camden thought perhaps she did, finally as one with her own her true tree.

In the rustle of the leaves, he heard her voice. "I love you...I will always love you."

Different was just different, not wrong.

GLINT STARCROST AND THE ICE PRISON

PAUL REGNIER

YOU'D THINK THE WORST THING ABOUT AN ICE PRISON WOULD BE THE frostbite, but at Cludmoor, the roaming horde of red-eyed, bottom feeders below was far worse.

My day started with the cold, metal claws of hulking guard droids yanking me from the landing pod, confiscating my beautiful Stinger 9 blaster, dragging me through the snow, and forcing me into a towering grey warehouse.

I no longer asked the question, 'how did I end up here?' The harsh reality of a star pilot for hire left little time for reflection. My mind immediately jumped to, 'how do I get out of here?'

The guards sealed me in a holding cell constructed of thick ice. My pleas of innocence and cries for mercy did nothing to slow their methodical cruelty. The impassive white glow of their electronic eyes appeared to take no remorse or joy in their work. It was just another line of code to follow.

Days like this made me question my life choices.

My cell was basically a giant cube of ice about ten-foot square with fist-sized holes in the sides and bottom. Besides the unforgiving floor, there was nowhere to lay down or even sit. Bathroom breaks were going to be rough.

Massive claws of iron descended on my cell like the hand of a giant and lifted it toward a suspension line above. A similar ice cell with another unfortunate prisoner was already attached to the line. I was just another convict in this automated assembly line.

The other cell hung about five feet ahead of me. Inside was a woman facing away from me with raven-colored hair that flowed down her back in tight curls. She hovered cross-legged near the base of her ice cell, her fingers pressed against her temples. A golden glow shone around her forehead.

"Hello?" I called.

There was no answer. She didn't even flinch.

I cupped cold hands over my mouth, speaking through the holes of my ice wall. "Yoo-hoo? Floating lady?"

Still no answer.

The assembly line jerked forward, and I slid back into the unforgiving cell wall. My fellow prisoner seemed unaffected by the abrupt motion. She continued to hover, unmoving.

Another prisoner was attached to the suspension line behind me. He was a scraggly looking mouse of a guy whose blond beard and hair looked like a mess of frayed wires. His thin frame was swallowed up by a brown trench coat about two sizes too big for him.

"Hey." His wild eyes connected with mine. "You a cyborg?"

"Cyborg?" Was he trying to insult me? "No."

"Oh." He looked me up and down. "Then what's with the outfit? Lose a bet?"

It was just my luck that the prisoners I ended up between were a hovering mute girl and a mangy little punk.

"Listen, skrid," I pointed a threatening finger. "This is the uniform of the Moon Men Alliance. I wouldn't insult them if I were you."

He chuckled. "They're still around? I heard the Satellite Seven took out all but three of them. Not much of an alliance."

Unfortunately, he was right about everything. Even the bad outfit. The three remaining Moon Men hired me for a life-threatening mission they claimed was "easy money," assigned me all the dangerous duties, then kept my cut of the profits, and ejected me onto this prison moon in a barely functional escape pod.

My only takeaway from the experience was their wretched, glossy black uniform with raised muscle padding in all the wrong places. It was as if an alien with only rumors of the human anatomy designed the suit.

"Oh yeah?" I narrowed my eyes. "You got an alliance behind you? Or are you just eager to get on my bad side?"

"Whoa, easy now." He took a step back, shrinking into his trench coat. "I thought that was cyborg exoskeleton. No offense. It just looks a little odd. And snug. Is it hard to breathe in that thing?"

"Listen here you little rat, when I get outta this cell–"

"I'm sorry." He put up his hands. "I can't help it. I talk too much. It angers a lot of people. That's how I ended up here. Got double-crossed by some mercenaries. Probably the same thing happened to you with the Moon Men, right?"

I gritted my teeth, growing tired of his spot-on guesses.

He smiled. "Uh-huh, I knew it. Hey, such is life in this thug-run universe. Don't worry, we'll get our shot. One day, we'll have the money and power on our side, right?"

I scanned the thick ice walls surrounding me. "Not today."

"Don't be too sure. I'm Pek by the way. What's your name?"

"Glint."

The suspension line jolted forward once more, and I was thrown to the side of my cell. Pek collapsed in a crumpled heap on the floor of his cube, his trench coat swallowing him up like a blanket.

"You okay?" I called out.

He grunted. "I hate this place already."

The suspension line continued forward, gaining speed as it moved. The line exited a rectangular opening in the warehouse wall. The light of the overcast sky flooded our cells and painted the featureless horizon in a bleak grey.

We rose about twenty yards above the frozen tundra. Roving bands of sickly-looking humanoid creatures populated the icy ground below. There must've been hundreds of them.

"Bottom Feeders." Pek fumbled onto his knees, scanning the landscape below. "They're a nasty bunch. Deterrence for early prison escapes."

Monotone grunting rose up from a passing group of bottom feeders causing a sickening twist in my stomach. They had red eyes, corpse-like skin, and no detectable signs of personal hygiene.

"Whew." Pek waved a hand in front of his nose. "They reek."

I couldn't argue. The rising odor was somewhere between mold and rancid meat.

Pek stood and moved to the front of his cube, closer to me, his eyes fixed ahead. "Who's the girl?"

I shrugged. "No idea. I tried to talk to her. She didn't answer."

He pursed his lips. "Why is she hovering? And glowing?"

There were so many oddities in the universe that a hovering woman with a glowing ring around her forehead seemed pretty tame. "Who knows?"

He scratched his head. "You think she's into short guys?"

I raised a brow.

Something ahead caught his attention. "There it is."

I followed his gaze to a castle-like structure in the distance.

He gave a low whistle. "The ice prison of Cludmoor."

The thick walls of the castle prison were daunting.

"I've heard the only life forms in there are the prisoners."

"Yep," Pek said. "Built by the Murgeret Kingdom before they got wiped out by disease. They made it so high tech it could run itself. Bet they never thought it would outlast them. Now it's just a drop-off spot for people you want to get rid of." Pek pointed to himself, then me.

"Then escape is just a matter of outsmarting the machines."

"Oh, is that all?" He chuckled. "Outsmarting ever-vigilant supercomputers, sleepless guards, and full sensor sweeps every freem of the day? Even if by some miracle you manage to escape the walls, bottom feeders wait right outside for their next meal."

I scowled at him, trying to ignore my rising panic. "What are you trying to do, scare me?"

He spread his hands wide. "There I go running my mouth again. It's all because of this." Pek turned his head and lifted up a fake ear. Underneath it was a computer panel embedded in his scalp with rows of blinking lights and buttons. "My head's too full of data."

A swirl of queasy went through my gut. "You're a cyborg?"

"No." He shook his head. "Tech-enhanced. My brain is awesome. I can jack into most systems and exploit vulnerabilities."

I paused, not sure how to respond. I'd heard my share of cyborg cautionary tales.

His brow furrowed. "You don't like cyborgs, do you?"

"Um," I fumbled. "I've heard stories."

"Pffft." He waved a dismissive hand. "First off, I'm not really a cyborg. I'm tech-enhanced. Second, don't listen to space bar tales. Bad programming causes glitchy cyborgs. Blame the faulty human programmers."

I gave a hesitant nod.

"I'll make it easy for you." He put his hands forward as if offering something. "I have skills. Mental skills enhanced by digital information. This prison is completely automated. For me, it's a simple escape."

Suddenly my opinion of being stuck next to the chattering, mousy guy changed. "Wait, you know how to escape?"

He huffed a laugh. "Easy. Tell you what, I'll bring you along. Would that change your opinion of cyborgs?"

My cold sense of doom thawed with the hope of escape. "Well, yeah. Of course."

"Great because I need help and we need to work fast." He pointed down to a large metal structure just ahead. "That's a control point. I can jack into the system from there and unlock grounded spacecraft inside. Stand back."

I took a step back in my cube, still trying to absorb everything he said. Pek lifted his false ear and his fingers adjusted something on the computerized side of his head. There was a high-pitched tone followed by a sharp splintering sound. A series of spider-web cracks formed in our ice cells. Even the hovering woman's cell bore cracks.

Nearby bottom feeders took notice. A few of the gruesome creatures headed our way.

"Whoa." A heavy thrum of adrenaline rushed through my chest. "You sure about this?"

"Well, not a hundred percent," Pek spoke casually. "I don't have exact charts of this particular installation. I'd say about seventy-two percent."

"Seventy-two?" My heart sped up. "Those bottom feeders will tear us apart."

"If we end up in the main prison, we don't stand a chance," Pek said. "We have to escape now."

"Hold on." I was second-guessing his whole plan.

"There's no time." The high tone sounded once more. My cube broke apart in a shower of ice fragments and the floor gave way beneath me. There was a sudden drop where my stomach felt like it leapt into my chest. I hit the snow below in a painful rush.

Black specks clouded my eyes like I might pass out, then dissipated. I shook off the snow and swayed to a standing position.

A field of bottom feeders ambled toward us. They were far more menacing now that I was on their level. Their red eyes were fixed on me. Their mouths hung open revealing sharp, stubby teeth. A strong desire to sprint in the opposite direction welled up. Unfortunately, the creatures were advancing from every direction.

Pek was on his knees, holding the side of his head. I rushed over and helped him up.

"What now?" I gripped him by the shoulders, wanting to shake him into action.

He blinked a few times as if waking up. His eyes fixed on the metal structure nearby. "Control point. Come on." He took off, his long trench coat trailing behind.

I started after him when I noticed the woman prisoner a few feet away. She lay collapsed in the snow, her head no longer glowing yellow. Bottom feeders were closing in on her.

Despite my nagging survival instincts, I ran to the woman and lifted her up. She winced as if in pain, her eyes closed. This was the first time I'd actually seen her face. She was a vision of beauty, even with her eyes all pained and squinty. Her high cheekbones, brown skin, and full lips were like something out of a dream. My daily struggle for existence usually left me surrounded by grizzled star pirates and smelly thugs. For a moment, all the dregs of the universe faded away. She was an oasis in a lonely desert.

Grunts from the approaching creatures snapped me out of the daydream.

"We have to move!" I tried to rally her to action. "Now!"

She stumbled into me, looking dazed. She wasn't going to recover in time. I wasn't a hero. My code of ethics was squishy. But there were times I had to act or I couldn't live with myself.

I hefted her over my shoulder and ran to rendezvous with Pek. My adrenaline must've been pumping overtime because I reached the structure while he still fiddled with a control panel by a metal door.

I set my dream girl down with her back to the structure and scanned the area for any kind of weapon. Nothing. No metal pipes, not even a broken stick.

"You can get in, right?" My question came out as more of a growl since I was fueled by extreme terror at the moment.

Pek had a cable running from his head into the control panel. "This code structure is ancient. I need some time."

Dozens of bottom feeders were ten yards away. They looked angry ... and hungry.

"We don't have time!" I said. "I thought you said you could do this."

"I can," he said. "Eventually. Wait, I found something. This should help."

A metal panel in the structure wall next to him slid away revealing a row of energy pistols. It was a beautiful sight.

"Now you're talking." I lunged for the first one and powered it on. Nothing happened. I hit the activator a few times and it remained dead.

An unholy chorus of moans sounded from the approaching mob. I dared not check to see how close they were. I grabbed another pistol. Dead. Another. Also dead.

"None of these work," I shouted.

"Maybe it's been too long and they drained," Pek said. "Living guards evacuated long ago."

"Fantastic. Then we're all dead!" I fumbled through the row of energy pistols with the same result until I reached the last one. With a hum of energy that sent an electric thrill to my core, it powered on ... then shut off.

"Work, blast it!" I hit the side of the pistol with the palm of my hand and it powered back on.

I turned to find the closest bottom feeders only steps away. My grip closed on the trigger sending a blistering array of energy blasts into the approaching fiends. Their ashen bodies crumpled to the ground with gurgling shrieks.

The advancing ranks slowed, unsure of this new challenge to feeding time. My confidence surged and I let loose another volley of blasts, taking out several more.

"How's it coming, Pek?"

"Any moment now."

"Okay, I'll hold them off." As soon as the words left my mouth, the pistol went dead.

"Oh, come on!" I hit the side of the gun with no effect.

The creatures rallied and pushed forward. Soon they were only a few feet away. I backed toward the structure trying to smack the weapon back to life.

"Pek!" I yelled.

Sickly grey hands reached for me. I braced for my final battle, my fists tightening, ready to throw their last punches.

A bright flash of golden light filled the area and the nearest group of bottom feeders were hurled backward as if hit with a powerful gust of wind. Their screeching cries faded away as they careened to the ground in the distance.

Beside me, the woman I'd left slumped against the building walked forward, her hands outstretched. A thin headband glowed brightly against her forehead.

A group of bottom feeders to our right closed in. She waved a hand toward them and a golden stream of light flung them away. Who was this woman? She was amazing. She turned and locked eyes with me. Her face looked golden in the warm light emanating from her headband. What was her story? Was she single?

"I can't hold them much longer." Her voice resonated, somewhere between speaking and singing.

As if in response, my pistol powered back on. "I'm with you." I fired once and the gun promptly died.

The woman turned to me, her face tight with concentration. "What are you doing?"

I held up the gun. "It keeps dying."

The horde surged forward once more. The woman glowed and thrust her hands forward. A golden wave of power swept away the front line of bottom feeders, their gangly limbs flailing as they hurtled backward.

She took a few steps back, breathing heavily. "I have to rest."

The creatures advanced toward us. We were out of options.

"Pek!" I yelled.

"Got it!" he called.

The door of the metal structure slid open. Without a word, we bolted after Pek into the doorway. On the other side, his fingers raced across the access panel. A blaring alarm echoed inside.

Dozens of enraged, red eyes glared at me through the doorway. I covered my ears to minimize pain from the alarm and took a few steps back, hoping the door wouldn't jam.

The creatures gathered at the door, reaching in with their diseased grey arms. Suddenly, the alarm went silent and the door slid closed with a metallic clunk, severing a few bottom feeder arms in the process.

"Take that you filthy beasts." Pek broke into a gleeful chuckle.

The woman's nose crinkled, studying Pek with a look of disgust.

I breathed deeply, realizing I'd held my breath for a long time. We were in a narrow entryway with a closed steel door on the other end.

"Can someone explain to me what's going on?" The woman leaned over, hands on her knees.

"We just saved you from a life sentence in Cludmoor." Pek grinned and made his way to the next door. "You're welcome."

Her brow furrowed, watching him pass by.

"You get used to him after a while." I smirked. "I'm Glint. Glint Starcrost. Thanks for the help out there."

"Velitia." She wiped a drip of perspiration from her temple. "Where are we?"

A series of ascending beeps sounded as Pek set to work on the next control panel.

"This is a control point," I said. "There should be a ship here we can use to fly outta this nightmare. Pek knows how to hack the system. He's a cyborg."

"Tech-enhanced," Pek called back.

I rolled my eyes. "Sorry, tech-enhanced."

She exhaled deeply. "Praise God. Once they sealed me in that ice, I thought that was it. But I never gave up. I prayed that I would never reach Cludmoor. That something, someone would help." Her rich, brown eyes were filled with warmth. "And I prayed that I could help someone else escape the same fate."

It'd been a while since I heard anyone speak like Velitia. In my teens, I piloted my missionary uncle from planet to planet to spread his faith. He was always trying to interest me in the Bible, telling me how every soul is precious to God. But after he died, so did my connection with faith. I had to admit, hearing her words brought back warm memories and stirred something powerful inside that I hadn't felt in a long time.

"Whatever works, I guess." I shrugged. "I don't do much praying these days."

"But you did at one time?" she asked.

"Sort of. I guess the harsh universe kind of beat it out of me."

She put a hand on my shoulder, her eyes searching mine. "I understand. I just lost someone very close. But faith can offer hope and strength, even through the pain."

The far door slid away with a clunk.

"We're in." Pek rushed into the next room.

Velitia and I were close behind. The next room was a landing bay, big enough for two ships. One bay was empty. A dusty freighter filled the other bay. It looked like it had been through an interstellar war. My guess was it hadn't left this hanger for some time.

"Yikes." Pek grimaced at the old freighter.

"You think it's operational?" I said.

"Let's hope so. Guards are on the way to check the alarm trigger. We gotta move." Pek rushed toward a pedestal control panel near the ship and plugged his head cable in.

I leaned over to Velitia. "You might want to start praying again."

"Already on it," she said.

"So," I tried to sound smooth. "If we get this ship running, where you headed? Home planet? Space station? Your boyfriend's place?"

She lifted a brow. "I don't have a boyfriend if that's what you're getting at."

"Well then, perhaps–"

"Glint." She put a finger to my lips. "I appreciate the interest. I can't entertain that right now. I almost just got eaten by bottom feeders. You're cute but your timing is terrible. Maybe later?"

"You're right." I put my hands up. "Escape first, romance later."

She smirked. "I said maybe later."

"I got something," Pek said.

We hurried over, gathering on the opposite side of the pedestal.

Pek shook his head. "These records are bizarre. Apparently, this freighter was grounded because of a quirky Artificial Intelligence. No major damages recorded." His eyes were wide with excitement. "This is our ticket out of here."

"Great!" I said. "Start it up."

"Okay." He widened his stance and gripped the sides of the pedestal. "Lots of technical information required. I'm switching to voice command." He pushed a button and steadied himself. "This might look a little weird. Don't judge."

Velitia shot me a worried look.

He cleared his throat. "Computer. System download."

Pek's body seized, then started to tremble. His head went into a shaking rhythm like he was experiencing his own personal earthquake.

"Is he okay?" Velitia's eyes squinted with concern.

"He's fine." I couldn't help but share her unease. "I think."

Another disturbing moment of shaking went by before Pek's body relaxed.

His eyes snapped open. "Got it. Watch this." His fingers danced across the control panel. There was a sudden whirring of energy from the freighter. Lights blinked to life around the ship and the engines powered on. A landing ramp lowered, and the roof of the building slid open, granting access to the sky beyond.

"Yes!" I shouted. "Great work, Pek."

"We're all set. I've disabled the exterior weaponry of the prison grounds for a clean getaway. Everything seems good for... Wait... Oh, this is interesting." His eyes jittered back and forth as if reading at an accelerated pace. "Not only are we free, but we're going to be rich."

He definitely had my attention now. "I'm listening."

"This place needs supplies. Several key systems are running low. Their days of self-sustainability are over," he smiled. "The computer is asking for help. Supplies in exchange for resources."

I was eager for specifics. "What kind of resources?"

"Precious gems. Lots of 'em. Apparently, prison construction dug up a nice little stash." He gave a mousy little chuckle. "The machines stored them, calculating this need would arise. Talk about being at the right place at the right time."

Most of my star pilot career put me in the wrong place at the wrong time. This was a nice change of pace. A hope sprang up that my days of scraping by for existence were at an end.

"Hold on." Velitia put a hand up. "Running supplies for this prison? This place is horrible. We can't help this atrocity continue."

Pek spread out his hands. "Hey, it's all relative. I'm sure there are reasons we all ended up here."

"I was sent here by thugs who killed my best friend." Velitia pointed to herself, her eyes bright with indignation. "There's no court here. No rule of law. If these machines are finally winding down, that's the only justice I see."

Pek's eyes slid over to me. "Glint, you wanna help me out here?"

My waffling moral code battled with self-preservation. I'd been waiting for an opportunity like this for a long time. But Velitia's integrity made me feel sick inside for entertaining the thought.

"Maybe we can change something here," I attempted to play both sides. "If we start running shipments, maybe we can fix the systems. Find the people wrongly imprisoned and free them."

Pek motioned to me. "There you go. Problem solved."

"Nothing is solved." Velitia seemed more upset than ever, casting an angry glance my way. "How are you going to assess prisoners? Ask them if they're innocent?"

"For starters," Pek said.

"This is wrong." Her headband lit up with a golden glow. "Enough innocent beings have suffered in this place."

"And plenty of criminals are probably here too." Pek narrowed his eyes. "It's not our call. Let's just run the supplies for a while and–"

"No!" she said. "I won't let this continue."

Pek let out a long sigh. "And there's no way I can convince you otherwise?"

She shook her head. "Not a chance."

He pursed his lips. "Okay, I tried."

In a flash he lifted his hand toward her, the fingers splitting apart to reveal a metal barrel concealed within. An energy blast fired from his hand, hitting her in the stomach. She doubled over with a cry of pain.

His hand swiveled toward me with lightning speed, just as I began to lift my pistol.

"Don't do it, Glint," he said. "That gun is probably dead but if you lift it toward me, I can't take a chance. I'll take you out too."

An ache radiated through my chest. Everything had happened so fast. I'd gone from the height of triumph to tragedy. Velitia lay on the ground, groaning. She barely stirred.

"You sick freak!" I glared at Pek. "She saved us out there."

"Spare me your lecture," he said. "I know the kind of jobs the Moon Men Alliance does. You're as guilty as I am."

"I never did the dirty work," I said. "Nothing like this."

"But you were a part of it, right?" he said. "Part of a corrupt system just like this prison. You're a survivor like me. That's the bottom line."

I shook my head. "I'm no saint but I'm not like you at all."

He shrugged. "Whatever. Bask in your moral delusions. I've gone through the pain of being physically modified to get an upper hand in this universe of thugs. I've paid my dues. I'm tired of getting pushed around. It's time to push back. If you want to help me, fine. If not, say the word and you'll end up with her."

I glanced down at my pistol. Did it have any life left?

"Don't try it," Pek shook his head. "That's a third-tier beta cannon. Even at full charge it's unreliable."

"Look," I held up my free hand, keeping a grip on the pistol in the off chance it would spring back to life. "I get it. You want this. It's all yours. I just want off this moon. Let me take this ship and–"

"Forget it." He angled the barrel of his blaster from my chest to my head. "You're not going anywhere. The system needs us. It needs this ship." His head twitched to the side repeatedly, his eyes flickering. "The system needs supplies."

The computer was gaining control over him. There was a storm of anxiety in my chest.

Velitia gave a weak groan. Her eyes partially opened, connecting with mine. A subtle glow came from her headband. She looked down at my pistol. A soft glow emanated from the weapon.

Pek regained his composure. "Last chance. Give me your answer, Glint."

"Okay," I shrugged. "It's not worth dying over. I'll join you."

He grinned, relaxing his weaponized arm. "I knew you'd come around."

One thing was for sure. He wasn't getting away with this.

"I just have one question."

"Shoot," he said.

"Computer. System download!"

Pek went rigid, then his whole body started to tremble.

"This is for Velitia." I lifted the pistol and squeezed the trigger. A series of bright energy blasts hit his chest, lifting his feet off the ground, his head cable snapping with the force. He flew backward and slammed against the floor with a metallic clunk. His body lay still like a lifeless pile of rags. Thick streams of smoke rose from his chest.

I kneeled by Velitia and grabbed her hand.

A weak smile formed on her lips. "Nice work."

"There's probably a med unit on board. We'll get you fixed up."

She gave a light shake of her head. "Glint, do me a favor."

"Sure, anything."

"Take this ship and find a good crew. Make a difference in this universe."

I nodded. "I'll try."

"And don't give up on God. He'll never give up on you." She smiled then arched back with a pained expression.

"Velitia." I grabbed her hand tight. Her grip went slack, and her body sagged to the side. The soft glow in her headband faded away. I waited for a moment, not wanting to accept the truth. I'd known her for such a short time but the warmth of her presence and purity of her convictions made my life feel wretched in comparison. I kissed her hand and placed it across her chest.

I walked to the fallen body of Pek, feeling numb. His eyes were wide open as if frozen in a state of shock. He had no pulse. I lifted the false ear. All the electronic lights were off. I was sickened by what he'd done. He'd turned a victory into disaster. I yanked the trench coat off his body, wanting some additional sense of recompense for the pain he'd caused. I threw it over my shoulders. The coat was a perfect fit. I snapped the lapels and headed for the ship.

As I entered through the landing ramp, an electronic voice sounded.

"Greetings," a female voice said. "I am Iris, the computer of this star freighter. Are you the new captain?"

"Um, yeah." Hearing captain before my name was definitely something I could get used to. "Captain Glint Starcrost."

I took the lift up to a shabby looking bridge. The upholstery was faded and ripped. Half of the lighting was out and some of the control panels were broken. It was far from ideal but it was a starship. My very own starship.

"What is our destination, Captain?" Iris said.

I took my seat in the captain's chair. "As far away from this moon as you can get us."

"My pleasure. I never liked this horrid place, anyway."

The freighter trembled for a moment, then lifted off the landing bay. The viewing screen flickered to life displaying the grey atmosphere. There was a wonderful sensation of speed as we powered through the clouds, the vast array of stars slowly coming into view.

Hard's Watcher

Kerry Nietz

I'm in my apartment by the window and my eyes are open. I see the silvers and golds of the multilevel buildings around mine—towers and temples—and the mesh of the downrider transport strings that span the upper stories. Two spherical downriders, one on my left, and another on my right, zip their way deeper into the city. They could be racing, their movements are so parallel.

They aren't, though. Downriders don't race. And even if they could, the debuggers that direct them couldn't. That would be a rule violation, which would produce a quick and sudden brainstrike. That's the way it always is.

There's a plant next to the window. A bushy fern set in a purple pot. It was given to me shortly after my implantation. I'm not sure who sent it. Only that it was in my apartment when I arrived, along with a note that said, "Congrats and welcome!"

Cheery, that. Girl gets a metal teardrop shoved into her cranium; someone gives her a plant. A little greenery for the slave.

At least the thing grows. Even if I don't water it for weeks. Still grows.

Those first few days, the ones immediately following implantation, seemed miraculous. Like being plunged into an invisible river. As if the lights suddenly turned on one morning, and I was surrounded by new toys. Everything, every single machine within streamsight of me, was alive. Millions of data points. Warm technical goodness waiting to be caressed and explored.

All that is muted now. After four years, I've reached the point where all that really interests me is the task in front of me. Occasionally, one of the other debuggers, one of the low levels, does something that amuses me. But other than that, it's all routine now. Over explored and overdone.

Imagine that, the only female debugger in the world, and I'm bored.

I get a message via the stream, a chore from my Master. The message is live and vid-enabled, so I shut my eyes and flick it open. My master's face appears inside my head. He's elderly, and rarely shields himself from me. I see every wrinkle. Every misplaced whisker.

He smiles. "My second son has need of you."

I send back the traditional head bow, but I'm troubled. I don't go on loan. Too many risks with that.

Master's eyes remain fixed on me, or at least, the representation of me he can see...from wherever he is. It looks like one of his offices. The one with the green walls.

I don't send anything more. I only receive.

"You have nothing to say?" he asks. "Always my HardCandy has something to say."

Maybe he senses my malaise. Maybe that's what brought this new assignment. Because it's impossible to believe that there's nothing in his entire domain that needs my attention. He owns thousands of bots, and even more stream-sensitive toys. Something always needs fixed.

I send him a head shake, but my unease remains.

"It will be perfectly fine," he says. "You'll have no problem with my son, Aahil. He has only one wife, and five children. My most honorable son. Nothing to fear."

"All right..."

"You're a debugger! No man desires a debugger."

He speaks the truth. With my slight build and bald head, I'm as undesirable as they come. Most think I'm a man. All debuggers *are* men, except me.

I receive his son's physical address and thank him. A few seconds later our talk is over, and I open my eyes again. I wipe my face nervously. Touch the sides of my head. Smooth as ever. Warm, burning even.

I don't like this. I collect my debugging bag and head for the downer station.

Twenty minutes later I'm at Aahil's residence. It is modest compared to Master's. Only two stories high and four pillars before the door. The houses on either side are within walking distance, each with a similar-size square of green in front. They're fancy, but not master-fancy.

I'm greeted at the front door by the wife. I can only see her eyes through her black coverings, but they seem kind. I think she's smiling. She even bows a little. Probably out of reflex.

"We're glad you've come," she says, backing away into the home. The place has a wooden entryway, and the room beyond has simple decoration. Light-colored walls adorned with bright watercolors. There's a stone fireplace in one corner with a vase full of flowers on top. My comfort level increases.

The place smells good too, like bread just out of the oven. I detect a scattering of bots on the premises. Most are specialized, like those used to clean floors and manicure lawns, but there are general-purpose bots lurking around. One upstairs and one on the bottom floor, somewhere to my right. That one is due for a tune up soon, but it isn't throwing warnings yet.

I notice traces of children too. The place is generally clean, but even servbots can't find all the coloring sticks or building blocks. Kids toss them everywhere. I see two of the latter on my left, between the sofa and the wall.

I hear muted children's voices somewhere upstairs, and a loud thump nearby.

I frown. I'm not okay with kids. They're messy and smelly. Plus, they break things.

I don't think about my own childhood. It isn't worth re-membering.

"Smiling Wife" stretches a hand to touch me, before correcting herself. "I'm sorry. I'm not sure how to greet you."

"No greeting is necessary," I say. "Just show me where to go."

She bows again. "Of course—"

A middle-aged man enters the room through an archway on the left. He's a head taller than me, dressed in a dark blue shirt and beige pants. His hair is black and salted with grey. He smiles when he sees me. Shows every tooth. "It is HardCandy!"

I raise an eyebrow but say nothing. When surprised, it's best not to talk. That's my rule.

"You don't recognize me?" he says. "We met when my father first acquired you." He glances at his wife, then looks at me again. "What has it been...five years?"

"Four," I say. "Four and two months."

He nods. "Father always praises your accuracy." He raises a hand toward the archway, then actually touches my shoulder. "I'm sure you're ready to work. This way." He moves forward, but his hand lingers behind him, invitingly.

I follow, but step so the hand leaves the area of my shoulder. When surprised, I definitely never touch. I place my arms straight against my sides.

The hand finally lowers. He doesn't look back.

After the arch, I follow up a long, darker hallway. Pictures hang everywhere from top to bottom. All family members, I think. I recognize Master's face in many of them, plus a lot of people that sort of look like him. Same smiles, similar eyes.

We enter what appears to be a spare office. There's a desk and lots of stacked boxes on the sides and in the corners. There is a small window, shaded, that lets in a little light. There are even shelves of bound books—something I haven't seen since grade school—along two of the walls.

I sense nothing here that I can sing to, nor do I see anything. I feel nervous again.

Aahil crosses the room to a second, shorter, door. He holds it open for me. The room beyond looks like a storage room. The walls are rough and unpainted.

"What's in there?" I ask.

He smiles. "Something for you to handle, HardCandy. Only a little work."

I don't want to go in there. Technically, Aahil doesn't have access to my controller, so I could just bolt away. I'd probably get shocked later, but I might be fine with that. I think I'm fine with that.

Hesitantly, I move forward. He still holds the door, waiting.

I wave him ahead. "I'll follow," I say. "Go on."

He looks a little irritated, but nods and steps through. I pause at the door and look in. I see nothing but boxes. The ceiling is low, and the walls are narrow. There's light, but it is diffused. Dimmer than I like. Nothing about this is comfortable.

He's smiling, though. Waves. "Come. Come in! It is all right here."

"Tell me what it is," I say. "I can't really—"

"Please." He comes out again, and standing by the open door, directs me inside. "Father said you were stubborn." He smiles. "But I never thought that. Now go, please. I want to keep this secret."

I feel a ripple of dread. Dampness on my palms. I could pull security on him at any time, but given he's Master's son, that could get uncomfortable. Pulling security is always complicated.

Finally, I harness my fears enough to walk inside. The room smells of disuse. Not unclean, but dust-filled. There's a small oval window and no other way out. Otherwise, the room is boxes and shelves. There's a stacked pile of the former in the center. A metal leg sticks out the top of one.

Aahil walks inside and now. Rails, can I smell him. It isn't unpleasant. He seems washed. There's a hint of cinnamon— possibly his shampoo or sweat reducer. But it is uncomfortable. I retreat a bit and try to look as disinterested and unpleasant as possible. It isn't much of a stretch for me, really, but a girl needs defenses.

Thankfully, he's more focused on the boxes. He lays a hand on the top one—the one with the leg. "There's a bot in here."

Never would've guessed.

"It is very old, but it has sentimental value. Is that something you can fix?"

I shrug and walk behind the boxes, peering inside. "What model is it?"

He bows his head. "I'm sorry. I don't know."

I wipe my palms together. When that doesn't help, I use my jumpsuit legs. "Difficult to tell from here. I'll need to take it all out and look." I flash a weak smile. "Since it isn't together, no power." I point to my left temple. "No connection."

"Yes, of course. Would you like me to leave you alone with it?"

Please, yes. Please leave. "That would be fine. I'm sure you have things to do." The quicker I get to this, the quicker I can go.

"I have chores, yes. Many chores for my father." He smiles again. Too much. "He keeps everyone around him busy. I'm sure you agree."

I nod, then move behind the stack of boxes and rest a hand on the top one. "I'll get started now then."

He bows and leaves the room. I listen until I hear his footsteps on the hall outside. Just to be certain he's gone.

I cross the room and shut the door. There's no lock, but I guess that'll have to do.

Next, I drop my tool bag and tear open the boxes. Doesn't take much before I know what I'm into. It's a humanoid servbot, though just barely. A model from at least forty years ago. Back when there was no effort to make them seem human at all. Lots of metal and hard plastisteel. Heavier, clunkier, and uglier than even today's budget bot. It's a burgundy color.

I'm amazed someone saved this thing. Even more amazed that there's so much of it. I empty the boxes and lay the parts out on the floor. Two arms, two legs, a torso, chest, and head. All the majors, but none of them together. The disconnected bot.

I pick up the head and look at it. It's slightly pointed and has a slit for a mouth. The eyes are simple, reflective circles. Possibly small screens. Real ugly.

I turn it so I can see the connection points. There is a wrapped bundle of wires and pseudo-paths tucked inside. I pull that out, unwrap it and inspect every linkage. Using my implant, I scan the worldwide stream for specs on this bot. Takes a while to find them. The maker is long since gone—bought and absorbed—and even the absorber doesn't talk about this model anymore. I find partial specs on a collector's site. They'll have to do.

I move the head close to the torso and start connecting. Path to path, wire to wire, conduit to conduit. Everything matches up.

I get the feeling I'm being watched. At first, I think it's because the bot's head is facing me—those shiny circles staring my way. But when I turn the head around, I realize that's not it. Someone is observing somehow.

I glance around the room. I don't see any cameras—don't sense any on the stream either. That's doesn't mean they aren't there.

Sons of masters have ways of hiding things. From workers, wives...
from everyone.

I shift my position, moving closer to one of the bot's arms. At
the same time, I think I hear motion. In the room outside. A glance
shows me that the door is cracked open now. A chill snakes down
my spine and my palms dampen again. Who is out there?

Maybe Aahil is a watcher. I know the type exists. Techno-
voyeurs that spy on debuggers. Post images on the dark alleys of
the stream. Pictures of the only female debugger would light up
the alleys, I'm sure. Nasty little men.

"Hello?" I see a flicker of movement through the crack and hear
more motion. Moving away this time. Leaving me. That doesn't feel
any better.

I pick up the bot's left arm. I probably can't use it as a
weapon—my implant will stop me—but it feels good to hold it.
Something concrete I can swing, or at least block with.

I check the arm's shoulder and notice some of the connectors
have been snipped off. I know I don't have any of those with me. I
don't have a forming tool that could make them either. Not parts
this old. Best chance is to grab some at a clink and clank. A tech
shop.

Nearest one is Billy's, only a block over. It would be nice to step
out, anyway. Leave this room. Leave the eyes.

Takes maybe thirty minutes to get to the shop and back.
When I return, I'm greeted by a late model servbot. It's a better
approximation of humanity than my current chore. Synthskin,
full movement, and dressed like a man in beige pants and shirt.
I don't have to explain myself. It simply bows its head and
waves me by.

I sense a change in the storage room right away. Everything is
in generally the same place, but some of the boxes have shifted
slightly. More noticeable, though, is the change to the air. There's
a hint of cinnamon again, but also something else. A floral something. Takes a second before I discover the source of that scent.

Slid into the slot of the bot's mouth: A single red rose. It is
pretty, sure, but its presence flips me. Sparks my intestines to a
new level of unease. I'm not a potential paramour. Nor am I a
possible wife. I'm a debugger. A sex-less, emotion-less, hair-less,
tool head. I fix things and that's all.

This is weird behavior, even for a watcher.

I grab a pair of tweezers out of my bag, pluck the rose from the bot's mouth, and toss it aside. I set to work on connecting the arm, but that lasts only a few minutes, because the flower's scent is still everywhere.

The little window opens fine. So, out goes the rose.

Can't throw out my discomfort, though. I want to be done and out now more than ever. Despite what Master says, apparently, some men *do* have designs on debuggers. I'm not okay with that.

I get the bot's left arm connected to the torso, and then its right. I pull the bot up on its waist and look it in the eyes. I see my silhouette there. The smooth circle of my head.

The bot should activate now. Specs say it has a startup switch tucked beneath its chin. I feel around for that and flip it. There's a gurgling sound, the head shifts left and right, and the eyes light up. I feel the bot's presence on the stream too. It is a slow, dim presence, but it is there just the same. "How are you doing?" I ask.

It doesn't respond verbally, but it feeds me a list of problems via the stream. Most notably, its legs are missing!

I feel a trickle of joy. "Yeah, I'll get those for you." I power it down and lay it on the floor.

The watching eyes return. I don't look at the door, but I'm sure it's cracked again. I want to call him out. To run over and throw open the door. Maybe catch his nose in the process. But I can't do that. Violence will get me tweaked. Even thinking about it hurts some.

Then I get a notion. The guy likes flowers, right? What if I order him some? Send a big bundle right to his front door? That'll get the attention of his only wife. Especially if I put a female name on them. The beauty of the stream. For the right implant, the possibilities are endless.

I smile and dig at my plan while I work. I find a nearby shop, a plausible paramour name, and the right bouquet. Lots of roses. Red ones like the one I threw out. My implant almost stops me along the way, but I get around that. I'm only returning a favor here. Flower for flower.

I get the left leg connected. The right one takes a bit more effort. The connectors are intact but one of the pathways is clearly clogged. I get out my slenderest probe and slide that into the path's aperture. Work it around. Not sure what the gunk that oozes out is. Something black and sticky. I feed in a new nanopack and sing to them. Get them moving like they should. Then I close everything up.

I hear movement behind the door and glance that direction. The door shivers slightly. It wasn't my imagination, there's someone out there. I stand, walk to the door, and heave it open.

I see no one, but I feel the movement of air. Smell cinnamon.

That cinches it. I order the flowers, to be delivered within the hour. I buy a double shipment using my food allowance. I can skip a meal.

What if this escalates? What if he tries to...? I shiver and wring my hands together. I'm more vulnerable than I like. More vulnerable than I should be.

I return to the room. Only a few more things to do, then I can get out and go home. Maybe stare at the skyline again. Be alone.

I finish up the leg and stand the bot up. It almost looks good. I mean, it's still ugly, but for its age and model—not bad. I turn it on again and stream it a diagnostic test. It begins to check itself. There are lots of warnings and a few errors. The bot has been asleep a long time. Things get shaky when you're away that long. Out of touch with the world.

The watcher is back again, I'm sure of it. I put my back to the door and have the bot face me. Behind it is the window. The sky looks mostly grey. Very little blue.

Look at the door, I stream the bot. *Can you see it?* The bot's eyes are reading "operational," so I hope it can.

I see the door, yes.

Great. Is there someone beyond it?

Yes.

That settles that. The Master's trusted son is a watcher. A messed up little man. Is that the "chore" he mentioned? Spying on me?

Pitiful.

What's he doing? The person at the door.

Looking, the bot streams back.

Rails! Is that all?

I can only see an eye and part of a nose. The bot's head shifts so it stares at me. "Did I describe it wrong?" it says. "Looking?"

"No," I say. *Of course*, I stream. *Yes. That's fine.* I contemplate checking again myself, but then get a weird feeling. Like I might have something completely wrong. Misread the situation.

How old is the person at the door? Can you tell?

The bot nods. *A child*, it streams back.

My anxiety melts into a puddle. Replaced with a big, shallow emptiness. A large void of stupid.

I crouch, and slowly pivot toward the door.

The eye disappears.

"Wait!" I say. "Come back."

Nanoseconds of uncertainty pass before the child returns. His eye is only a little higher than mine in my crouched position.

"You don't need to hide," I say. "I won't hurt you."

The door swings slowly open. Beyond it is a young boy, roughly eight years of age. He's dressed in beige and blue, like his father. His hair is dark—and his eyes—they could be Master's eyes. "Peace be to you," he says, bowing his head. "Am I bothering you? I'm not supposed to."

Kids. I don't really like them, but I wouldn't hurt them either. Plus, I was on his side of this situation once. Hiding out. Watching a debugger at his work.

"You're not bothering me." I point at the bot. "I'm almost finished here. He almost works."

The boy smiles. Nods.

I roll forward onto my knees, then sit down. "Is it for you?"

He shakes his head. "For Momma. Dad is surprising her. It was her family's when she was little."

I nod. Another situation I misread. Rails stupid. "So, you're in on the secret," I say.

"Yes."

I glance at the bot, then at the window. "That's nice of him."

The boy takes a step forward. His eyes search the room. "I gave you a flower. Did you like it?"

I smile, uncomfortably. "I did. Thanks. I—"

He bows his head. "I think you are beautiful. The most beautiful woman I've ever seen."

My face gets warm. My palms too. "Well...that's...unusual." I can't look him in the eyes, so I seek solace elsewhere. Boxes. Lots of boxes. Finally, I glance at him. "Most people don't think that. Most wouldn't say it."

"But it's true. You're beautiful, kind, and smart."

I pat my hands together. Unsure of where to go next. "I'm... um...why do you say that?"

He comes closer, then takes a seat a meter away. "It is inside of me." He touches his chest. "I had to let it out."

Flipping wild, this kid. "You know I'm too old for you, right?" I half-smile. "Plus, I can't be married. I have this thing in my head and—"

A look of panic takes his face. "I'm too young to get married." He shakes his head. "We're not getting married."

I can't help but smile. "Rails, then. Okay. We're not. We're fine." I stand and walk behind the bot. There are warnings to fix and tests to perform. Don't want the boy's mom disappointed. Or the boy, for that matter.

He scoots closer and lays a hesitant hand on the bot's leg. He follows the surface all the way to the knee. His eyes get wide. "It is hard."

"That's how they used to make them. With a really hard shell." Like me.

He looks at me. "Can we be friends?"

"Of course."

He bows. "My name is Haadee. What's yours?"

"Hard..." I feel uncomfortable again. "Um...HardCandy."

He doesn't seem to make the "hard" connection. That the reason it's part of my name is because I maintain a shell too—an emotional cover. He only nods and sticks up a hand. "Nice to meet you, HardCandy."

I nod but don't take the hand. "We..." I shrug. "We don't touch usually. Touching is complicated."

He lowers his hand, and nodding again, stands up. "I will go."

My chest feels hollow. Like I'm back in that void of stupid again. This kid seems different. Almost like I was at that age. Authentic and real.

"Um...wait." I retrieve a small diagnostic sheet from my bag. I step around and smooth it over the bot's chest cavity. The sheet makes the inside visible. A ten-centimeter square of activity. A rainbow of pathways, conduits and blinking lights. "Ever seen that before?"

His eyes go wide and his hands come together, as if in prayer. "Wow. It is beautiful. So much movement." He studies it for thirty seconds. "Hard on the outside. Beautiful within." He smiles. "Thank you for showing me this. I can't wait to tell my sisters."

"Sure, I—" I smile. "It was good to meet you, Haadee."

His mother calls from somewhere in the house. Haadee cocks his head to listen, then frowns. "I should go."

"That's okay. I need to finish."

With that, my watcher leaves. I feel a little lonely now, which is weird. I spend the next thirty minutes finishing the bot. It works flawlessly. Ugly, old, but flawless. Not a bad way to be.

I shut it down and collect my things. Amazed by the twist in it all. My watcher being a kid who seemingly has a big ole heart. Who, all things considered, might be one of my favorite people now.

I hear a chime from the front door and almost ignore it. Why should I care? Isn't my place. This house probably has lots of visitors during the day.

Then I remember Haadee and his father and my stomach churns.

Roses. I sent roses.

"Rails!" I dart out of the storage room to the hallway and down the hall. I arrive at the front door as the wife swings it open. Haadee is there too, hovering near her legs.

"What is this?" Then there's a bundle of two dozen roses in her hands.

I come up fast behind her, but she plucks the card from the flowers. Opens it.

"Who is Jadwa?" she says.

I move in close, bow. "Sorry," I say. "That's a name I sometimes use." When I'm trying to fool someone. To really mess with their life.

She gives me a quizzical look. "It says they are for my husband."

"It does?" I force a chuckle. "Well, rails, that's a mistake. Um... I didn't know who—" I notice Haadee standing there, eyes wide, and get this shine of an idea. A real lightning strike. "They are for

Haadee." I smile as bright as I can. "Just wanted to make sure that was okay with his father and you first."

Wife looks more confused now. She glances at Haadee, and then back at me. "Why would you—?"

I bow again. "He's my hero today." I step forward and place a hand on his head. It feels soft and warm. Real. "Thought he deserved a reward." I smile. "I would've sent sweets." I point at my mouth. "But you know, teeth, rot, that whole thing."

The door is still open. That's convenient. "Anyway, I need to go."

She still looks confused. She smiles and bows her head, though. Real polite. "The job...my husband's—"

I step outside and feel refreshed by the little breeze that's blowing. "All done. All finished here now." I wink at the boy. "Haadee knows all about it—right, Haadee?"

He gives me a questioning look, but then smiles. "Can I see the flowers, Momma?"

She smiles. "Of course. We'll put them in your room."

Haadee looks at me again.

I wave, he waves, and I walk away. Feeling good. A rainbow of colors on the inside. And on the outside?

Maybe not as hard.

THE LIBRARIAN WHO WOULD BE KING

TEISHA J. PRIEST

LILI SHIFTED A FEW SPARE PARTS, MAKING SURE NOTHING LOOKED AMISS. Sweat trickled down her back and she blew a strand of curly hair out of her face. She heaved the cart around the corner and smiled at the guard.

He glanced at the overflowing cart and asked, "Working late?"

She held out her ID clip. "You know how it is. Most of us don't get to keep the same hours as Parliament."

His laugh echoed off the metal walls. "Isn't that the truth!" He loaded his own ID clip into the access panel and the massive airtight doors to the hangar slid open.

"Thanks!" she called over her shoulder.

Lili checked the impulse to run to the fifth ship in the middle row. Scuffs and a scorch mark or two marred the dull gray alloy, but it was space-worthy. With a huff, she shoved the cart up the ramp and onboard the ship. She'd barely touched the panel to close the hatch when the Crown Prince clambered out of his hiding place, scattering spare parts across the deck.

"What took so long?"

She looked pointedly at his nicer than average suit and started picking up the mess. "I thought you were supposed to wear something that would blend in?"

"It was the best I could do." He eyed the ship. "Are you sure this thing is safe?"

She tossed the last of the scattered parts back in the cart. "If we get caught, they'll execute me. I'd rather blend in and not get caught if it's all the same to you."

He crossed his arms. "We'll get caught if this rust bucket breaks down in orbit."

"It may not be pretty, but it will get us out of orbit. Please tell me that you've had some flight training." She headed for the cockpit without waiting for his response.

"Of course I have. I served in the Commonwealth Navy!" he called out indignantly and followed her.

She was perched in the pilot's seat, running through an abbreviated pre-flight checklist. "Just because you were in the Navy doesn't mean you *flew* anything."

"In my case it does." He took the co-pilot's seat and started running through his half of the checklist.

"Really?" She glanced up at him.

He shrugged. "If I was going to be in the Navy then I at least wanted to learn something useful."

She slipped the flight straps over her shoulders. "Better buckle up."

He was snugging his flight straps when she handed him a miniature electronic tablet with a code displayed on the screen.

"What's this for?" he asked.

"I need you to enter this when the computer prompts us for the access code."

The deck plates shuddered slightly as she powered up the engines.

"How did you manage to get a Parliamentary access code?"

"I don't know." Her hands flew across the controls. "And I didn't ask. I'm already in enough trouble as it is."

The ship rattled as it lifted off. Lili held her breath. The massive overhead doors cracked open and finally retracted once the Prince entered the code.

"Huh. I was afraid it wouldn't work." She piloted the ship out into the atmosphere as soon as the opening was large enough for them to slip through.

"What!?"

"Little busy," she muttered, keeping her eyes on the readouts as she looked up the coordinates for the closest jump portal.

"If they'd caught us—"

"They didn't," she interrupted. "Can you bluff your way out of this with Flight Control?"

A metallic voice came through the communications console.

"Personal shuttle 3XV2, your departure is ahead of the scheduled flight plan you filed."

"I'll fly, you bluff."

He sent her a withering look and flipped a switch. "Flight Control, this is 3XV2. We have a Parliamentary access code granting us permission to depart early."

"Transmit access code, please."

"Transmitting now."

The sky grew darker as the ship ascended. If the code wasn't accepted, they didn't have a chance of making it to the jump portal before being shot down.

"Access code confirmed. Have a safe trip 3XV2."

"Thank you, Flight."

"That's all they needed? The same code we used to open the hangar doors?"

He shot her a look. "Of course it's all we needed. It's a *Parliamentary* access code."

They both shifted in their seats as the artificial gravity calibrated.

Lili sighed. "We still need to get you somewhere safe. Any ideas?"

"You don't have a plan? What kind of half-baked prison break is this?"

She raised a finger. "First off, you were hardly in prison—"

"They were going to execute me," he cut in.

"Which is the only reason why I got mixed up in this." She tapped her fingers on the console. "Lord Frederick only gave me the access code and told me where to pick you up. He insisted that no one could know where I took you once we were offworld."

The Prince slumped in his seat. "It's so he couldn't betray me if he was caught and interrogated."

Her head snapped up. "Is that likely?"

"More than likely," he nodded grimly. "Inevitable."

"Why didn't he come with us?"

"There was a better chance of me getting offworld if he stayed." He ran a hand through messy dark hair.

"He was the only one who was ever nice to me," she said softly. "Used to tell me about his grandkids and try to convince me to take up fishing."

"Frederick Halcion was nice to everyone. Didn't matter what title you did or didn't have." He studied Lili. "Is that why you agreed to help me?"

"When he begged me to help get you offworld, I couldn't say no. He cared so much about keeping you safe, and I thought that if your life meant that much to him, you must be someone worth saving."

"Not if that was the cost."

Every vid she'd ever seen showed the Crown Prince perfectly attired and coiffed. Never with dark circles under his eyes, wrinkled clothes, and drooping shoulders as he appeared now.

The navigation console beeped, breaking the silence.

"We're at the jump portal coordinates. Ready to make FTL?"

He tightened the flight straps one more time and nodded. "Where are we going?"

"The last place anyone would think to look for a Crown Prince."

"*This* is your idea of a good place for me to hide?" He waved at the outpost ID on the monitor. "Are you trying to get me killed?" He squinted at her. "You are."

She rolled her eyes. "If I'd wanted you dead then I would have left you back on the planet where they were going to *execute* you. This is the safest place. Just don't tell anyone who you are."

"Right," he scoffed. "No one will *ever* recognize me."

Lili typed out a landing request. "Put you in a pair of coveralls and smear a bit of grime on your face and no one will look twice. Trust me, the grease monkeys are pretty much invisible to anyone who's going to care."

"Are we just going to hang around with the maintenance crews? Someone will start asking questions."

She waved a hand dismissively. "I've got connections with the administrator here. We'll have a place to stay."

"What *kind* of connections?"

Before she could answer a voice crackled over the communications system.

"Lili Tychis, what in the ever-lovin' stars are you doing flying a decrepit cargo ship all the way to my outpost?"

A grin split her face. "You know how it is, Uncle Mav, I got homesick. Brought along a visitor this time, too. So, are you going to grant us permission to land?"

"Ah, you brought home a boy. About time."

The Prince choked and started coughing.

"Yes and no," she hedged. "Kind of a long story."

"You still have time to make it to dinner if you don't drag your feet. I'll tell your aunt to set a couple of extra places at the table. Landing request approved, 3XV2, Broen Outpost out."

"Your uncle is the administrator of a mining outpost that's decidedly not friendly toward the Commonwealth? And you think it's a good idea to take me to dinner? This is an even worse idea than I imagined."

"Hey!" she snapped. "My uncle is a fair man, and he wouldn't countenance you being executed when you haven't committed a crime. We may not exactly support the idea of a monarchy, but that doesn't mean we want to kill all the nobles. In case you forgot, me sneaking you offworld is the only reason you're not still stuck in your royal apartments waiting for said execution."

She turned her attention back to the flight controls and concentrated on landing. It wasn't until she was working through the post-flight checklist that the Prince spoke.

"You're right. I was wrong to be anything but grateful considering all you've risked on my behalf."

She blinked. "You just admitted you were wrong?"

"Because I was."

"Okay." She leaned back in her seat. "I'm sorry, too. I should have told you where we were going before we got here. Let's try this again. Lilian Tychis, it's an honor to meet you, Your Highness."

"Crown Prince Rylan Marchaves, and the honor is mine, Lilian." He took the hand she offered. "Please call me Rylan."

She smiled. "My friends call me Lili."

"Are we? Friends, I mean?"

"Considering what we've been through together? Sure." She climbed out of the pilot's seat. "C'mon, we need to find you something to wear."

They scrounged up a pair of worn, ill-fitting coveralls, but it would have to do.

"Just don't make eye contact with anyone," she warned.

He nodded and gestured to the hatch. "Lead the way."

They walked swiftly through nondescript beige corridors. The occasional window looked out on the purple-gray surface of the moon, and mining equipment could be seen coming and going. No one paid the Prince any mind.

Lili stopped in front of a numbered door and pressed the chime. It opened to reveal a man of average height with hair the same shade of brown as his niece's.

"Lili!" He enveloped her in a bear hug. "I didn't think we'd see you again until next year!" He released his niece and motioned them inside. "Come in!"

The door slid shut and he turned to Rylan. "Now, young man, I've been waiting to meet you..." he trailed off and looked carefully at Rylan, then back at Lili. "You brought the Crown Prince of the Commonwealth to dinner?"

She blew out a breath. "This is the only safe place I could think of. You've heard that the Queen was murdered. Rylan's the only member of the Royal Family left, and they were going to execute him. I was asked to help. I couldn't refuse when the life of an innocent person was at stake."

"You've managed to get yourself in over your head when it comes to Commonwealth political machinations." Mav shook his head and then addressed Rylan. "Do you deserve the punishment that my niece risked her life to spare you from?"

Rylan cleared his throat. "I've broken no laws of the Commonwealth. My only 'crime' is that I'm the rightful heir to the crown. Whoever killed my sister wants me out of the way."

"I've heard rumors," Mav leveled a frosty look at him, "That you were being executed because of your involvement in your sister's death."

"That's not true!" Rylan's hands clenched into fists. "I loved my sister more dearly than my own life!"

"Can you prove it," Mav countered.

The Prince answered quietly, "No."

"I think I can."

Both men looked at Lili in surprise.

She pulled a data clip from the chest pocket of her coveralls. "Lord Frederick gave me this. He said to guard it with my life because it held the truth. I thought it was an odd thing to say at the time, but if someone's trying to frame you, then it must be the proof of your innocence."

There was a slight tremor in Rylan's hand as he reached for the clip. "You don't know what's on it?"

"No, he just said that I'd know when to give it to you."

Mav sighed and rubbed his forehead. "You're both mixed up in the worst kind of trouble. If you're here to raise an army, Your Highness, then I'm afraid you won't find much support."

"The last thing I want to do is raise an army or endanger anyone else," Rylan insisted. "I have no intention of claiming the crown, anyway."

"What do you intend to do?"

"I thought," he swallowed, "I could just disappear. Start over somewhere where no one knows who I am." He looked at Lili. "You need to disappear, too. We'll both be hunted by the Parliamentary Guard, and they must know that you're the one who smuggled me offworld."

"You're probably right." She scuffed her foot on the floor.

Mav looked thoughtful for a moment. "I daresay you had no idea what you were getting yourself into by saving the Crown Prince's life, but he's right. I know someone. The kind of person who can make arrangements for people who don't want to be found."

Rylan looked stunned. "I'll never be able to repay you."

"Just make sure my niece stays safe," Mav said sternly, then smiled. "Now, let's see what your Aunt Pipa has in store for dinner. I wager she's a better cook than even the palace can boast!"

⋙⋘

Mav's study boasted a large window with an impressive view. He had an affinity for books, the old paper kind, and it was both his collection and the view that drew Lili. She sat on the bench that ran the length of the window, an open book in her lap, when Rylan found her.

"It's beautiful."

She motioned for him to have a seat. "It never gets old watching the planet from up here. It's even more impressive from outside. Looking up at the storms and the rings—it makes you feel small. Not in a bad way. Just a sense of awe and wonder at how much more is out there."

Rylan settled on the padded bench. "You sound like someone who'd like to explore it all."

"I would," she said wistfully. "Wasn't meant to be, I guess."

"Is that why you took a job in the Commonwealth? Wander-lust?" he asked.

"I could have signed on with one of the cargo crews based out of here and still seen a fair bit of the systems."

"But?"

"I wouldn't have known whether they hired me for me or for my uncle. He would never have interfered of course, but people like and respect him. I wanted to make it on my own merits."

"I know what you mean. No one ever sees me as anything other than the Crown Prince." He turned to rest his elbow on the frame around the window and stare out at the gas giant the moon orbited. "I just wanted to be a librarian."

"Really?"

"It's true," he said seriously. "I love books and everything they represent. Librarians are the keepers of history, philosophy, culture, legends—everything that makes us who we are. Think of all the knowledge contained in the great libraries lost through the centuries. What might history look like if they hadn't been lost? I can't think of a more noble thing than being the guardian of the books that should be treasured."

"I've heard you collect paper books. Is that why?" she asked hesitantly.

He nodded. "Of all the things I had to leave behind, that's what I think I'll regret the most. I wish you could have seen the library at the palace before we left."

Lili looked to the small bookshelves in Mav's study. "My uncle's books must seem like a poor collection in comparison."

"There's no such thing as a poor collection of books." He picked up the volume she held loosely in her hands. "It doesn't matter how many or how few. It's always a wonderful thing to see someone else treasuring them as I do. You have a soft spot for poetry?"

She took back the book that he held out to her. "Yeah, Uncle Mav used to read a poem to me every night before bed. After my parents died, I had trouble sleeping because of the nightmares." She ran her hand over the gold embossed cover. "He told me if my head was filled with beautiful poetry, that I'd have beautiful dreams."

"Did it work?"

"Sometimes," she said quietly. "But even when it didn't, I loved him for trying to help. I fell in love with the books somewhere along the way, too." She looked at him for a long moment. "You honestly would rather disappear, and not just because your life's in danger?"

"I've never wanted the crown," he admitted. "I still don't want it. Frederick died to get me offworld, thinking that I'd return and claim the crown. He shouldn't have sacrificed his life for me. I'm no king."

Rylan stared down at his hands, and Lili reached over to rest a hand on his.

"Maybe the best kings are the ones who take up their crown out of duty and not desire."

"I thought you weren't a monarchist?"

She chuckled. "I'm not. But there's more to you than I thought. You're not just another entitled noble. I think you'll be a good man whether you're a king or a librarian." She squeezed his hand once and let go.

"Not likely to be many libraries where we end up. It will be a hard life hiding in the shadows, and I'm sorry that you're stuck with it because you helped me."

"Doesn't matter." She shook her head. "It was the right thing to do."

They both looked back out into space, lost in thoughts of the past and the uncertain future.

⊱❦⊰

Morning at Broen Outpost looked the same as evening. Mining and maintenance workers pulled shifts around the clock so the hangar was never deserted. No one really noticed a woman in midnight-blue coveralls boarding a worn-out ship.

They hadn't brought any luggage of course, but she still combed the ship to make certain they hadn't left anything behind to betray them.

Lili lowered herself into the pilot's seat to pull up the navigational logs. While she waited for the computer to initialize, she ran a hand over the console. It wasn't anything special, just the dull gray metallic color of un-coated metal. Nothing about the ship was special, but it had been nice piloting it while it lasted. Maybe someday...

The computer beeped, jolting her out of her musings. She altered the logs to include a fictitious stop at the Valhalen Cluster. With any luck, the Parliamentary Guards would assume that she'd transferred Rylan to another ship at that point. With a lot of luck, nothing of the ship would survive when Mav towed it out into space and triggered the remote self-destruct she'd rigged up.

She'd barely shut the system down when she heard four pairs of booted feet on the deck plates. Lili's eyes slid shut and she smoothed a few loose curls out of her face before rising to meet the Parliamentary Guards.

"Lilian Tychis," the tallest of the Guards addressed her, "We have a warrant for your arrest on the charge of high treason against the Commonwealth. You are to come with us and turn over any and all information regarding the whereabouts of the traitor, Rylan Marchaves."

"I don't know what you're talking about. I just stopped here for supplies and maintenance."

Lili had no clue it was coming until her head snapped to the side and her face burned from the strike. She tasted blood and wiped the corner of her lip.

"Allowances can be made, but only if you tell me the truth." He gripped her chin between thumb and forefinger and forced her to look him in the eye. "Where. Is. The. Traitor?"

"I..." she said with a shaking voice. "They only paid me to take him to a rendezvous point, and I don't know where they took him after that. I just came here to hide because it was the closest outpost not part of the Commonwealth."

He released her chin and nodded to one of the other guards who quickly initialized the navigation system and started scrolling through logs.

"She stopped at the Valhalen Cluster, then headed directly here," he reported.

The officer raised an eyebrow. "She was telling the truth. Put her in restrains."

"Wait!" She tried to step back from the guards. "You said that allowances may be made. Please, just let me go. I'll disappear—"

His laugh sent chills dancing across Lili's nerves.

"I'm allowing you to retain a shred of honor by confessing to your treason. Lock her in the brig. I need to have a word with the outpost administrator."

Two of the guards dragged Lili to the hatch. She was tempted to resist, but there was still a chance that they wouldn't connect her to Mav. They didn't share a family name, and Broen Outpost records weren't included in the Commonwealth databases. If they found Rylan or discovered the connection with Mav, the Commonwealth Navy would show up in orbit and none of the families at the outpost would be safe. If she cooperated—and if Mav could bluff convincingly—there was still a chance that no one else would pay the price for what she'd done.

꙰

Mav found Rylan reading in the study.

He dropped into the chair behind his desk. "They've arrested her."

"The Parliamentary Guard is here?" Rylan closed his book and moved to stand.

Mav held up a hand. "Not anymore. Lili convinced them that she'd met another ship and handed you off before coming here. They didn't connect her to me or the outpost, so there was no reason to stay. They're taking her back to the Commonwealth."

"They'll execute her for what she's done!"

"I know." Mav scrubbed his face with his hands. "But there's nothing I could have done without endangering the whole outpost. It's the kind of impossible choice that leaders face every day, Your Highness."

"I'm not a prince anymore—" Rylan began to protest.

Mav cut him off. "What if it was the only way to save Lili? Would you claim a crown you don't want to save the woman who saved you?"

He sighed when Rylan didn't immediately reply. "I'll be in the kitchen."

Rylan looked out the window above the bench that he and Lili had occupied the evening before. Shades of green and blue swirled about on the planet surface. Mav didn't understand that Rylan was powerless to stop the events set in motion. If he tried to claim the crown, they'd execute him alongside Lili. He could try storming in to rescue her, but chances were he'd never get close. He wasn't a soldier any more than he was a king. He certainly wasn't the sort of person that anyone should be dying to protect, but that didn't seem to matter to people like Lord Frederick and Lili.

Rylan slumped back in the chair and crossed his arms. A small object in his chest pocket pressed against his wrist. He jumped out of the chair, fished the forgotten data clip out of his pocket, and loaded it into the computer terminal on Mav's desk. The documents and vid files that it contained made his eyes widen and his blood boil. It did more than prove he was innocent, it implicated the Prime Minister who served as head of the government in his sister's place. He tucked the data clip back into his pocket, zipped it shut, and strode out of Mav's study.

"I need your help if I'm going to save Lili."

✥

They'd skipped the trial. Lili was an anti-monarchist commoner accused of high treason. She wasn't entitled to anything but a very swift, very public execution—beheaded on the steps of the palace. Prime Minister Lynton himself presided over the occasion and the courtyard was crammed with people calling for her death.

They read the list of crimes aloud, and she absently wondered how they managed to make it so long. The white stone pressed cold against her knees when she was ordered to kneel. A black hood obscured the executioner's face. The sword he held was ancient and terrifying, forcing Lili to bite her lip to keep it from trembling. Closing her eyes and bowing her head, she held her breath, waiting for the blow to land. Her eyes flew open at the ring of metal blade clashing with metal blade.

A champion stood between her and the executioner, wielding a sword even more ancient—one heavy with the weight of royal history.

"This woman is under my protection," Rylan's voice carried across the courtyard.

"The protection of a traitor?" The Prime Minister stood and pointed at him accusingly. "Arrest him!"

"Not a traitor!" Rylan's eyes flashed and he stood firm. "I am Rylan Alaric. Son of Galen Essius. Brother of Valencia Celinia. Rightful heir of the House of Marchaves."

"It doesn't matter who you are, Rylan," he sneered. "Treason is still treason, and what else would you call plotting to kill the Queen?"

The most senior member of Parliament, Lady Delayna, stepped forward. "Proof of his innocence has been presented, *former* Prime Minister. Interestingly, the same proof implicates you." She held a rolled paper aloft as guards restrained Lynton. "Parliament has issued a warrant for your arrest. Furthermore," she turned to address the crowd, "We hereby recognize Rylan Alaric Marchaves as next in line to the crown and the rightful King of the Commonwealth. God save the King!"

"God save King Rylan!" echoed thunderously from the assembly.

The new King faced his people, rested the tip of his sword on the white stone, and placed both hands on the hilt. At that moment, he looked every inch the King.

"I pledge to wield this sword in defense of the people of the Commonwealth of the Seven Systems. I will stand always for justice and truth, leading by the grace of God."

He turned and helped Lili to her feet, pulling her to stand beside him.

"My first act as King is to issue a full pardon to Lilian Tychis. At great risk to herself, she saved my life and has proven herself worthy of the highest honor."

A cheer rose up from those assembled, and Rylan squeezed her hand. Lili tried to smile. She couldn't help but feel a little unsettled that this was the same crowd of people who had called for her head.

***

White stone arches supported two levels of balconies circling the room. Warm sunshine poured through the skylights, illuminating the library. It was filled to the brim with books. Honest-to-goodness paper books.

"Uncle Mav would cry at the sight of so many beautiful books."

Rylan held out a handkerchief. "It appears he's not the only one."

Lili's face flushed. She wiped a stray tear from her cheek and tried to hand the cloth back.

"Keep it." He smiled. "Memento of the time you saved the King."

She laughed. "I seem to recall him saving my life in return. Doesn't that make us even?"

"Lili," he took her hand, "I can't ever repay you for what you did. You took a far greater risk than I did, but maybe this will go a little way toward making us even." He dropped a data clip in her hand. "It's the title to a ship of your own. At least one of us should have the chance to pursue our dreams."

She threw her arms around him and then jumped back as if burned. "I'm sorry, Your Majesty! I don't think I'm supposed to hug the King."

"Certainly not in public," he chuckled, "But maybe when it's just the two of us we can still be friends. As your friend, I'd rather you call me Rylan, and I don't mind a hug now and then."

He stepped closer and she wrapped her arms tight around him as he did the same.

"Thank you, Rylan. For everything."

"And thank you, Lili."

They let go and she looked at the data clip with wonder.

"So, where are you headed first?"

Lili chewed her lip. "I guess I'll go see Uncle Mav first to let him know that I'm okay and everything. Then?" She shrugged. "I don't know. Somewhere I've never been! What about you? What's next for you?"

He rubbed the back of his neck. "Librarian is out, at this point. I'm the King now, for better or worse, so I don't have much choice in the matter."

"I don't know about that." She looked around at the collected books. "Looks like you have a pretty impressive library right here. Maybe there could be others."

"That's an idea." His gaze wandered the full shelves thoughtfully.

"I should be going." Lili turned to the door.

"Maybe stop in for a visit now and then?" Rylan asked hopefully.

"Visit the King, or visit my friend?"

"Who says you can't do both in the same trip? Perhaps you'll be the guest of honor at the opening of a new library one of these days."

"I could arrange that." She smiled warmly. "Since I have a ship of my own now. Speaking of which, walk me to my ship? I'm not sure where it's parked."

"Of course." Rylan winked. "As long as I'm not stuffed in a cart of spare parts this time."

THE BRICK

JEFFREY LYMAN

"WHERE'S THE *TOBIACK*?" JACQUETTE RASPED OVER THE BOOMING thump of detonations up and down the ship's hull. Ange cranked down on a tourniquet around the spurting ruin of Jacquette's leg.

"Down in a ball of flame," Ange yelled back as he checked her thready pulse, fingers against her throat. "We are on our own. Where else are you hurt?" Her entire left side was a raw mess from hairline to tourniquet. Her pilot's seat was twisted metal and scorched plastic.

"Something's broken." She gripped his arm in pain.

"I'm gonna to put this neck brace on you."

Her eyes were going hazy. "Take control of the ship, you idiot, before we crash." Her grip went limp and her arm fell to the deck.

The refugee ship shook violently from another too-close blast and Ange glared up through the scarred, front windshield, seeing another pulsing gun battery approach. "Darn it!" He slapped a clotting patch on Jacquette's leg, flipped the promised neck brace around, and strapped her against the smoking wall of the cockpit.

He scrambled back to his copilot's seat, slid the command cable into the jack at the base of his skull, and took over skimming the station surface. He couldn't do this! He wasn't half the pilot Jacquette was, and their escort tugs, the *Jade* and the *Tobiak*, were gone. Video feeds and damage reports flashed across the insides of his eyeballs. "Mayday! Mayday!" he projected through the data stream. "This is the *Curious*. We are under heavy bombardment on the L7 Spoke. We have lost our companion ships."

"We have you on radar," crackled a reply from the new colony. "We are scrambling an escort. Hold your heading, *Curious*."

Ange nervously nudged the ship around an oncoming spire. Jacquette had brought them down very close to the station hull before the explosion that knocked her off her seat, but now they were flying too close. The *Curious* was practically dragging her belly. Ange triggered the starboard repulsers, pushing the ship into a hard bank between derelict structures, looking for dark gaps between newly activated gun towers. He couldn't imagine the bouncing the fifteen hundred refugees were taking in the back. Not to mention the livestock.

The Verj were not fully up and running in this old, abandoned sector, that was the only reason the ship was still flying, but what were they doing here at all? How had the big bugs expanded so far beyond their borders?

He increased power to the repulsers, pushing against the station's artificial gravity, gaining altitude over the mass of steel under them.

A line of explosive spheres arced out of a distant battery, homing in on the ship. He took evasive maneuvers, as evasive as the 9,000-ton ship could manage, and the spheres exploded close. He felt a lurch and alarms blared.

Calling up the belly-view of the ship, Ange watched as one of his port repulser modules tore away from its stanchion in a flash of sparks, tumbling to the surface. It punched through the station deck in a bright flash, and debris-filled atmosphere puffed out of the gash. He hoped a whole squadron of Verj had gotten sucked out in that venting. Five tons of electromagnets had to be good for something after they separated from the ship, didn't they?

For a moment, the bombardment eased. Were they past the last of the operable gun towers? He switched to the intercom to the rear of the ship. "How are you doing back there?"

"The secondary hull's holding, but the outer hull's in tatters," came back the response from Hale. "We got injuries. Where's the captain?"

"Captain's down, but we're almost through this." Ange could see a dwindling of the Verj's reenergized station lights.

"She alive?"

"She is, but we've got to get her to the medics."

"The weather report said this sector was safe!"

"It's not."

"The Verj can't have much of a presence here yet."

"They will soon enough. We won't make it across this sector many more times if they're already bringing the old defenses back online."

"We have too many people trapped back there to give up."

Hale was right, which terrified Ange. They needed a new path across. Where? The Verj were rushing into abandoned sectors of the giant station too fast, and this had been the last, best route between the old human colony and the new one. How did the Verj do it? How fast did they breed and mature soldiers?

The bugs fought to hold onto the territory they were taking at nearly every front. The Mai had brought them to a stop to the west, and the United Peoples of Mucky Mucky, or whatever the hell those birds called themselves in their weird chirps, fought them to the east. The human colony was surrounded now, trying to evacuate as best they could before the xenophobic Verj slaughtered and ate them.

How many refugee runs had he and Jacquette made in the last four months? Twenty? The *Sanctuary*, a sister ship, had gone down crossing the Trench of Liatta two months ago. Thirteen hundred people. Captain Nya was a good woman, and it was a bad loss. *Fundamentum* had gone down five weeks ago in a great, slow skid that saved most of the refugees. Captain Epanchin had walked twelve hundred people across fifty kilometers of station dead zone, uncontrolled and unpowered, and got more than six hundred of them through alive. All in all, the transportation ships had evacuated nearly a hundred thousand people, but still, thirty thousand remained behind.

This ship, the *Curious*, and its sister ship, the *Falcon*, were the only two big ships still flying. The Brick, a new ship so named because that's exactly what it looked and flew like, should be up and floating on repulsers soon. Its cavernous holds could theoretically lift fifteen thousand at a shot, but with the maneuverability of a, well of a brick, it would need an open path across the contested zones. The path they'd just lost.

"Thirty thousand left to rescue," he muttered angrily as he swooped around a half-lit tower that had been dark and cold on the last run. Blasted nitrogen-breathing bugs.

Human ground troops were holding the old colony's barriers against relentless assaults, but they couldn't replace their losses and the enemy seemed limitless. The Verj had taken the docks where transport ships had landed up until a month ago, forcing the engineers to cobble together a new dock. If the Verj ever reached the greenhouse module, the remaining refugees would starve within a week.

He reached back and touched Jacquette's shoulder, reciting Psalm 23. Valley of the Shadow indeed. He had to get her to the hospital.

As the Verj consolidated their hold across this sector of the station, the odds of the old colony holding grew worse. Evacuation flights became increasingly desperate. The Senate had hundreds of converted wreckers and tugs transporting citizens a dozen at a time, but that wasn't making a dent.

Thirty thousand people. It would take twenty or twenty-five more runs between the *Curious* and the *Falcon*, unless they could fly the *Brick*. They needed that lumbering behemoth, otherwise they'd never get everyone out, not even half.

He forwarded the new Verj information to the weathermen so that the *Falcon* wouldn't fly this route blind.

The ship bucked from a final near-miss and he breathed a long sigh as they crossed the terminal line of lights. The dark zone stretched beneath them to the curved horizon of the ancient station. He increased power to the repulsion magnets and brought the ship up higher to avoid black towers or spires in the dark, feeling the loss of the lower repulser in a new list to the deck.

He leaned back and pulled his cramped hands free of the yoke, shaking them, then increased the air filters to high. The smoky cockpit stank of ozone, burnt plastic, blood, and the acrid stench of sweat.

"Lt. Tsia, Status," a voice crackled from the receiver. It was Mark, at the new colony.

"This is Lieutenant JG Luriel," Ange said, gazing through the forward window. Nothing above but the bright stars, nothing below but scavengers and squatters from hundreds of species who didn't have enough surviving members to hold any real territory. "Lt. Tsia is down but alive and we have crossed the clear mark. Where's my escort?"

"Lt. Commander Naddom should reach you shortly."

"I think I see their headlights."

"The top brass have convened to sort through the data you sent. The old colony is under renewed assault as well. How quickly can you take off? Can you and the *Falcon* get through again?"

The colony was under renewed attack? How the hell were the Verj pushing so many fronts at once? "We took a pounding. The outer hull is a mess and we lost the #8 repulser on the lower port stanchion. *Falcon* might get through if she leaves right now. They used up a lot of their artillery on us."

"Lt. Luriel," interrupted a new voice. "This is Lt. Commander Naddom. Follow us to new landing coordinates."

"Roger, sir," Ange said, acknowledging his field promotion from Lieutenant JG to Lieutenant. He didn't want it, not on the back of Jacquette. "We are following you in."

He flicked off the transmitter and sat in the near-silence of the cockpit, listening to Jacquette's wheezing breath, the smell of burnt flesh thick in his nostrils.

"This was your last run, Captain," Ange said to her. "Congratulations, you're one of the few captains to have lived." He fell silent for a few beats, then laughed softly. "Is this a bad time to ask you out on a date? Yeah? I thought so. You have other things on your mind."

Six escort ships fell in around him, floating on small mag-lev engines, light and fast, armed with just a few hull-breaking projectiles. He adjusted *Curious's* repulsers to alter his trajectory.

Even though he'd done this terrible run over and over, Ange knew he was afraid of dying. Deathly afraid? But every successful run saved between a thousand and fifteen hundred. The last humans anywhere, as far as anyone knew, stuck on this inexplicable, abandoned, alien space station with a lot of other orphaned species. How did the Verj even find the energy to try and make an empire out of it?

He switched to ship-wide intercom. "Passengers and crew, this is Captain Luriel," he said into the mic. "We have passed into the safe zone and are under escort. We should be landing in about thirty minutes. The Red Cross will be waiting to receive you. Crew, please prioritize injured passengers for the medics."

He wiped his forehead. His shaking fingers came away coated with filth and blood.

❧❦❧

"Lt. Luriel," someone shouted as Ange dropped down the pilot's elevator tube at the nose of the ship.

He didn't know the woman in the gray uniform striding toward him; he didn't know this area of the colony at all. It had only recently been resealed to handle atmosphere and then repowered. It was still heavily under construction to make it comfortable for humans, and the walls bore sprawling pictographs from the original inhabitants a hundred thousand years ago.

There was a big, noisy throng around the ship—medics for the wounded; Red Cross for the terrified, stunned, passengers who crowded down the gangway; scores of fork-trucks for personal effects and rescued assets, all mashed between the temporarily dormant construction cranes. Loaders were already pulling crates of dirt from the rear of the *Curious*—a hundred salvaged tons of it for the expanding crop-fields. The first of fifty cattle was led cautiously down a gangway built for them. There were pigs and chickens in pens farther back in the hold, he knew, and four camels. Data techs in green waited anxiously to check over the server farm he and Jacquette had brought out, one of the four data hubs still at the old colony. So many things they wouldn't be able to replace for years if they got left behind.

Above him, mechanics already clambered over the badly damaged ship to assess and estimate repair times.

"Lieutenant," the woman said as she reached him.

"Petty Officer?"

"The generals and admirals are in conference, and you're wanted. They're waiting for you."

"Now?" He looked toward the medical bus bearing Jacquette Tsia toward the emergency center. "I have to check over my people, make sure..."

"We'll handle that. They're waiting."

He looked at his ash-coated, bloody uniform, then back to her steady gaze, feeling the exhaustion of the flight catch up to him all at once. "Right. Lead the way."

She brought him to an electric cart next to a massive transformer, built to reduce the old station's voltage down to something usable. Just beyond, the new, vaulted ceiling of the landing dock dropped to the original, claustrophobic six-foot ceilings of the station. At six-foot-three, Ange was happy to ride and not have to walk with his head hunched down.

"This is about the old colony being under attack?"

The woman flipped on the cart's rotating red light and lurched into the wide corridor, beeping insistently to get people out of their way. "*Falcon* launches in about fifteen minutes. This is about the *Brick*."

"The *Brick*?"

"She's preparing for launch."

"But she's not ready!"

"I know that, but we're out of other options."

About twenty minutes later, far across the colony base into the military complex, they swung to a stop in front of a gray-slab building beside a dozen similar carts. Col-Comm. A steady stream of foot traffic came and went through the front doors with a sense of urgency.

"This way," she said, hurrying with everyone else.

They waved their badges over the security readers at the door, and then three more times as she led him deep into the building, far past any section he'd ever been in before. The rebuilt ceilings had been pushed up to about seven and a half feet and racked with pipes and conduit, so he didn't have to duck while hurrying.

At last, they were both escorted into a crowded conference room. A map of nearby station sectors glowed on the wall, lit up with newly expanded Verj territory.

"Lt. Luriel," called an imposing woman in a white dress uniform beside the map. Several command officers stood around her.

Talk died down and Ange and his escort both saluted. "Admiral Kirark," he replied. He'd never been within speaking distance of the Admiral, but he knew her. Everyone did. She could have been the colony president in a heartbeat if she wanted it.

"At ease. I'm sorry to have called you here without a chance to wash up and change, but things are urgent. We all send prayers for Lt. Tsia."

"Thank you, ma'am."

She swept her arm to the map beside her. "Your new information in red overlaid with ship's scans of the launching platforms the Verj have reactivated."

Ange frowned. They'd been peppered from start to finish, so he'd assumed it was a mass attack. The map showed launchings from only a dozen staggered towers, mostly along the forward edge of the new Verj territory. "Their hold of the zone looks thin, ma'am."

"Thin as can be. We've been in contact with our new friends, the Kthoia, who have people trapped inside there. The Verj swept through the zone swiftly and established a forward boundary. They flooded the whole sector with nitrogen, wiping out most of the non-nitrogen breathing squatters. They energized the forward gun batteries, but the vast interior of that zone is still empty. The Kthoia have a big cluster of several thousand citizens trapped behind bulkheads, and they'd very much like to get them back."

"You want me to fly a rescue mission?" he asked, incredulous.

"Absolutely not. We still have thirty thousand of our own people behind bulkheads to rescue. Major Arramu here will be leading ground troops into the zone on a hard strike before the Verj get too well established, and the Kthoia will ride beside him. The goal is to open up a corridor of breathable air and evacuate the trapped Kthoia on foot. It's going to be dirty and ugly, and it'll distract the hell out of the Verj for a day or two. Hopefully, it'll pull their gunners off those twelve launch towers and their soldiers off our colony wall. We've asked Commander Epanchin," she pointed at a portly man to her left, "to fly the *Brick* during that window of distraction, and we want you to copilot. The *Brick's* equalizers aren't programmed yet, so we need two pilots working together to control the fore and aft repulsers. We need a pilot with your experience. Can you do this?"

Ange stared at the glowing screen and the twelve blue enemy launch platforms, and then met Captain Epanchin's hard eyes. He'd been expecting something like this, but it still took his breath away for a moment. The colony was in serious trouble. "The gun turrets will still be active, ma'am, at least partially," he managed. "At the Brick's flying speed, we're going to be an easy target."

"Yes, you will, Lieutenant, and you'll be carrying a precious cargo of fifteen thousand people on your return trip, right when you've lost the element of surprise. We're increasing your odds with an aerial assault. We're sending in the wreckers to take on those towers while you make your run. It's imperative that we silence them."

"Yes, ma'am."

"And then, no matter how badly you're damaged, we're turning the *Brick* and the *Falcon* around and doing it a second time. We have an extremely limited window before the colony collapses. The Kthoia and our ground troops will push back the Verj forward line as far as they can."

"We're going to mine the hell out of the station at that location and then fall back," one of the generals spoke up. "Blow a chasm twenty levels deep and take their front line with it."

Ange turned to Commander Epanchin. Michael Epanchin who had walked twelve hundred civilians across fifty kilometers of hostile, frozen station and been hailed as a hero when he brought half of them home. "When do we launch, sir?"

"Eighteen hours. We're powering up the mag-levs now, and there are a lot of them. We'll have to top them off at the other end while we're loading because fifteen thousand people will be a lot of inertial mass to overcome. We'll need all the juice we can get for maneuverability."

Ange almost laughed. Maneuverability? Then he met and held Captain Epanchin's eyes, and understood that the man didn't expect to survive both runs.

❧

Twelve hours later, Ange sat in the busy hospital ICU, wedged in beside Jacquette's bed. She was dozey, barely awake after surgery, bandaged from head to her remaining toes.

"Captain Epanchin's a good pilot," she said.

Ange's hands shook and he pressed them to his knees. He'd showered and gotten a new uniform, even napped a bit, but he was tired. "There's no way in hell we're running this twice," he said. "And when we go down, we'll take all those people with us." He choked up for a moment.

"The *Brick*'s meant to be a battering ram," she mumbled, looking over at him with half-focused eyes. "It'll take a pounding if you can keep the nose up. And you'll have to keep the nose up if you go into a skid. A slow skid's what you need to aim for if you start losing too many repulsers."

He smiled and took her good hand gently. "Thanks for not saying it'll all be fine."

She smiled back. "Where's the *Falcon*?"

"She's at the old colony right now, loading up, almost ready to return. She took a beating on the way out, but smaller than the one we got. She's trying to turn it around fast before the Verj reset. They packed two of the last three server farms into her holds and two hundred llamas. That's a ridiculous number of llamas, isn't it? She's got maybe a thousand people. That's all she could fit after they loaded up the dirt."

"Dirt's vital. What about the ground troops at this end?"

"Swinging into position. You ever seen a Kthoia? They got eight legs. They sort of run on six of them and bring the front two up like arms. They're bright red, too, like a berry. I heard the red is armor, but it doesn't look like they're wearing anything. The head's a mess of sensory organs and anemone feelers."

He fell silent, looking around. There were a number of people in the ICU who had been bounced around on the *Curious* and broken bones. This whole hospital, and four others like it, had been lifted from the old colony on the early runs.

"I should come with you," she said. "We hardly have any pilots left who can mesh with the big ships."

"You're too doped up to mesh with anything, and you've lost too much blood to talk sense."

She closed her eyes. "Remember to keep the nose up," she said firmly.

He stood on tired legs. She was raw and swollen from bruising and the hair had been shaved on one side but she was beautiful; fierce and smart and nimble at the helm. "It was an honor serving with you."

"You're not dead yet."

"Not yet."

Ange accompanied Commander Epanchin across the vast, busy construction hanger that housed the nearly completed *Brick*. The rust-colored ship hung from a series of gantries but was slowly taking its own weight as repulsers powered up. It was easily three times the length of the *Curious*, and four times as tall.

"Captain Tsia, Jacquette, says good things about you," Cmdr. Epanchin said.

"She's an amazing pilot."

"She says you're solid. Calm in a fight. I need that."

Ange was pleased. Jacquette was talking about him? "I'll do my best, sir."

"We'll get through the first run. We'll get shot up, no doubt, but the *Brick* can handle it. Second run will be harder, no bones about it. They'll have adjusted to us, and we'll be flying damaged and heavy. That's when I need your calm grip on the aft controls."

"Yes, sir."

Cmdr. Epanchin stopped and faced him. "Compartments are going to be breached, and you're going to see bodies spilling into the vacuum. You've got to ignore them and focus on incoming fire and what limited evasive maneuvers you've got at your fingertips. Can you do that?"

Ange swallowed hard, thinking back on Cmdr. Epanchin walking all those people out. "Yes, sir." It was all he could say.

"Then let's do this, Lieutenant. The ground troops are in position and are waiting on us."

Ange shoved his hands in his pockets and hurried toward the aft lift tube.

⧫⧫⧫

The first run was, in fact, easier than Ange had expected. The booming explosions were clearly audible, but didn't rock the ship so much as they had the Curiosity, and running empty, he found the repulsers to be responsive. Cmdr. Epanchin, in the forward cockpit, brought them through as fast as he could, keeping to the darkened paths of the sector, passing above the limping, dinged-up *Falcon* somewhere in the dark.

Ange listened over his neural link as the ground assault made progress toward the trapped Kthoia colony, pushing against strong resistance. Beyond that, he couldn't follow what was happening below the station surface. Fifteen thousand pre-selected people were waiting for him anxiously at the loading platform. There were riots among the other half of the refugees scheduled for a later pick-up; there were attacks on the livestock that were so precious to the new colony but took seats from humans; there were soldiers diverted from the defense of the perimeter to keep peace amidst the panic; there were deaths.

"Coming through the atmospheric shield now," Cmdr. Epanchin's voice barked back from his own armored roost. "Prepare for docking."

Ange guided the aft repulsers to swing the end of the ship around broadside to the final approach. A cluster of his electromagnets were sparking from a close explosion on the flight in.

"Ground control," he radioed down, "I need a check on 17 through 21. They got rattled."

And then they were docked, long starboard side lined up with the docking station, doors open from fore to aft on three levels. The crowds came pouring in, running, fearful, filling one bulkhead chamber after another, dropping into seats, clutching a single lap bag of possessions to their chests. The crowds beyond the landing dock on the approach ramps fought like mad to break in. Ange could see soldiers firing smoke grenades full of sleeping gas into the violence. Camera feeds from the lowest deck showed him wranglers dragging the last of the livestock up into hundreds of pens, and showed desperate people outside with grinders trying to cut their way through the animal gates. The wranglers closed the ship doors as soon as they could and hunkered down with the frightened cows and pigs and, oddly enough, a score of ostriches. Several dozen soldiers who'd been defending the animals also boarded. Ange wasn't sure if they were under orders or had just failed to exit the pens when the doors closed, but he couldn't blame them if they had. He was fairly certain that five mechanics had sealed themselves up in the service boxes of the five damaged repulsers, and he hoped their oxygen would last the return trip.

"We are clear to leave," Cmdr. Epanchin said as fork trucks stacked the last of a hundred crates of dirt. The fork trucks and their drivers didn't back themselves off.

Ange brought his aft electromagnets up to full power and had to use every single one of them to shove away from the tower. "We are very heavy back here," he radioed forward.

"Like a pregnant whale," came the response. "We'll ride low to the surface, as fast as we can. Now push with everything you've got."

Ange did push, angling back every repulser, but there was tremendous inertial mass to overcome. Internal cameras showed the crew struggling to get thousands of people strapped into seats. Internal bulkhead doors continued closing, partitioning the vast holds into smaller and smaller spaces. Animal wranglers fought to tie down terrified pigs.

Slowly, the station surface below them began to move by. They rose back into the vacuum and crossed the colony boundary where Verj and humans fought tooth and nail. He tracked incoming explosive projectiles almost immediately and did his best to execute lumbering evasive maneuvers.

Cmdr. Epanchin flew them so low to the deck that they bashed through thin, station antennae and the Verj bombardment around them ripped great holes in the station's hull, venting nitrogen and debris. Echoing booms of explosions traveled up and down the hull in waves and the ship quivered from impacts.

Ange kept his focus on the controls through the burning smoke and shrieking alarms. Hold #23 ripped open from end to end, simultaneously suffocating and freezing several hundred people, who remained strapped into seats in orderly rows. Fourteen repulsers overloaded and blackened. A muskox broke lose, charging into a wall and breaking its neck after trampling two sheep and a young woman.

At the same time, gun towers were going dark all around them as wreckers swung thousand-ton hunks of debris like wrecking balls; there were explosions that rippled the station hull from the inside with fighting going on below; there were whoops and hollers over the link from ground commanders as they finally reached the trapped Kthoia.

Still, for every gun tower that fell dark, another sprang to life, and the *Brick* flew over a surface cratered with the wrecks of tugs and small fighters.

They came in for a gentle docking at the new colony.

"It'll take eight hours to recharge the batteries," Cmdr. Epanchin's weary voice cut across the intercom. "Crew to eat and sleep, and get ready for the return run."

Ange acknowledged, then disconnected from the neural link. He staggered off the ship to get some air and shake the ringing from his ears, feeling used up. How long had it been since he'd slept? Before the *Curious's* last run.

People and animals poured off the ship around him, stunned joy and relief on their faces, but his eyes were drawn up to the scarred and scorched hull above the crowd. Rippled, blackened gouges covered every inch of the *Brick*. Crews were already craning sheets of steel over the through-holes into Hold #23, preparing to seal the chamber again before they'd even removed the bodies. Underneath the ship, several electromagnetic drivers were being cut from their struts while new ones waited on tractors below. He wondered if the five stowaways in the old modules had made it.

Pushing through the crowds being checked over by medics and logged in by security, holding up his badge, he requisitioned a cart and drove through endless tunnels to Jacquette's hospital. He needed to see her, even though she was sleeping in the embrace of painkillers. Sitting in the same, uncomfortable chair he'd occupied a few hours ago, he told her, "I'm not dead yet." A nurse he recognized waved to him and he waved back. "We got most of the refugees through alive. This batch, at least. That's half the people who were still there." He wondered who those people were in Hold #23. Parents of children who'd gone on earlier, probably. Or grandparents.

"Fifteen thousand to go, though the Falcon is due to lift a thousand or so of those on her next run. I'm amazed she's still flying. We'll follow her in about six hours, so I was wondering if you'd have dinner with me while I'm waiting. A date?" He gazed at her bandaged, tranquil face, the wall-lamp illuminating laugh lines. "This joke's getting old. If I make it back, I promise to ask you out while you're awake."

He bought some chili in a cup at the hospital cafeteria before heading back to the *Brick*. The landing dock was cleared of refugees and animals now, while loaders trundled along in lines with crates of dirt. Ostrich feathers and piles of cow dung lay trampled on the cold floor. Looking up once again, he watched sparks pouring down like beautiful waterfalls as hundreds of welders patched breeches. Clean-up crews swarmed the interior.

Two mammoth repulser drives rose slowly on lifts toward their waiting stanchions.

Ange finished his chili and took the nose-lift to the forward cockpit. The air in the ship smelled stale, though they had exterior vents running at full blast.

"Permission to come in, sir?" Ange said from the door.

The cockpit was dark and Cmdr. Epanchin seemed draped in his chair, staring into the distance through the forward window. Sparks showered brightly past the glass from time to time. He startled suddenly and looked over at Ange. "Oh, yes. Come in. Four hours until the batteries finish charging."

"All you all right, sir?"

"We lost two-hundred-and-ninety-two people. Hold #23, plus a few more here and there. That poor girl who got run over by the muskox. She lived for a bit, but I got word that she died on the transport to the hospital. Mara Babbage was her name."

"If we lost two hundred-and-ninety-two, then we saved four-teen-thousand, seven-hundred-and-eight, plus stowaways, right?"

"That's why we do this. They'll call you a hero, you know. Even if you save five thousand, Hell—four thousand, and lose the rest, they'll thank you." He pushed back in his seat. "I can still see all those people I lost on *Fundamentum's* last run. Some nights they shout louder than the survivors."

Ange frowned, gripping the edge of the door so hard the metal lip cut into his fingers. "Sir, are you all right to do this again?"

"I'll be fine," he said coolly. "Always was, no matter what. That's why they brought me out of mothballs. Now go take that nap I ordered."

Epanchin's far-away eyes stayed with Ange as he made his way back to his stuffy cocoon at the rear of the ship and tried to doze on the floor next to his chair.

He listened instead to the incoming reports of the battle. All the triumphs and losses of the ground troops beneath the tranquil surface of the station. They led thousands of Kthoia out on foot; they lost hundreds of Kthoia to savage attacks that burst up through the floors of ancient corridors; they fought to go lower, claiming deep levels abandoned and empty for countless centuries so long as they were getting under the Verj and could lay explosives. From within the claustrophobic, six-foot-high tunnels of the station, Ange watched video feeds of soldiers and bright red Kthoia shooting from behind make-shift shields of their own, piled dead or, more frequently, the massive, tangled carapaces of the Verj. As at the old colony, the Verj sacrificed themselves with inexplicable abandon, paying dearly for each human or Kthoia casualty but still pushing forward nonetheless. Frequently, the battles shifted between levels and corridors simply because the path was too corked up with Verj dead.

And on the surface, the battle between the wreckers and gun towers continued unabated like cosmic whack-a-mole. For every tower that the wreckers brought down in a thundering collapse of metal, another popped to life and spewed explosive shells in waves at the small ships.

"Thirty-minute countdown to launch," came Cmdr. Epanchin's voice over the intercom. "Get to your positions and check all bulkhead door latches. Check all air masks."

Ange took that to mean that their outer hull was riddled with more holes than eight hours of patch welds could fix.

⊰⊱

Their second run progressed much as the first had, with less armor. The *Brick* was down ten repulsers and wallowing, and Ange could swear he heard welds cracking at every hit, but as Jacquette had promised, the ship was a battering ram. It took everything the Verj threw at it, and the Verj were still too distracted by their substation contest to amplify their gun tower attacks.

He leaned hard on his remaining repulsers as he shoved the stern around at the old colony for docking, and briefly worried that he would overshoot as the ship drifted badly. When the mooring clamps dragged them in the last few feet, he had to remind himself to let go of the controls. His shoulders had cramped into rigid knots and he stood to try and shake them out. He was sweating.

Outside, a repeat of the frantic loading of people, equipment, and dirt commenced. Battle reports coming in from the Kthoia fight signaled that the allied ground forces had pushed the Verj back as far as they could, and casualties were mounting. Demolition crews had started laying explosives along their forward line, struggling at times to hold onto what they'd fought so hard to take the hour before.

His link pinged from Epanchin. "Lieutenant?"

"Commander?"

"I got word that the *Falcon's* down."

"What?" Ange's breath caught and anger swirled beneath his shock. His knew her crew.

"She dropped into an ugly skid right at the far edge of hostile territory but managed to keep many of her compartments intact. She's been ordered to sit tight while Central Command mounts a rescue. We're to fly clear."

"A rescue? With what?"

"They're putting the *Curious* back in the sky. She's going to transfer survivors."

"The *Curious*? Who the hell's left with the neural jacks and experience to fly her? One of the old-timers?"

"It would seem that Captain Tsia has come out of retirement, with a full medical staff to keep her alive during the attempt. Admiral Kirark herself is riding copilot, but her old neural jacks aren't advanced as Tsia's."

"Jacquette's barely out of surgery! She's missing part of her leg."

"And the *Falcon's* a sitting duck out there on the surface. Now concentrate on getting *this* ship home. We've got a lot of territory to cross."

Ange felt like he'd been kicked in the stomach. Jacquette had survived the explosion. She'd gotten out alive, and here she was galloping back to the rescue. It was exactly the sort of thing she'd do. With Admiral Kirark riding shotgun, no less.

He checked his camera feeds from inside the holds—all those people tensely holding hands; all those soldiers who'd volunteered to come home last.

"How's our hull integrity?"

"Inner hull is still intact. Outer hull took as much as it could take on the starboard side. I'll be flying us on a thirty-degree angle on the way back, leading with the port side as the better armor. You'll have to adjust your repulser angles."

Ange dropped back into his still-warm seat, having worked out none of his tension, as damaged reports scrolled past his eyes. His thoughts were still far away, though. The *Falcon* was down, the survivors trapped on limited oxygen, and the *Curious* was going to come under heavy fire during a rescue. He wanted to ping Jacquette but knew she was probably concentrating with everything right now and couldn't handle the interruption.

He prayed her concentration and stitches would both hold together.

"Get ready to shove off," Epanchin continued. "They're loading on about three hundred wounded soldiers into the cattle pens. When they're on, the remaining ground force is going to attempt a controlled retreat. We've got to keep bay doors open."

Ange looked to the lower video feeds as military medics drove in cart after cart of men and women on stretchers. Very quickly, they had a mobile medical unit under construction among the empty animal stalls. Above, some of the internal bulkhead doors had started closing, isolating the crowds of civilians trying to find seats. Other holds lay empty, awaiting the soldiers.

Thousands of soldiers began to fall back, collapsing the colony in around the elevated landing platform at a walk, remaining orderly. Verj bugs scrambled over each other trying to get to them, firing their own bulky guns.

Ange nervously brought the power levels up in his repulsers, nudging against the docking clamps as medics hurried on with the last few dozen wounded. He'd never been so close to live Verj soldiers before. Five data techs, rolling heaped servers on carts, trailing wires, ran on after the wounded.

Lights cut out in the colony as the Verj line overran the last of the transformers. Emergency batteries kept every tenth lamp lit, throwing the landing dock into twilight. The soldiers began running in groups as their commanders pulled them off the line and sent them scrambling up the ramps, many carrying heavy equipment between them.

"C'mon, c'mon," Ange said, leaning forward in his seat, every muscle taut.

Bright tracers of bullets flew back and forth in the gloom between the oncoming Verj and the human retreat. Soldiers zigzagged between stalled vehicles and station steel for cover, defending the ramp. The first soldiers to reach the *Brick* formed a line on the edge of the landing dock, shooting down on the Verj below. The soldiers sprinting up the ramp became a controlled rout under this new cover-fire, and men and women poured through the bay doors of the ship. Grenades were lobbed, hurling

Verj and body parts into the air, but never slowing the river of armored carapaces wearing nitrogen breather masks. Freshly wounded soldiers were dragged up the gangway at a staggering run. Sparks from projectiles ricocheted around inside of the ship as the Verj drew close enough to target the loading bays. The final defensive line ran.

"Here we go," Epanchin called tightly. "Releasing the clamps."

"The doors are still open, sir."

"Closing them now. Get me some thrust."

"I'm pushing, Commander, but this is what I've got."

Below, the old landing dock disappeared under swarming Verj and the bugs targeted the belly of the *Brick*. Ange watched the repulser modules nervously as sparks chattered across their skin from small-arms fire.

Below decks, soldiers filled all available seats and crouched on the floor. Field medics worked over the wounded, taking them down to the livestock deck.

"We're moving at a crawl," Epanchin snapped as they lifted free of the colony's atmospheric shield and into the vacuum. "Rotate all repulsers thirty degrees to starboard and let's present our port side to oncoming fire. We'll be a bigger target, but at least it's still got its armor. Incoming!"

Claxons sounded, but Ange had already seen the spray of bombs arcing toward them across the surface of the station and was maneuvering to present their strongest remaining hull to the impact. The ship bucked, as there were fewer electromagnets to counteract the force from the blast. Ange looked for signs that there were still wreckers attacking the towers, but couldn't see anything. In the distance, another tower spewed out a spray of bombs.

"We got a bigger problem," Epanchined called back. "General Hannu says his ground troops can't hold their position. They have to blow the mines, and we're on the wrong side of the line."

A cold chill swept across Ange's skin. "We can't free-fly across the trench they'll make!" He pictured the *Sanctuary* going down over a trench two months ago. Without something for the repulsers to push off of, the *Brick* would drop like a rock under the giant station's artificial gravity. "Can they give us another half hour?"

"They already gave us half an hour, and more. They can't hold, and if they don't blow the line immediately, the Verj will break through. I'm taking us west around the explosion zone, right to the edge of Snee territory."

"The Snee should be allies."

"After the Verj advanced into the abandoned zone yesterday, the Snee packed their border with artillery. Command is trying to buy us safe passage. Now give me speed!"

"Aye, aye, Captain." But there was no more thrust to give. All of Ange's repulsers were struggling at full power.

Another impact shook the ship so hard that it rattled Ange's teeth and almost knocked him out of his chair. Alarms shrieked and he shut them down with a slap of his hand, righting himself. Thousands of people in the holds were picking themselves up off the deck.

"Where were we hit, Commander? Commander! Do you copy?"

Altitude gauges registered a starboard drift to the ship. Port and starboard exterior feeds showed him a storm of debris and bodies tumbling down the ship's damaged hull on both sides from some point at the bow. Forward repulsers weren't working in concert.

Numb, terrified, Ange entered his code into the central operating system and assumed command of the whole ship. For a moment he saw double, as the fore and aft systems weren't synchronized, but he quickly learned to toggle between the two systems. Two of the forward repulsers were knocked out of alignment and wouldn't rotate on their stanchions, so he killed power to them. How many repulsers did he need to fly?

He pushed the damaged motors hard as more bombs exploded close and more debris rattled down the sides of the ship. The bow had taken a direct hit.

"Mayday, Mayday," he called. "Commander Epanchin is not responding. I have assumed control of the *Brick*." How many more times would he have to make that call? "We are flying low on limited thrust."

"Explosives are set to go in 90 seconds," came back the urgent voice of Mark at the colony. "Can you make it past their position?"

"Negative! Commander Epanchin was angling west when he was hit. What is the status of Snee negotiations?"

"No-go on the Snee. The Snee and Verj are battling along their border and Snee artillery is targeting anything that swings too close."

A strained, familiar voice echoed across his feed. "Lt. Luriel."

"Jacs? Lt. Tsia?"

"I need you to calm down and keep your head, you hear me?"

"Are you really back out in here?"

"We will be docking in about two minutes. Admiral Kirark is proving a deft hand at unorthodox docking maneuvers. *Curious's* armor will shield us both for the time being and we've got a couple of tugs running interference, so don't worry about us."

"You're going to get pounded!"

"And you're going to jump the gap."

"There's no way. I don't have enough repulsers left to make that kind of a jump."

"Four...Three...Two...One," came Mark's voice.

All along the horizon, the station puffed up in a silent eruption of metal and atmosphere in a dense cloud of debris.

"Get height now," Jacquette barked. "As much as you can. Then freefall when you hit the gap—and keep your nose up like I told you! Give your forward repulsers everything you've got when you hit the other side. Long, shallow skid, you hear me? You'll be in the abandoned zone. I'll come for you."

Ange rotated the repulsers down, gaining height, lifting above the next wave of bombs but making himself a higher target for following waves. He watched the glittering debris-field hanging over the newly formed trench warily as it began to fall back to the station surface.

He toggled to the ship-wide comms. "In a couple minutes, we are going to have to jump a gap. Landing will be rough, so everyone strap in and place your head between your knees. Secure the wounded."

The *Brick* continued rising, charging forward as the trench rapidly approached. They were higher than the darkened towers and spires now, the highest Ange had ever flown, and he could see the distant curve of the station highlighted against the brilliance of the stars.

There was an enormous beauty to it, and he wondered why there was no sunward side. Why did the ancient aliens choose to build a massive station within no known system, or had it once been in a system and broken free? It made him uneasy with inexplicable awe that struck him at odd moments. They were all trapped here, with no fuel to escape the artificial gravity but more than enough electricity to skim like waterbugs across its surface. Someday they would all die here.

The trench was beneath them now, and without something for the repulsers to push against, they began to fall, rattling through small debris-impacts. The new hole was deep and dark and surrounded with bristling towers on all sides like the hairs on a dog. They were all just fleas, burrowing beneath its surface. The surface was self-healing too, and this gap would be gone in twenty years. The towers that their tugs had brought down would grow anew. What did any of it mean? What did any of it matter?

A spray of bombs swept up from behind and struck them aft, shoving the ship. Chunks of armor fell away.

"Come on!" Ange snapped, furious that they couldn't get one moment to coast. The far edge of the trench was approaching fast and they weren't going to make it.

"Brace for impact," he called back to the refugees.

Repulsers began a stuttering grab onto the rough, rising pile of debris leading to the trench-wall, shaking the ship. He poured energy into them, trying to slow their fall. He brought the two damaged repulsers online at the bow for additional lift.

"Hang on." He brought the nose up hard as soon as the front repulsers found firm footing, and they skipped over the edge of the rift, striking somewhere amidships and ripping off half a dozen repulsers to the deafening thunder of tearing steel. The ship gyrated wildly, threatening to tip over onto her side while Ange held on for dear life and let the auto-gyros correct for roll. Then their tail smacked down again, tearing away the remaining aft repulsers. Forward momentum was still tremendous, pushing them across a quarter mile of station at each skip, and he fought to thread the needle between looming towers and spires down in the dark valleys.

He diverted more and more energy to the front repulsers as aft repulsers fell away, struggling to keep afloat. They settled into a forty-five-degree tilt, dragging what was left of their tail, cutting a deep furrow into the station hull. As the belly of the *Brick* had been designed as one giant skid-plate, the lower compartments filled with wounded soldiers remained intact, save for those at the point of impact against the rift-wall and those at the far stern.

Gradually, they slowed to a stop and blessed silence fell. Ange was panting, pressed way back in his seat. The front array of repulsers still held the bow of the ship high, bobbing like a child's balloon.

He checked for compartment integrity. The Brick had lost four compartments along the bow, and two along the belly. Five hundred people to a compartment. A scattering of other compartments leaked atmosphere through shrapnel-holes and the crew were racing to reseal them with high-expansion foam, picking their way across the sharply tilted deck.

He toggled over to Jacquette's feed. "We made it across and my nose is still up, but there isn't a single aft repulser left."

A flood of emotional joy pinged across the feed, surprising him. "I'll come for you," she said.

"Secure the *Falcon*. I might be able to get mobile if I take it slow."

"Let me know. And Ange?"

"Yeah?"

"About that dinner? I'd love to."

He couldn't stop the grin that took over his face. "Aren't you wrapped in bandages and hanging on an IV pole?"

"I'm missing a foot too. What about it?"

"We could order take-out and I'll bring it to you in the hospital. I know a pizza place that just reopened. In fact, I think we carried it across a couple of months ago."

"Pizza? That's your idea of a first date? What are we, fourteen?"

"There must have been static on the line and you misheard me."

"That's better."

Filled with joy for her and also with sadness for the people they'd lost, he gave the forward repulsers everything he had left. The tail of the *Brick* slowly lifted up out of the furrow it had made.

He activated the ship-wide comm. "We are in the clear and heading home. Bad news is we'll be flying at this tilt the whole way, so try to make yourself comfortable."

Back at the new colony, docked with the help of damaged tugs, Ange stood in the huge landing bay and looked up at the mangled mess that was the *Brick*, wondering how they'd made it back at all. The outer armor was almost entirely flayed away, and the tail was a deeply crumpled mess. The bow looked like it had been punched in.

Cmdr. Epanchin still sat at his post in the forward cockpit, frozen solid and gripping the yoke.

Throngs of people poured down the gangplanks and at least fifty medical trucks waited on the wounded. A mobile medical station had been erected off to the side to triage the flood of wounded. Red Cross workers spread out through the crowds.

"I think you've earned your rank, Lieutenant."

Ange turned to face Admiral Kirark three feet away. Her silver hair was rumpled and there was a burn under her eye.

He saluted. "It wasn't pretty, Admiral."

"The *Brick* was never going to fly pretty, and I ordered you into a tough situation."

"I lost over three thousand people!" He felt tears blurring his vision and fought them off.

"On a flight that had slim odds. Celebrate what you managed to do, not what went wrong. We didn't expect the ground commanders would have to blow the trench early."

"We lost Commander Epanchin."

'I know. He told me he was going to die on this run and I told him he'd be fine." Her expression seemed to crumple in on itself a little.

Ange smiled a tight, sad smile, and looked toward the *Curious* at a nearby docking station. It was also surrounded by disembarking refugees and medical trucks. A single medical bus hovered by the nose doors.

"Is she out yet?"

"Almost. She was a fragile mess going in, so they're being gentle bringing her out. She's stubborn as hell. She's got quite a future here."

"We have a date tonight."

"I heard. Pizza? How about I requisition some steaks and baked potatoes and maybe a few greens. I think I've got enough seniority to override the rationing."

"Thank you, ma'am."

"I'll have it sent over to the hospital. Both of you eat, and then sleep for a week. No hanky panky, that's an order."

"Thank you for flying with her, ma'am."

"We watch each other's backs out here, Lieutenant. And I'm far rustier than she let on. Embarrassingly so. Good night."

Ange saluted again then headed for the Curious and the medical bus, feeling every bit of his exhaustion through to his bones.

Our Heroes

KATHY TYERS - Growing up, I had a string of literary heroes: Peter Pan, Robin Hood, Francis Marion, Frodo Baggins, Luke Skywalker, Lord Peter Wimsey, Miles Vorkosigan, and yes, Brennen Caldwell. I also had a longish list in this world. Probably most pertinent to Ashling's story is Brigid of Kildare, who lived in sixth century Ireland. Her father threw her out for giving away too many of his possessions to the poor. She developed a reputation for working miracles. She definitely administered a double monastery for both men and women, and she founded a school for the arts, but the miracles are more fun to contemplate. Who wouldn't want to meet a gal who could multiply butter, convince a wild fox to do tricks for the local king, and hang her cloak on a sunbeam?

L. JAGI LAMPLIGHTER – Esther was a young Jewish woman who became queen of Babylon. A day came when violence was planned against the Jews. Esther was asked to speak to the king and beg for the lives of her people. But by law, if she approached the king, and he did not acknowledge them, the penalty was death. She found the courage. The king did acknowledge her, and she was able to save her people. I truly admire her courage.

JAMES CHAMBERS – I don't do heroes. Does that sound odd? If so, it's only because I long ago learned it's better to admire accomplishments, deeds, and ideas than individuals. When we make someone our hero, we idealize them and inevitably must face the fact that they, like everyone else, have feet of clay and are less than perfect. A letdown. True heroism, for me, lives in the everyday, the people who struggle day after day but never lose hope, the sick who refuse to let their illness control how they live their lives, the ones knocked down who get up and try again, the ones who stick to their principles even when it costs them. My heroes are people who find the best in life even when it throws the worst at them.

STEVE RZASA – There's many heroes who are in or who have left my life. But there's one whose advice comes to mind frequently. David Grima was the assistant editor at The Camden Herald weekly newspaper in Camden, Maine, when I started working there in the early 2000s. He was that rare journalist who wasn't a workaholic. Oh, he took his job seriously, and he was an adamant advocate for the public's right to know, and insisted local government work for the voter. He was not, however, a fan of working insane hours, since we weren't going to get paid overtime. He also prioritized family and friends. His balance is what I try to emulate. The most important words I learned—outside of Scripture—was his adage, "I work to live. I don't live to work." Many others have said it. David lived it. And I've always taken it to heart.

GABRIELLE POLLACK – My parents are heroes of the everyday sort. They fostered my imagination when it was young and wild and took joy in my stories when they were silly. They proofread many a blog post, listened to more than a few writing-related rants, and embarrassed me with their pride over my achievements. Their investment in my life has influenced every word on my pages, and though they may not be storytellers themselves, they taught me more than Shakespeare or Austen ever could.

WAYNE THOMAS BATSON – My hero is my father, Thomas Charles Batson. He was not a perfect man, nor was he built like a superhero, but he had a quiet iron about him. He had wisdom in the midst of any storm. Like a bulkhead, he absorbed the storm's wrath and held steady for everyone else around him. He loved my

Mom and my family, worked hard, and found joy in the simple things of life. He showed me the value of a quiet evening with a good book, and he taught me how to fish.

DANIELLE ACKLEY-MCPHAIL – My hero is Brad Phillips, my youth group leader growing up. He is a man of love and faith and honor. He stood up for me and others in so many ways and supported us in becoming upstanding adults equipped to make the right choices in life, showing us by example that the choice between right and wrong doesn't have to be difficult, even when it's hard.

PAUL REGNIER – CS Lewis crafted beautiful stories that set my childhood imagination free. As a child, I was a Narnian. When I grew older, his Space Trilogy was there to continue the journey. His books on theology and philosophy challenged and inspired me as an adult. One day, when I get to heaven, I'll be able to tell him, "Your words meant a great deal to me. Thank you from the bottom of my heart. You're my hero."

KERRY NIETZ – One hero of mine is Joseph from the book of Genesis. Betrayed by his family, sold into slavery, taken from his home. Then, when things seem to be improving, he resists temptation—only to be falsely accused and sent to prison. For eleven years! If anyone had a right to be vengeful and bitter, it was that guy. If anyone had reasons to lose faith, it was him. But he never wavered, and even when released from prison and given power over his enemies, he didn't seek revenge. He instead counted all his experiences, good and bad, as part of God's plan of salvation for him and his family. Perseverance, faith, grace, and honor—character traits of Joseph and qualities everyone could use more of.

TEISHA PRIEST – Nate Saint initially dreamed of becoming a military pilot. When illness cut that dream short, Nate found a new way to use his talents and love of aviation—as a missionary pilot. His life did not turn out as he first planned, but rather than becoming bitter about lost dreams, he followed Christ anyway. Ultimately, he sacrificed his life in following this new path, but not in vain. Nate Saint's example has ever challenged me to let go of my own lost dreams, and look for the new path that I may better serve and follow my Savior—wherever that leads.

JEFFREY LYMAN – mine is about all of the unsung heroes who put themselves selflessly out there. Could be ministers or drug councilors or psychologists or police officers, who seek to bring us from an old, bad (but comfortable place) to a new, scary, but potentially much better place. And its about helping other, different/alien people along the way who might be going through the same thing. We're all in this together.

About the Authors

Kathy Tyers is best known for her Star Wars Expanded Universe novels, *The Truce at Bakura* and *New Jedi Order: Balance Point.* Besides her classic "Firebird" series of five novels, she has published five other science fiction novels and a travel book, and co-authored a book with classical guitarist Christopher Parkening. Her most recent publication is *Writing Deep Viewpoint,* published by the Christian Writers Institute. Kathy lives in southwestern Montana. www.kathytyers.com

L. Jagi Lamplighter is the award-winning author of the YA fantasy series: *The Books of Unexpected Enlightenment,* the third book of which was nominated for the YA Dragon Award in 2017. She is also the author of the Prospero's Daughter series: *Prospero Lost, Prospero In Hell,* and *Prospero Regained.* She has published numerous articles on Japanese animation and appears in several short story anthologies, including *Best Of Dreams Of Decadence, No Longer Dreams, Coliseum Morpheuon, Bad-Ass Faeries Anthologies* (where she is also an assistant editor) and the Science Fiction Book Club's *Don't Open This Book,* and she also helps to maintain several websites, including one covering magical schools called *Fantastic Schools and Where to Find Them.*

She also has a collection of her own works: *In the Lamplight.*

When not writing, she switches to her secret identity as wife and stay-home mom in Centreville, VA, where she lives with her dashing husband, author John C. Wright, and their four darling children, Orville, Ping-Ping Eve, Roland Wilbur, and Justinian Oberon.

Her website and blog: http://www.ljagilamplighter.com/

James Chambers is an award-winning author of horror, crime, fantasy, and science fiction. He wrote the Bram Stoker Award®-winning graphic novel, *Kolchak the Night Stalker: The Forgotten Lore of Edgar Allan Poe and was nominated for a Bram Stoker Award for his* story, "A Song Left Behind in the Aztakea Hills." *Publisher's Weekly* gave his collection of four Lovecraftian-inspired novellas, *The Engines of Sacrifice*, a starred review and described it as "...chillingly evocative...."

He is the author of the short story collections *On the Night Border* and *Resurrection House* and several novellas, including *The Dead Bear Witness* and *Tears of Blood*, in the Corpse Fauna novella series, and the dark urban fantasy, *Three Chords of Chaos*.

His short stories have been published in numerous anthologies, including *After Punk: Steampowered Tales of the Afterlife, The Best of Bad-Ass Faeries, The Best of Defending the Future, Chiral Mad 2, Chiral Mad 4, Deep Cuts, Dragon's Lure, Fantastic Futures 13, Gaslight and Grimm, The Green Hornet Chronicles, Hardboiled Cthulhu, In An Iron Cage, Kolchak the Night Stalker: Passages of the Macabre, Qualia Nous, Shadows Over Main Street (1 and 2), The Spider: Extreme Prejudice, To Hell in a Fast Car, Truth or Dare, TV Gods, Walrus Tales, Weird Trails*; the chapbook *Mooncat Jack*; and the magazines *Bare Bone, Cthulhu Sex*, and *Allen K's Inhuman*. He co-edited the anthology, *A New York State of Fright: Horror Stories from the Empire State*, which received a Bram Stoker Award nomination.

He has also written and edited numerous comic books including *Leonard Nimoy's Primortals*, the critically acclaimed "The Revenant" in *Shadow House*, and *The Midnight Hour* with Jason Whitley.

He is a member of the Horror Writers Association and recipient of the 2012 Richard Laymon Award and the 2016 Silver Hammer Award.

He lives in New York.

Visit his website: www.jameschambersonline.com.

Steve Rzasa is the author of many novels, novellas, and short stories of science-fiction, steampunk, and fantasy, with a bunch more in progress. He was first published in 2009 by Marcher Lord Press (now Enclave Publishing). His third novel, *Broken Sight*, received the 2012 Award for Speculative Fiction from the American Christian Fiction Writers. *The Word Endangered* (2016) and *Man Behind the Wheel* (2017) were both finalists for the Realm Award in recent years. Steve grew up in Atco, New Jersey, and started writing stories in grade school. He received his bachelor's degree in journalism from Boston University, and worked for eight years at newspapers in Maine and Wyoming. He's been a librarian since 2008, most recently earning his Library Support Staff Certification from the American Library Association. He is the library director in Buffalo, Wyoming, where he lives with his wife and two boys. Steve's a fan of all things science-fiction and superhero and is also a student of history.

A long time ago in a land not so far away, **Gabrielle Pollack** fell in love. Not with coffee or epic instrumentals (though those things are never far from her side) but with storytelling. Since then, she's been glued to a keyboard and is always in the midst of a writing project. During the rare moments she's not working on a novel or finishing articles for StoryEmbers.org, she's pursuing an English degree, failing at poetry, and admiring storm clouds. She hopes to infuse her fiction with honesty, victory, and hope, and create stories that grip readers from the first page to the last.

Wayne Thomas Batson was born in Seabrook, MD in 1968. He had an adventurous childhood and adolescence that included: building forts in the woods, crabbing and crayfishing in bays, ponds, and bayous, playing lead guitar in a heavy metal band, and teaching tennis lessons at the local recreation center. He attended Gabriel DuVal Senior High School where he wrote for the school's newspaper and literary magazine. He was voted "Most Talented" in his senior year, and wrote this for his Yearbook Senior Goal: "To become a published author." Little did he know that God had even greater plans.

Having successfully completed the rigorous Holmes English Literature Curriculum, Batson graduated from the University of

Maryland, College Park in 1991 with a BA in English and Secondary Education. In 1996, he earned a graduate degree in Counseling and has continued his studies with 36 credit hours of graduate-level Reading courses.

Wayne Thomas Batson has spent the last twenty-four years teaching Reading and English to middle school students. He pioneered the active instruction of Strategic Reading in Anne Arundel County. Most recently, he helped develop the Challenge Reading Curriculum for advanced readers in Howard County, Maryland. Wayne Thomas Batson lives in Eldersburg with his extraordinary wife of 21 years and his four amazing (and challenging) teenage children.

Batson's writing career began in 2005 with the publication of fantasy epic, *The Door Within*. Since then, *The Door Within, The Final Storm, Isle of Swords*, and *Isle of Fire* have all appeared on the CBA Young Adult Bestseller List, including #2 for *The Final Storm* Fall 2007. To date, Batson has penned or coauthored seventeen novels and has sold well over half a million copies.

Batson's works have garnered many awards and nominations including: Mom's Choice, Cybil, Lamplighter, Silver Moonbeam, ACFW Book of the Year, and The Clive Staples Award. Mr. Batson and *Isle of Swords*, his pirate adventure novel, were featured on the front page of The Washington Post, and he was interviewed live on Fox's nationally televised morning show. But most importantly, all of Batson's works are "student approved," meaning that, over the years, the middle school kids in his classes have given each novel a rigorous critique and enthusiastic thumbs up.

Wayne Thomas Batson gives thanks to God for the abundant life he's been given. He continues to write for the kids he cares so deeply about because he believes that, on a deep level, we all long for another world and yearn to do something important.

Award-winning author and editor **Danielle Ackley-McPhail** has worked both sides of the publishing industry for longer than she cares to admit. In 2014 she joined forces with husband Mike McPhail and friend Greg Schauer to form her own publishing house, eSpec Books (www.especbooks.com).

Her published works include six novels, *Yesterday's Dreams, Tomorrow's Memories, Today's Promise, The Halfling's Court, The*

Redcaps' Queen, and *Baba Ali and the Clockwork Djinn*, written with Day Al-Mohamed. She is also the author of the solo collections *Eternal Wanderings*, *A Legacy of Stars*, *Consigned to the Sea*, *Flash in the Can*, *Transcendence*, *Between Darkness and Light*, and the non-fiction writers' guide, *The Literary Handyman*, and is the senior editor of the *Bad-Ass Faeries* anthology series, *Gaslight & Grimm*, *Side of Good/Side of Evil*, *After Punk*, and *In an Iron Cage*. Her short stories are included in numerous other anthologies and collections.

In addition to her literary acclaim, she crafts and sells original costume horns under the moniker The Hornie Lady, and homemade flavor-infused candied ginger under the brand of Ginger KICK! at literary conventions, on commission, and wholesale.

Danielle lives in New Jersey with husband and fellow writer, Mike McPhail, and three extremely spoiled cats.

Her newest book, *Eternal Wanderings*, release at the beginning of April. An elven mage joins a Romani caravan to help a friend fight his inner demons, only to be confronted with ancient demons of a more literal sort.

To learn more about her work, visit www.sidhenadaire.com.

Paul Regnier is the author of the *Space Drifters* science fiction series. He is a technology junkie, drone pilot, photographer, web designer, drummer, Star Wars nerd, recovering surfer, coffee snob and a wannabe Narnian with a fascination for all things futuristic.

Paul grew up in Orange County, CA and now lives in Treasure Valley, ID with his wife and two children.

To connect with Paul Regnier and discover the full extent of his nerdhood, please visit his pages on Facebook, Instagram, and Twitter.

Kerry Nietz is an award-winning science fiction author. He has over a half dozen speculative novels in print, along with a novella, a couple of short stories, and a non-fiction book, *FoxTales*.

Kerry's novel *A Star Curiously Singing* won the Readers Favorite Gold Medal Award for Christian Science Fiction and is notable for its dystopian, cyberpunk vibe in a world under sharia law. It is often mentioned on "Best of" lists.

Among his writings, Kerry's most talked about is the genre-bending *Amish Vampires in Space*. AViS was mentioned on the *Tonight Show* and in the *Washington Post, Library Journal,* and *Publishers Weekly. Newsweek* called it "a welcome departure from the typical Amish fare."

Kerry is a refugee of the software industry. He spent more than a decade of his life flipping bits, first as one of the principal developers for the now mythical Fox Software, and then as one of Bill Gates's minions at Microsoft. He is a husband, a father, a technophile and a movie buff.

Visit his website at www.KerryNietz.com

Teisha J. Priest is slightly obsessed with astronomy, aviation, space exploration, and Star Trek. When she's not writing space opera, she homeschools four kids, blogs, and knits while watching sci-fi with her husband. She's a regular contributor to Family magazine, writing about homeschooling, family, and faith. Her family lives in rural Maine where the dark night skies provide a brilliant view of the stars. Visit her website at www.teishknits.com.

Jeffrey Lyman is an engineer in the New York City area. His work has appeared in the anthologies *Sails and Sorcery* from Fantasist Enterprises, *New Blood* from Padwolf Publishing, and *Breach the Hull, So It Begins, By Other Means, Best Laid Plans,* and *Dragon's Lure* from Dark Quest Books. He was co-editor of *No Longer Dreams* and all four volumes of the award-winning *Bad-Ass Faeries* anthology series. He is a 2004 graduate of the Odyssey Writing School and won 2nd place in the fourth quarter of the 27th Annual Writers of the Future Award.

ABOUT THE ARTIST

Through the years **Kirk DouPonce** has designed well over a thousand covers. He's won a few awards and has been published in art magazines and annuals including Communication Arts, Imagine FX, and Spectrum Fantastic Art. Kirk lives within the Rocky Mountains of Colorado with his wife, their four children, three cats, a dog, and a ferret. You can see some of his work at www.DogEaredDesign.com

Our Heroic Backers

A.C. Williams
Alisa Hope Wagner
Allen Brokken
Amy Brock McNew
Andra Marquardt
Anna Tan
Annaliese
AslansCompass
Becky B
Ben Harris
Beth
Bethany A. Jennings
Brian D Lambert
Brianna Tibbetts
Brodie Media
C. S. Wachter
Carol H
Cathrine Bonham
Chad Bowden
Chand Svare Ghei
chasvag.com
Christopher Shupe
Cindy Emmet Smith

Cindy Koepp
Cora Anne Hurst
Curtis and Maryrita Steinhour
Dagmar Baumann
Danielle Ackley-McPhail
Darbie Pelachick
David Jung
Doug Triplett
Emily Gellhaus
Erik T Johnson
Ernesto Pavan
eSpec Books
Esther LoPresto
Evan Miller
Fernando Autran
Gerald P. McDaniel
Ginny Huckins
Her Royal Highness,
    Pam Halter, Queen of Fairies
Ian
Ian Harvey
Ivan Donati
J F Rogers

J. L. Ender

Jason C. Joyner

Jennifer L. Pierce

Jeremiah Johnston

Jhannah de Castro

Johne Cook

Joseph Ely

Josh Hardt

Josh R Smith

Joshua C. Chadd

Josiah DeGraaf

K.A. Cummins

Kailey & Emily

Kara Jaynes

Katherine Briggs

Keith A. Robinson

Kerry Nietz

KL Wagoner

Kristen Stieffel

Kyle ?aroban

Lark Cunningham

Laura A. Grace

Laura VanArendonk Baugh

Laurin Boyle

Lelia Rose Foreman

Lena Karynn Tesla

Lisa Godfrees

Marian A. Jacobs

Mark Featherston

Mark Griffin

Mark Lukens

Melinda Dixon

"Michael ""Skipper"" Adams"

Mike Skolnik

Morgan L. Busse

Nathan Cowick

Pat Hayes

Paul Regnier

PJ Kimbell

Pyxis Gate Library

Rachel Hastings

Rae Graham

Ralene Burke

Rebecca Crawford

Richard Ohnemus

Rob Voss

Robert Claney

Ronie Kendig

S. E. M. Ishida

Sara James

Scott Schaper

Sharon Rose

Sophia Hansen

Stephanie H. Warner

Steve Rzasa

Steve Thomas

Stuart Vaughn Stockton

Teddi Deppner

Teish Priest

Timothy Hicks

TLC Nielsen

Tracy L Snyder

Wendy McLouth

Xavi H.

Zackary Russell

CPSIA information can be obtained
at www.ICGtesting.com
Printed in the USA
BVHW032329210619
551700BV00002B/2/P

9 780996 271844